ANGELA CARVER

The Mafia Boss's Pregnant Bride

Copyright © 2024 by Angela Carver

All rights reserved. No part of this publication may be reproduced, stored or transmitted in any form or by any means, electronic, mechanical, photocopying, recording, scanning, or otherwise without written permission from the publisher. It is illegal to copy this book, post it to a website, or distribute it by any other means without permission.

First edition

This book was professionally typeset on Reedsy. Find out more at reedsy.com

Contents

1	RIP Julian	1
2	In for a Treat	7
3	Oops!	12
4	Accidental Father	20
5	You are NOT the Father	25
6	His Dad	29
7	I am Not Joking	36
8	I won't Marry You	43
9	The Baby isn't Mine	50
10	Silly Man	56
11	Let Me Handle It	63
12	A Family	69
13	Men are Great Idiots	77
14	You are Hurt	84
15	Live With Me	91
16	Is it to your liking?	98
17	Men Like Him	105
18	Dinner Date	112
19	Sweet Old Lady	119
20	A Kiss	126
21	Lying to Herself	134
22	You are Crazy	140
23	I Am No Gentleman	147
24	Breakfast With the Mafia Boss	155

25	Sweet Wine	163
26	Wash My Hair	170
27	In Control	177
28	Lovely Sight	186
29	The Necklace	194
30	Special Day	202
31	Shiny Things	209
32	Beautiful and Elegant	218
33	Birthday Celebration	225
34	Nightmares	231
35	I Need You	239
36	You Can't Say That!	245
37	Lullaby Type	253
38	He is Sick	261
39	Photographs	267
40	Sleep with Me	272
41	Spending Time	280
42	Tell Me His Story	286
43	Marry Him	292
44	Accept Me	300
45	Approval	306
46	Tell Me Everything	314
47	What Do You Want to Do?	322
48	Rip Them Apart	330
49	Secret Talent	337
50	What to Wear	344
51	Wedding Night	352
52	He Will Pay	359
53	Take Care of Them	368
54	I Love You	375
55	Forever	385

56	Who Helped You	395
57	Happy Birthday	403
Book 2 in this series		414

One

RIP Julian

"You are Valerie Foster?" Antonio Costello asked in a thick Italian accent, his deep voice surprisingly gentle.

Valerie looked at him, studying his features slowly and carefully. He appeared to be in his late thirties with jet-black hair and eyes so dark they seemed almost black. His face, while almost handsome, had a deep scar running from his forehead down to his cheek on the right side, making him look intimidating, to say the least.

He sat with an air of confidence, his posture tall and regal, indicating a man of power and strength. Even seated, his broad shoulders and the powerful build of his chest and arms hinted at his impressive height.

The Mafia Boss's Pregnant Bride

He looked absolutely terrifying, Valerie thought.

One look at Antonio Costello and Valerie could tell he wasn't a man to be trifled with.

"Yes," she replied briskly, holding her stomach protectively as if to protect her baby from the predator in front of her. She was sitting on a couch in front of him with one of her brother's men standing behind her. He had his eyes glued to her just as he promised he would.

"Hmm," Antonio said. He narrowed his eyes at Val's pregnant belly. "And that's Julian Sinclaire's child."

"Yes."

The man made a face as if he had eaten something bitter. "You decided to have a child with that Russian sleaze bag? Could've done better, Bella."

Val rolled her eyes. Why did everyone, including her mother, just assume she could've done better than Julian? Sure, he was a douchebag and a cheating bastard at times, but he was at least nice to her. He took her in and protected her when she needed it the most!

Not to mention he had gifted her with her unborn son. RIP Julian.

"Is there a point to this conversation?" Valerie asked impatiently. "Why did you bring me here?"

Antonio's black eyes flashed. "A little impatient, are we?" he remarked, his tone laced with amusement.

Val bristled at Antonio's condescending tone but forced herself to stay composed. "I didn't think you brought me here to make small talk," she said.

He chuckled, a deep, rumbling sound that sent a shiver down her spine. "Of course, of course. Pregnancy does tend to make women a bit…testy."

Val clenched her jaw, resisting the urge to snap back at him. Instead, she forced herself to remain calm and focused on him. "Let's get to the point. What do you want from me?"

Antonio leaned back in his chair, steepling his fingers together as he studied her with those intense black eyes. "Straight to business, I like that," he mused. "Very well, Signorina Foster. Like I said to your brother, you have something that belongs to me."

"What would that be?" she asked.

"A series of codes. I won't go into details, but they are written on a piece of paper," he paused and leaned forward. "I have reasons to believe that you have it in your possession."

Val narrowed her eyes. "And if I did have these codes, why would I give them to you?"

Antonio's smile was like a predator's, confident and unnerving. "Because, mio amore, you don't have a choice."

"What? Are you going to kill me? With my unborn baby?" Val asked, struggling to keep her voice steady.

His eyes widened. "Kill you? Oh no. I am more decent than that."

Valerie snorted loudly at that.

He frowned at her. "Do you have something to say?"

"If you are a decent human being, I'm the Virgin Mary." She paused and pointed at her swollen belly before continuing. "And this… here… is baby Jesus ready to be born."

The muscle in his jaw twitched, and for a moment, she thought he might smile. But his face stayed serious.

"You seem to have a sharp tongue, little lady," he said, his voice low and dangerous. "I guess what they say about red-headed girls is true."

Valerie rolled her eyes.

Antonio's gaze narrowed, his demeanor shifting from playful to intense. "But let's not forget why we're here," he continued, his voice low and commanding.

"I don't have your stupid codes," Val barked.

Antonio's expression remained unreadable for a moment before he leaned back in his chair, seemingly unfazed by her outburst. "That's a shame," he replied calmly. "Because I have reason to believe otherwise."

Val had something smartass to say. It was at the tip of her tongue but she stopped.

Because the room suddenly felt hot. Val gripped the edge of the chair. Sweat broke out on her forehead, and her heart pounded in her chest.

Antonio leaned forward, placing his elbows on the table between them. "Is there a problem, Signorina?" he asked, a dangerous gleam in his eyes as he watched her squirm. "Did I catch you in a lie? You know where the paper is, don't you, Bella?"

Val shook her head vehemently. "No, no, I don't, asshole."

"Then why do you look uncomfortable?" Antonio pointed out.

"Just hot, that's all," she mumbled, wiping her forehead with the back of her hand. The room was suffocatingly warm now, and she glanced around helplessly.

Was it her imagination, or was everything beginning to sway?

Suddenly, a sharp pain ripped through her abdomen, making her gasp and clutch at her stomach. Her dress was suddenly wet, and she looked down in shock.

Her water had broken.

Two

In for a Treat

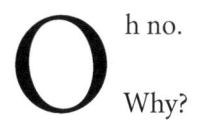

Oh no.

Why?

Why now?

Of all the times to go into labor, now was definitely the worst. Valerie could already feel the first contractions coming on, a sharp pain that made her grit her teeth and clutch at her belly.

Antonio looked at her with raised eyebrows, his smug smile quickly disappearing. "Err…Valerie?" he asked, suddenly sounding less confident and more… worried?

She ignored him, breathing heavily as she tried to ride out

the pain. Caught up in the moment, her mind focused only on getting through this ordeal. She couldn't give birth in front of this man! What if he tried to kill her? She could feel the liquid seeping down her legs and onto his plus carpet.

It served him right for forcing her to be here!

"Is she…is she having the baby now?" one of Antonio's goons stammered. He looked pale and terrified, his eyes darting from Val to his boss in panicked confusion. If Valerie wasn't in so much pain, she would've giggled at his goofy expression.

Antonio stood abruptly, his chair scraping loudly against the floor. "Get the car!" he roared at one of his men, who disappeared from the room like a shot.

Her brother's man, Samuel, was by her side in a flash. "I… I will call Boss and take you away, Val."

"There's no time for that, you fool!" Antonio barked at him. "I am taking her to the hospital. You come with me so Foster doesn't think I am harming his sister."

Despite the pain, Val couldn't help but let out a bitter laugh at Antonio's expense. His confident facade had wholly shattered, and he looked utterly helpless now. His intimidating aura now ceased to exist.

But damn…she could finally see how tall he was, and he was a motherfucking giant! She wondered how his mother felt while giving birth to him. Was he a big baby or was he…

In for a Treat

"Ouch!" Val cried as another contraction interrupted her thoughts.

"What's wrong? Are you going to die?" Antonio squealed.

Jeez…he looked like he was about to pass out.

"Is this your first time witnessing childbirth?" she asked through gritted teeth. A fresh wave of pain hit her then and her body convulsed.

Antonio looked at her with wide eyes and nodded mutely. "I have seen death," he admitted quietly. "But never life."

"Well," Val gasped out between contractions, "you're in for a real fucking treat."

Antonio watched her for a moment longer before he stepped toward her hesitantly. He reached out slowly and placed his hand on her arm. It was a comforting gesture but not nearly enough to take away the pain.

And besides, Valerie wasn't exactly expecting to be comforted by a murderous Italian giant.

"The car is ready, Capo," Antonio's goon informed them.

Valerie yelped as Antonio scooped her up in his arms and strode toward the front door. "Breathe, Amore," he urged as he settled her into the car.

She held onto Antonio's suit jacket, her fingers digging in as another contraction made her vision swim. His usually calm exterior was ruffled, his dark eyes wide and a frown creasing his usual smile lines.

"Drive faster!" he barked at the man behind the wheel.

"I'm trying!" the man snapped back, urgency clear in his voice.

As the car sped through the streets, Valerie tried to focus on breathing as her doctor had instructed. Antonio's hand had been warm against her shoulder, but somewhere between the hospital entrance and being rushed into a room, his touch left hers. The sudden absence felt strange, though she should have been relieved he wasn't near.

A nurse leaned over her. "Oh dear, you made it just in time."

"Yeah, just in time," Valerie gritted out, her breath hitching as another contraction rocked through her.

In a whirlwind of motion, doctors and nurses rushed around her. Valerie was lifted onto a gurney and wheeled down the hospital corridor at an alarming speed. The lights above her blended into one long, glaring strip as they whizzed by.

A doctor appeared in Valerie's line of sight, her eyes full of kind concern. "You're doing great, Valerie. Just keep breathing."

In for a Treat

Valerie nodded, clenching her teeth against the next wave of pain that roared through her.

Suddenly, the door burst open again, and Antonio was there.

Wait…why was he here?

"You'll need to gown up," the doctor told Antonio, handing him a sterile set.

Antonio blinked at her, a look of bewilderment flashing across his face. But then he squared his shoulders and nodded. "Okay," he said, disappearing behind a curtain to change into the sterile gown.

"Wai… wait…" Valerie tried to protest when another contraction hit her. Words failed her as she rode out the wave of pain. By the time she recovered, Antonio had reentered the room, garbed in sterile scrubs.

Was he seriously planning on helping her deliver her child?

Valerie cursed out loud. This could not be happening to her!

Three

Oops!

Antonio Costello had never been so frightened in his life.

Here he was, apparently helping a woman give birth to her child, and he wasn't even the real father!

All he wanted to do this morning was to meet Julian's woman, get her to give him the codes Julian stole from him, and send her on her way. But instead, he was doing…this.

Madness.

Absolute madness.

Antonio burst through the sterile doors, his breath catching in his throat. He was in the delivery room, and in front of

Oops!

him was Julian's little redheaded girlfriend, screaming her head off.

Valerie Foster was a thing of beauty with her fiery red hair and large green eyes. Her skin was pale, right now, paler than usual had sprinkles of freckles all over. Antonio didn't particularly have a type when it came to women, but looking at Valerie, he suddenly realized he was a sucker for redheads.

"Cara mia," Antonio started, his voice stuttering, "I'm here."

"Here? Here!" She spat the word like venom, her emerald eyes blazing with a fury that singed his very soul. "Antonio, you bumbling fool! What are you even doing in this room? Why…are you here?"

The medical staff circled around her like a well-oiled machine, their movements precise, their focus unwavering. They must have seen this play out a thousand times, indifferent to the personal drama unfolding before them.

"Helping" was all Antonio could muster, but it was lost, a mere whisper against the storm of her anger. Why was she so angry? Was it because she was scared of him?

"Helping?" Valerie's laugh was sharp. "What the fuck for? Get out!"

God, she was beautiful when she cursed!

I should get out, Antonio thought to himself. What the hell

was he doing anyway? He wasn't the father of the baby. It was Julian, who was now dead. Antonio had no right to witness the birth of Julian's child. This whole situation was absolutely absurd.

"Stand next to her, Sir. I will tell you what to do next," the doctor said, and all thoughts of leaving fled Antonio's mind. He wanted to stay and see this through, for whatever reason.

Valerie's curses didn't wane, but he tuned them out, focusing on the rhythm of her breaths and the clenching of her fists.

Should he hold her hand? He remembered seeing in a movie once that was what you were supposed to do when helping someone give birth.

"Deep breaths, Valerie," one of the nurses said, though Valerie likely heard none of it.

"Shut up, just shut up!" Valerie's voice broke, raw and ragged.

Antonio leaned in closer, his hand hovering above her arm, unsure if his touch would be a comfort or a spark to more fury. "You're doing great," he murmured, dodging another volley of verbal daggers.

"Great? You think this is great?" The sneer in her voice could slice through steel.

He smiled at her. Mamma Mia, he had never seen a woman get so angry!

Oops!

"Focus, Valerie. Almost there," he said.

"Focus?" She spat the word like venom. "When I am done with this, I will kill you."

Oh, she is feisty! Antonio thought.

"We can revisit that after you are done, mio amore," he said gently.

"Look!" A nurse pointed, and Antonio shifted his gaze. Time stopped.

There it was—the baby's head, crowning, a sliver of new life fighting its way into the world.

"Keep pushing!" The command came from the doctor.

"Pushing! That's all I've been doing!" Valerie retorted angrily.

Antonio watched, every muscle tensed, as the top of the baby's head emerged further with each of Valerie's Herculean efforts.

"Push, mi amore, you can do it!" he encouraged, suddenly feeling joy erupting from within him. He had taken many lives before but never helped bring one into the world. The feeling of this was... exhilarating.

"Shut up, Antonio! Just... shut up!" Valerie's fingers gripped the front of his gown, knuckles white, her body convulsing with the effort of each push.

Antonio took her hand in his and squeezed it. He wanted to hold her and maybe kiss her a little, but he knew kissing her now would be a bad idea. She might bite his tongue off.

"Almost there," a nurse said, her eyes fixed on Valerie's progress.

"Can't... can't do this..." Valerie's voice wavered.

"You are doing it, cara mia. You're incredible." The words fell from Antonio's lips with sincerity that surprised even him.

"Feels like... punishment...for letting that asshole Julian fuck me," she managed between gritted teeth.

Finally, something they could both agree with. He couldn't imagine what a magnificent woman like Valerie was doing with a man like Julian.

"Ah, si, I agree," Antonio said and nodded, earning a death glare from his little redheaded firecracker.

"Here comes another one, deep breaths," coaxed the doctor, his hands poised and ready.

"Deep breaths," Antonio echoed, feeling useless next to the professionals yet compelled to stay by Valerie's side. His heart hammered against his chest.

Oops!

He was Antonio Costello, and he never got nervous, but this... this was the most nerve-wracking moment of his entire life.

Valerie gave out a final outcry, and soon, he heard the sound of a baby crying.

"Congratulations," the doctor announced, his voice a beacon of triumph amidst the chaos. "It's a beautiful baby boy."

Valerie's head lolled to one side, her face ghostly pale against the stark white of the hospital pillow. Her eyes fluttered shut, and she slipped into unconsciousness, a silent surrender to the exhaustion that claimed her.

Antonio watched as the nurse cleaned the baby and bundled her in a blanket. Then, she walked toward him.

"Here you go," she said, her words clipped as she thrust the bundle into his arms.

His hands, which had thrown punches and shot bullets, now cradled something far more delicate—a tiny, fragile baby. His skin was red and wrinkled, his head full of black hair.

"Careful," the nurse instructed, her gaze scrutinizing his awkward hold. "Support her head."

He adjusted his arms. She was light, nearly weightless.

"Err... ciao," he murmured to the baby, his voice unsteady.

Her tiny fingers, impossibly small, grasped at the air.

"Keep him warm," another voice commanded. Someone was moving in his peripheral vision, but he barely registered their presence. All that mattered was the infant in his arms, the steady rhythm of his breathing syncing with his own.

"Is the boy... is she okay?" he stuttered.

"Perfectly healthy," the doctor replied, a smile in her voice as she turned her attention to Valerie.

Antonio looked down at the baby, her eyelids fluttering like butterfly wings, innocence personified. In that instant, he understood the depth of Valerie's pain and how strong she was.

"Sign here, please," the doctor said, sliding a clipboard with a birth certificate toward him. Her hand hovered over a line marked 'Father's Signature'.

He blinked, the sharp scent of antiseptic stinging his nostrils. His gaze flickered from the document to Valerie's unconscious form, then down to the baby cradled in his arms.

"Uh," was all he managed, his brain scrambling. The pen was put into his hand, a gentle nudge against his palm. Without a thought, his name flowed across the paper—Antonio Costello—in ink as black as the uncertainty that filled him.

Oops!

"Congratulations," the doctor said, but her voice seemed distant, like an echo in a vast, empty hall.

He stared at the signature, his signature, on the line meant for someone else. It was done. A simple act of confusion, and suddenly he was... what?

A father?

Questo è folle!

"Ha!" The sound burst from him, a mix of disbelief and irony. He looked at the baby—his baby? No, not his. But he signed the damn birth certificate like he belonged to him.

Oops!

Four

Accidental Father

River Foster, the leader of the Red Vipers, rushed to the hospital as soon as his henchman Samuel told him his sister Valerie was going into labor right in front of that damned Antonio Costello.

Jesus Christ, how could this be happening? What was Valerie doing visiting one of the most dangerous men in the city and, not to mention one of his enemies?

His wife Ellie grabbed his hand and squeezed it, and he looked at her. Her eyes were wide with worry, mirroring his own.

"Valerie is going to be okay, River. Don't worry," she said in an attempt to comfort him.

River nodded but didn't say anything.

Accidental Father

The drive to the hospital felt like an eternity for River, his mind racing with worry for Valerie. He couldn't shake the image of her in pain, with that smug bastard Antonio standing over her. The thought of him witnessing such a vulnerable moment made River's blood boil.

As they pulled up to the hospital, River barely waited for the car to stop before jumping out. Ellie followed closely, her hand still tightly holding his. They rushed through the sliding doors and straight to the front desk.

"Valerie Foster," River said urgently to the nurse behind the counter. "She was brought in a few minutes ago. She's in labor."

The nurse nodded, quickly scanning her computer. "Room 304," she replied, pointing them in the right direction. "Follow the signs for maternity."

They hurried down the hallway, River's heart pounding in his chest. Ellie kept pace beside him, her presence a small comfort amidst the chaos.

When they finally reached the room, they were greeted by an unexpected scene.

There he was, the notorious Antonio Costello. In his hands, he held a small bundle wrapped in a blanket, which River could only assume was Valerie's baby.

"Antonio!" River roared.

The Mafia Boss's Pregnant Bride

Antonio's head shot up, and his black eyes locked with River's. "Hush, Costello. You will wake up the baby."

River blinked in confusion, the adrenaline of the drive and the chaos of the situation crashing to a halt. His eyes darted around the room, searching for Valerie. But she wasn't there.

Ellie gripped River's arm tightly, her eyes wide with shock. "River," she whispered, pulling him back to the present moment.

"What the hell are you doing with my nephew?" River demanded, his voice a harsh whisper as he stepped closer.

Antonio's expression was unexpectedly gentle as he looked down at the infant in his arms. "Holding him."

"Why?" River asked.

"Because babies need to be held. It's science. Something about needing skin-to-skin contact, etcetera, etcetera. I read it on Goo*le," Antonio said dryly.

The absurdity of the situation momentarily stunned River into silence. Antonio Costello, his enemy, was standing in a hospital room cradling a newborn and citing Google as his source for childcare advice.

River took a deep breath, trying to calm the raging storm inside him. "Where is Valerie?" he asked, his voice still tense.

Antonio nodded towards a door at the side of the room. "She's in there. The nurses are taking care of her because she passed out. But don't worry, she is stable. She was just dehydrated. Didn't you give your sister water at your house, Foster?"

River glanced at Ellie, who was still holding onto his arm. Her expression was nothing short of amusement. Reluctantly, she moved toward Antonio.

"Can I hold him?" she asked, extending her arms.

Antonio hesitated for a moment before carefully placing the baby into her arms.

As soon as Ellie held the baby, her face softened with awe and tenderness. The baby gurgled softly, her tiny fists waving in the air.

"He is so adorable," Ellie whispered, her eyes misting over as she gazed down at the newborn.

River stepped closer, his heart finally starting to calm as he looked at the baby. He had pitch-black hair and big brown eyes with a hint of green in them.

"He is quite beautiful. Hopefully, he won't have her father's ugly mug when he grows up. I'd rather not have my son grow up looking like that Russian sleazebag," Antonio declared.

River slowly turned to him. "Excuse me. Did you say your

son?"

Antonio shook his head vigorously, a grin spreading across his face. "Si. I …may have accidentally signed the birth certificate."

"What the actual fuck!?" River exclaimed.

"Hush, I prefer you didn't curse in front of my son," Antonio said.

Would it be so terrible to shoot this bastard right here? River wondered.

Five

You are NOT the Father

~~~∽༶∾~~~

Ellie Foster stared at Antonio Costello and then back at her husband. Antonio and River had been rivals for a while now, and she knew River was itching to kill him right now. Or at least, badly hurt him. But unfortunately, he had his sister and her newborn baby to think about.

But did Antonio just say he signed Valerie's baby's birth certificate?

Ellie's eyes widened, and she instinctively tightened her hold on the baby. "What do you mean, accidentally?" she asked, her voice a mix of incredulity and disbelief.

Antonio shrugged nonchalantly, the grin still plastered on his face. "When Valerie was being rushed in, there was a lot of confusion. The nurses asked me to fill out some forms, and I…well, I might have put my name down as the father." He glanced at me, his expression oddly proud. "So, it seems I am now officially the father of this adorable bambino."

Ellie was speechless, and River looked like his anger was momentarily eclipsed by sheer shock. "You…you can't just do that," River stammered. "That's not how parenting works!"

Antonio raised an eyebrow, his demeanor suddenly serious. "Relax, Foster."

"Don't tell me to relax, asshole!" River growled. "Get the doctor in here and fix this mess right now!"

But Antonio dismissed River's anger with a dismissive wave of his hand. "Why the fuss, Foster? The deed is done. And let's be honest, I'm a far more respectable figure than that pitiful excuse for a father Julian could've been."

Both Ellie and River stood dumbfounded, staring at his nonchalant posture as he leaned against the wall with his arms crossed over his chest. Ellie knew River had half a mind to punch that smug grin off his face. But he knew better than to start a fight in the hospital.

"Respectable?" River repeated incredulously. "Antonio, your history of trouble is longer than your family's lineage!"

He snorted at this, still looking oddly amused by the whole situation. "At least I am here, Foster. I didn't choose the fatherhood. The fatherhood chose me."

River moved forward, and Ellie could tell he was planning to hit Antonio.

"River, don't," Ellie warned, her voice tense with apprehension.

It was at this point that the doctor finally arrived. Clearly unaware of the tension in the room, he glanced between Antonio and River.

"Is everything okay in here?" he asked, his professional demeanor at odds with the awkward atmosphere.

"No," River stated firmly before Antonio could interject. "There has been a mistake. This man is not the father of the baby."

"Sure I am," Antonio interrupted, stepping closer. "How is the mother doing?"

"Yes, is Val awake?" Ellie asked anxiously as she cradled the baby boy.

The doctor looked at everyone, clearly perplexed by the tension in the room. "Valerie is stable and awake," he said, addressing Ellie. "She did very well considering the circumstances. She'll need to stay hydrated and get some rest. She is requesting to see the baby now."

"Yes, of course. Let's go," Ellie said.

Antonio nodded before he turned his attention back to River. "See, Foster? Everything is fine."

"No, everything is not fine," River shot back, stepping closer to Antonio. "You need to get your name off that birth certificate. Because once Valerie finds out what you did, even I wouldn't be able to save you from her."

"Please, let's not keep fighting," Ellie warned. "Valerie must be waiting."

River and Antonio began to argue in hushed tones, but Ellie was determined to keep the peace and prevent any further escalation.

With a deep breath, she stepped between them and placed a calming hand on each man's shoulder.

As they approached Valerie's room, the atmosphere in the hospital hallway seemed to lighten, and the tension that had been palpable just moments before began to dissipate.

Ellie let the nurse take the baby first then motioned to River and Antonio that it was time to see Valerie.

The doctor had managed to secure the privacy of the room, and as the door opened, a small gasp of surprise escaped Valerie when she saw them.

Six

His Dad

Valerie's eyes flickered open. Blurry ceiling tiles came into focus above her, and the sharp scent of antiseptic burned her nose. Where was he? Where was her son?

She heard his faint cry before she passed out, so she knew he was alive.

She craned her neck, peering around the small hospital room. Empty. Panic bubbled in her chest. Where was her son!?

"Nurse!" Her throat was raw. She winced, swallowing hard. "Where's my baby?"

A woman in pink scrubs hurried to Valerie's bedside. "Please try to relax, Miss Foster."

"Relax?" Valerie rasped. "How can I relax? Where is he?"

"Oh god, did something happen to him? But the doctor said he was healthy when they checked last time. Is he okay?" Valerie breathed.

The nurse checked Valerie's IV, avoiding her gaze. "The baby is perfectly healthy. He is in the nursery with his dad."

His dad?

"My baby doesn't have a dad," Val said.

Heck…he didn't even have a name yet.

I want to see him," Valerie struggled to sit up, clutching the thin blanket. "Bring me my baby. Now."

"I understand you're eager to meet your son, but you need to rest," the nurse said firmly, laying a hand on Valerie's shoulder and gently pushing her back down. "You just gave birth. Your body has been through a trauma. If you don't allow yourself adequate recovery time, it could be dangerous for both you and the baby."

Valerie batted the nurse's hand away. "If you don't bring me my baby right now, I'll get out of this bed and find him myself."

The nurse's lips thinned into a disapproving line. "Threatening to put your health at risk will not help matters." She

His Dad

checked Valerie's IV again. "But… I'll speak to your doctor about moving the baby to your room."

Valerie sank back against the pillows, clutching her blanket until her knuckles turned white. Any moment now, she would hold her baby in her arms.

Her heart hammered as she waited, counting each second that ticked by on the clock. Where were they? Had something gone wrong? No, she couldn't think like that. Her baby was fine. He had to be.

At last, the door creaked open. A nurse peeked in, an impish grin on her face. "Someone's here to see his mommy."

Valerie lurched forward, her arms already reaching out. The nurse stepped aside, revealing the rolling bassinet behind her. There, swaddled in a blue blanket, was the most beautiful creature Valerie had ever seen.

Her baby boy.

Tears welled in Valerie's eyes as the nurse brought the bassinet closer. She ran a gentle finger over the soft curve of her baby's cheek.

What should I call you? Valerie thought to herself.

The baby squirmed, blinking open his brown eyes, though Valerie had a feeling they would turn green as he grew older. A feather-soft whimper escaped his lips.

"Here now, none of that," Valerie whispered lovingly. She lifted him into her arms, settling him against her chest. The warmth and weight felt so right, as if he was made to fit there, as if he had always belonged there.

"My baby. My son," Valerie murmured, overwhelmed with emotion. "You are perfect. Wait until you come home. I will love you so much. And your uncle and auntie will be too. Your cousins can't wait to see you, did you know that?" she said, her voice filled with bliss.

The baby yawned, nuzzling closer. A surge of love and protectiveness swept through Valerie, fierce and all-encompassing. She would do anything for this tiny life, face any challenge to keep him safe.

Valerie brushed a light kiss over his forehead, breathing in her sweet scent. "Hello, my darling," she whispered tenderly. "I'm your mommy. And I will never leave you."

The newborn let out a contented sigh, his eyes drifting shut. Valerie held him close, marveling at how love could grow and bloom so swiftly. In that quiet, perfect moment, it felt as though they were the only two people in the world.

The moment was interrupted when Ellie and River burst through the door, their faces glowing with joy. Ellie rushed to Valerie's side, River close behind.

"Oh, Valerie," Ellie said, breathless. "You did so great."

His Dad

Valerie gazed down at the sleeping angel in her arms, a smile curving her lips.

"He is perfect," Valerie whispered. "Absolutely perfect."

River smiled warmly. "Yes, he is."

Valerie's heart swelled at the sight of them. Surrounded by love, her darling boy would never want for anything. He was the luckiest baby in the world—and so was Valerie.

A small part of Valerie felt a twinge of sadness, knowing her son would grow up without a father. But a larger part of her was relieved that Julian was no longer in the picture.

"Where is Lucas and Tiffany?" Valerie asked Ellie suddenly.

"I left them with Molly. I thought it would be safer for them. They are every excited to meet their cousin soon," River replied with a smile. "By the way, what will you name him? Most mother would already decide on a name BEFORE the baby is born you know." He chuckled heartily.

"Hmmm...I always liked the name Landon," Val said.

"Landon Foster, I like it," Ellie agreed.

"You mean, Landon Costello," a deep voice interrupted.

Valerie's heart jumped at that. A familiar figure sauntered into the room. It was Antonio.

"Why are you still here?" Valerie blurted out, embarrassment flooding her cheeks at the memory of Antonio in the delivery room, comforting her and even kissing her forehead.

Did he really kiss her? Or was that her imagination?

And did he just attach his own last name to her baby?

Antonio's smirk widened as his gaze settled on the baby. "Well, well. You're finally reunited with the little one."

Valerie grunted in response. "Seriously, Antonio. Why are you still here?"

Antonio raised his hands in mock surrender. "Such hostility! I brought you here safe and sound, and this is how you treat me?"

Valerie softened slightly. "Okay, yes. I appreciate you getting me here on time. And for helping in the delivery room," she admitted, her cheeks flushing again at the memory. "But you can leave now. I don't have your damn codes, and now is not the time to talk about it."

"Ah, yes. We can discuss the codes another day," Antonio agreed with a nod.

"Then you should just leave," Valerie insisted.

River cleared his throat awkwardly. "Do you want to tell her, Antonio, or should I?"

His Dad

Valerie looked at River in confusion and then back at Antonio. "Tell me what?"

Seven

I am Not Joking

Antonio's smirk faltered for a moment as he glanced at River. "Well, Cara," he began, rubbing the back of his neck awkwardly. At that moment, with that stupid expression on his face, he almost looked like a little boy who had done something wrong.

"What is it?" Valerie asked, feeling dread pulling in her stomach as she imagined the worst. Why did he look so guilty?

"There was a bit of a mix-up with the paperwork when you were rushed in. A… uh… misunderstanding." He hesitated.

Valerie frowned, her gaze shifting between the two men. "What kind of misunderstanding?"

I am Not Joking

River took a deep breath and stepped forward. "Antonio...he signed the birth certificate as the baby's father."

Val stared at the two men, uncomprehending. "He...WHAT?" she cried when she realized what was said, then quickly lowered her voice, remembering she was at the hospital. "I don't understand," she hissed.

"By accident," Antonio interjected quickly. "There was confusion, and the nurses needed the forms filled out. So, I may have signed my name where Julian's should have been. You know...on those dotted lines where it says father's signature?" He explained as if speaking to a five-year-old.

Valerie blinked. "You signed as his father?"

"Si. But I mean, not like Julian could sign. He is dead," Antonio reminded her.

Her heart pounded in her chest, a mix of anger and bewilderment surging through her. "You signed the birth certificate? My son's birth certificate?" she repeated, unable to believe what she was hearing.

"Si," he said again without a hint of guilt on his face.

Was this some kind of sick joke?

"Valerie," River said softly, stepping closer. "I know this is a lot to take in, but right now, the most important thing is that you and Landon are both safe and healthy. We'll sort out the paperwork. I promise."

But Valerie wasn't paying any attention to River. "Antonio. Y-you...are you an idiot!?"

"Oh, come on, Bella. You don't need to be rude," Antonio almost looked sad as he scratched the side of his face where his scar was.

If she wasn't holding a newborn, Valerie probably would have jumped out of the bed and kicked him in his family jewels. That would teach him! She couldn't believe how dismissive he was being about something so important. This wasn't just some random mistake – it involved her son's legal identity.

"Fix it right now!" Valerie said through gritted teeth.

Antonio raised an eyebrow. "Fix it? I don't know if I could."

"Why not?" she asked.

"Because I find that I rather like being Landon's accidental father," Antonio declared.

Ehh?

"Antonio, this is not a joke," Valerie snapped, her hands tightening around Landon.

"I'm not joking, mia cara," he replied, his dark eyes locked on hers. "I may have signed the birth certificate by accident, but

I am Not Joking

that doesn't change the fact that I am now Landon's father in the eyes of the law. And honestly, I don't hate it." He smiled innocently.

Well…as innocent as he could with that terrifying face of his.

Valerie couldn't believe what she was hearing. Was Antonio actually serious? Did he think this was some kind of game?

"I don't want you to be my son's father!" she exclaimed, her voice trembling with anger and disbelief.

"Valerie, calm down," Ellie said soothingly, placing a hand on her shoulder. "You are still weak."

"The boy doesn't have a real father," Antonio stated the obvious.

"That's because YOU killed his real father, jackass," Valerie hissed. She shivered at the memory of Antonio's men swarming inside Julian's club and open firing. Luckily, she was spared because she was at home stuffing her face with potato chips. "Did you think I'd just forgive you for that?" she barked.

Part of her was relieved that Julian wasn't alive to raise Landon, but Antonio didn't need to know that…

Antonio waved his hand dismissively. "I didn't kill him with my own hands. One of my men got overexcited. Anyway, it's neither here nor there. What's important now is that Landon needs a father, and I'm available. I have no children, and my name is attached to him now."

"Hang on a moment. Are you trying to adopt my nephew, Antonio? You got to be fucking kidding me," River growled.

Oh, thank god. At least River was still thinking clearly.

"I'm not joking," Antonio repeated, crossing his arms over his chest. "I can be a good father to Landon."

River snorted in disbelief. "You think being a kingpin makes you father material?"

"I have resources. I can offer her protection that no one else can," Antonio shot back. "And you are no better than me, Foster. So are you saying you won't be a good father either?"

River opened his mouth and then closed it.

"That's beside the point!" Valerie screamed, finally finding her voice again. "I am his mother! I get to decide who gets to be a part of his life!"

"Why, of course, mi amore," Antonio nodded. "No one is trying to take your baby from you. What I am suggesting is that…" He paused and smiled at her sheepishly.

Something told Valerie he was up to no good. "What are you suggesting?" she breathed.

I am Not Joking

His smirk widened. "I am suggesting that we get married."

For a moment, all she could do was stare at him, her anger replaced by sheer disbelief. Then she did the only thing that seemed logical at the time—she burst into laughter.

She couldn't stop laughing. Her sides hurt, her vision blurred with tears, and there were spots in front of her eyes. What a crazy, outrageous proposition!

Antonio was staring at her without saying anything, his lips curled up in an amused smile.

"Are you serious?" Ellie asked, as shocked as Valerie was.

"Yes," Antonio answered, his smirk never wavering. "I am as serious as a heart attack."

"Have you lost your damn mind?!" River exploded, making a grab for Antonio's collar, but Ellie held him back.

"You can't ask her to marry you," Ellie stated harshly, her eyes narrowed at Antonio.

"And why not?" Antonio retorted. "I mean, I suppose she could just come and live with me, but I'm a traditional man with traditional family values. If I am to make the boy my adoptive son, his mom should be my wife."

This man was insane.

"I won't let you marry my sister," River growled.

"Why ever not?" Antonio raised an eyebrow.

"Because you're my enemy!" River bellowed. "You're not fit to be a dog's parent, let alone a human's!"

"Oh, come on, Foster, you make it sound like I'm some kind of monster," Antonio chuckled darkly. "And we aren't exactly enemies. We just didn't have the chance to get to know each other. But don't worry. We will have plenty of chance once I become your brother-in-law."

River looked at Ellie. "Are you sure I shouldn't kill him here?"

Antonio ignored River and looked at Valerie. "How about you tell me your answer, yeah?"

"I...I..." Valerie's mind was spinning, and she felt dizzy with everything that was happening, but one thing was clear—there was no way in hell that she was marrying Antonio Costello.

Eight

I won't Marry You

E llie Foster didn't know if she should laugh or cry at the whole Valerie and Antonio situation.

This whole situation was absolutely ridiculous. Valerie looked at Antonio like she wanted to tear his dick off, but Antonio still stood there with a smug expression on his face.

And River…he was livid. Ellie stayed on guard in case River decided to make the hospital room into a battleground.

Oh boy.

"No," Valerie said. Ellie could tell she was trying to make her voice as steady and firm as possible, but it wavered slightly.

"I won't marry you, Antonio."

He cocked his head. "You sure?"

"I am sure."

"Well, that's a shame," Antonio murmured, feigning disappointment. His devilish grin never faded. "It would have been such an entertaining spectacle."

"You're one sick man, Costello," River growled, his hands balled into fists at his sides. "Do you think relationships are games?"

Ignoring River's comment, Antonio sauntered over to Valerie's hospital bed and looked down at Landon, who was sleeping peacefully in her arms. "He is an adorable fella," he said in a strangely sincere tone. He reached out his arms as if to hold Landon. "May I…"

"Stay away from my son!" Valerie exclaimed, instinctively hugging Landon closer to her chest.

Antonio chuckled at her defensive reaction and slowly backed away. "Don't worry," he quipped. "I'm not here to steal your baby boy. But my offer still stands."

"And I am still not interested," Valerie snapped.

"Then I suppose I should take my leave now. Goodbye, my Bella."

I won't Marry You

With one last smirk, Antonio made his way to the room's door. But right before he stepped out, he turned around and said with a playful wink, "I will call you tomorrow when you are more…stable."

Valerie made an odd squeaking sound as if the air was sucked out of her lungs.

With a final wave of his hand, he walked out of the room, leaving behind a stunned silence. River was the first to regain his senses and rushed towards the door, intending to chase after Antonio.

"I'm going after him," River declared with a stern set on his face.

"No." Ellie stopped him again.

"But Elle…" River began.

"No buts, River!" Ellie shot back. "We need to focus on Valerie and Landon right now. You can deal with Antonio another time."

River gave Valerie an apologetic look before resigning himself next to Ellie.

"Yeah, you are right. This is not the time or place," he said.

Suddenly, the room felt full again, full of warmth and joy despite what had just unfolded, thanks to Antonio's outrageous antics.

Valerie sighed, a mixture of relief and exhaustion washing over her. "I can't believe Antonio signed the birth certificate. And then proposed! That man needs some serious psychiatric help."

Or maybe he just needed a wife, Ellie thought.

"We'll get it sorted out," Ellie assured her. "River will take care of it, won't you, honey?"

River nodded, though his eyes still flickered with residual anger. "Absolutely. First thing tomorrow, I'll speak with the hospital administration and make sure everything is corrected," he declared.

"He is such a strange man," Ellie said absentmindedly.

That man almost sounded genuine when he said he wanted to be Landon's father. But that couldn't be right. Why would a man like Antonio want to raise a stranger's son? Ellie thought to herself.

Valerie sighed again, leaning back against her pillows. "I just want everything to be normal. I want Landon to have a stable life, free from all this craziness."

"We'll make sure of it," Ellie said firmly, squeezing her hand. "We're here for you every step of the way."

I won't Marry You

The room fell into a comfortable silence, each of them lost in their thoughts. Landon stirred in Valerie's arms, letting out a tiny sigh before settling back into his peaceful sleep. The sight of the newborn brought a sense of calm and hope to the room, a reminder of the love and support surrounding them.

River cleared his throat, breaking the silence. "I will go and discharge you so we can go home."

Valerie looked up, gratitude shining in her eyes. "Thank you, River. I just want to take Landon home and start our life together."

River smiled softly, brushing a hand through his hair. "We'll get you both home soon. Just sit tight."

As River stepped out to handle the discharge paperwork, Ellie sat down on the chair by the bed. "I'd have to admit, Valerie. When I arrived here, I didn't expect to see an Italian don cradling your son in his arms and declaring him as his adoptive son." Ellie giggled. "You have to admit, the situation is kind of funny and…adorable."

Valerie snorted. "Adorable? God…it's the most ridiculous thing I've experienced. What is wrong with that man anyway?"

"It's kind of sweet, though. Don't you think?" Ellie asked. "Him offering to be Landon's father I mean. Some men disappear because they don't want to be responsible for a child but he is trying to do the opposite. But I will say that the marriage proposal was insane." Ellie chuckled.

"Yes," Valerie said, suddenly going quiet.

"River did mention that the man is kind of…eccentric," Ellie continued, shaking her head with a chuckle.

"I guess so," Valerie said, a small smile tugging at her lips. "I suppose I shouldn't be surprised by anything anymore."

"At least we can look back and laugh about it someday," Ellie said, trying to lighten the mood. "One day, this will just be a crazy story we tell Landon."

"That a scar-faced Italian Don proposed to me right here at this hospital bed? He would never believe me." She laughed.

Ellie wrinkled her forehead. "How do you think he got that scar on his face? It looks pretty serious. Nearly covers half of his face."

Valerie shrugged. "He is in the Mafia, Ellie. He could've gotten it from an enemy. Maybe he was stabbed there. River has quite a bit of scars on his body, too, right?"

"Yes, but not like that," Ellie said.

"Julian also donned some scars. But I guess not like Antonio either," Valerie said thoughtfully.

I won't Marry You

Ellie frowned at the mention of Julian's name. Ever since Valerie moved in with them, she often wondered about him. Valerie told them about him but never in detail. She hardly ever mentioned his name unless someone asked. And if Antonio's men killed Julian, how come Valerie wasn't more hostile toward Antonio? Didn't Valerie love Julian? The father of her child? Ellie wondered.

She was curious but now was hardly the time to ask Valerie about that. Her thoughts were interrupted when River returned with a triumphant look on his face. "Alright, everything is set. You're officially discharged."

"Thank you, River," Valerie said, her relief palpable.

"Let's get you home," Ellie said.

Nine

The Baby isn't Mine

T he floorboards creaked under Antonio's feet as he paced back and forth in his room, unable to shake the feeling of confusion and disbelief. Valerie Foster had rejected him—at the hospital of all places, right after she gave birth to their child.

Okay…the baby wasn't actually his, but so what? His name was attached to him now, accidental or not. He was his son now. Because he had already claimed him to be!

"Can you believe this?" Antonio muttered to himself, throwing his hands up in the air. His heart raced with anger and frustration. And a bit of sadness. "I offered to make her son legitimate. And she just…rejected me."

The Baby isn't Mine

He couldn't comprehend it. The pieces weren't fitting together in his head. How could she turn down such a generous offer? It felt like a slap in the face.

He had never wanted to get married and had never cared about having children, but he had thrown himself out there. For her.

"Unacceptable!" he growled under his breath, clenching his fists at his sides.

"Bene," Antonio said aloud, determination coursing through him. "I won't give up just yet."

He believed that once Valerie was back at his brother's house and feeling healthier, she might have a change of heart about his proposal.

"Maybe she was just scared," he reasoned, trying to understand what had gone wrong. "She needs time to adjust."

He thought back to the hospital when he first held the baby in his arms. The warmth of his tiny body, his small fingers curling around his—it was a feeling he couldn't describe. A sense of fatherhood washed over him, solidifying his love for this child. He hadn't even known he was capable of such feelings.

Strange concept…love was. He had never thought he'd love something, let alone someone. He hadn't even known what love was until…

Until he held that tiny human in his arms. As soon as the baby opened his eyes to look at him and gave him that tiny smile, he knew…he knew what love meant.

"See?" Antonio murmured to himself, picturing the moment vividly in his mind. "I can be a good dad. Valerie just needs to see that."

"Who're you talking to?" a voice cut through his thoughts, making him jump.

"Jesus, Sam!" Antonio exclaimed, turning toward his right-hand man, who had snuck into the room without him noticing. "Don't sneak up on me. I could've shot you in the face!"

"Sorry, Capo," Sam grinned sheepishly. "But seriously, what's going on? You've been acting weird ever since you came back from the hospital."

"Nothing," Antonio said grimly. "What news do you have for me?"

Sam gave him a rundown of how his businesses were going, but Antonio barely listened. His mind was occupied with thoughts of the child and the mother. He had proposed to Valerie Blackwood on a whim so he wouldn't have to let the child go, but now that he thought about it, he wouldn't mind having her as his wife either.

She had a fiery attitude that matched the color of her hair

and those intense green eyes that seemed to pierce into his soul. And her lips…those full pink lips…

He wanted to bite them.

"Enough," he muttered to himself, trying to stop daydreaming.

To distract himself, he decided to go check on his grandmother. She had raised him and was the only living relative he had left. No one could understand him better than her.

"Nonna?" he called out, turning the corner to find her sitting in a cozy armchair. Her fingers worked nimbly, knitting a small scarf of some sort.

"Ah, Toni, my darling," she smiled gently, her eyes twinkling behind her glasses. "You look troubled, nipotino. What's on your mind?"

"Nonna, I need your advice," Antonio said, his voice cracking slightly. "Valerie…she rejected my proposal."

Her eyes crinkled in confusion. "Valerie? Who is that?"

Right…he should've started from the beginning.

Antonio took a deep breath and sat down on the floor beside his Nonna's chair. She continued knitting, her needles clicking rhythmically, a comforting sound that had always soothed him as a child.

"Nonna, there's this woman… Valerie. She just had a baby, and there was a mix-up with the paperwork at the hospital. My name ended up on the birth certificate as the father."

His grandmother's eyebrows shot up, but she didn't interrupt. He continued, "I thought it would be a good idea to propose to her, to make things right, you know? But she turned me down."

Nonna paused her knitting, her sharp eyes studying him. "Toni, amore mio, you can't force someone to marry you, especially not in such a situation. And you say the baby isn't yours?"

"The baby isn't mine," he replied.

"Then why do you want to adopt it, amore mio?" she asked, confusion evident on her face.

He shifted uncomfortably. "I… I don't know, Nonna. When I held the baby in my arms, I felt something I'd never felt before. A sense of responsibility, maybe even love. But…"

She put her knitting aside and reached out to cup his face with her wrinkled hands. "Toni, you have a good heart. But love isn't something you can rush or force."

"Hmph…"

"Sometimes, Antonio, life doesn't go as planned," Nonna continued softly, resuming her knitting. "But if your intentions

The Baby isn't Mine

are pure, then perhaps this Valerie will come around."

Antonio's mind wandered back to the moment in the hospital, holding the baby girl and feeling her tiny fingers curl around his. He smiled. "Yes, you are right."

"Of course I am right," she nodded, her eyes never leaving her work. "Just remember, love takes time and patience. Don't force it."

"Grazie, Nonna," he whispered, his heart swelling with gratitude. He knew what he had to do now.

She finally looked up from her knitting, a small smile teasing her lips. "Now, Toni. Care to tell me how you came to sign the birth certificate by accident?"

Ten

Silly Man

"It's raining," Valerie whispered to Landon as she stared out the window.

It had been three days since she had brought Landon back home. Lucas and Tiffany were overjoyed to see their cousin, and they were eager to help her put Landon to sleep or tell him stories that they had just heard from their mom.

The house felt warmer with the sound of the kids' laughter and Landon's tiny coos. Despite the storm outside, there was a sense of peace within these walls.

Valerie glanced down at Landon, his tiny hand curled around her finger. "Your cousins are quite the storytellers, you know," she murmured, smiling. "We are going to be very happy here."

Silly Man

As if understanding her words, Landon gave a little yawn and closed his eyes, drifting off to sleep. Valerie gently placed him in his crib, tucking him in snugly. Standing there, watching him sleep, she felt a mix of overwhelming love and fierce protectiveness. Landon was her world now, and she would do anything to keep him safe.

The past few days had been a whirlwind. Antonio's unexpected proposal still lingered in her mind. Why would he, a man with no apparent ties to them, want to claim her son as his own?

Silly man...

A soft knock on the door pulled Valerie from her thoughts. "Come in," she called softly, not wanting to wake Landon.

Ellie stepped in, her face lit with a warm smile. "How are you holding up, Valerie?"

Valerie sighed, running a hand through her hair. "I'm managing. What did River say about the birth certificate? Can he take Antonio's name off of it?"

Ellie walked over to her, her expression turning serious. "River's been working on it. He spoke with the hospital administration, but it's going to take some time. Apparently, there's a lot of paperwork involved, and they'll need to verify the details before they can make any changes."

Valerie let out a frustrated sigh. "This is such a mess. I never wanted any of this confusion for Landon."

"I know," Ellie said, placing a comforting hand on Valerie's shoulder. "But we'll get through it. River is determined to fix this, and we'll make sure everything is set right for Landon."

Valerie nodded, grateful for Ellie's reassurance but still feeling the weight of the situation. "It's just hard to understand why Antonio would do something like this. It doesn't make any sense."

Ellie gave her a sympathetic look. "People can be unpredictable, Valerie. Antonio might have his reasons, even if we can't see them right now. Maybe he feels some kind of responsibility or connection."

"Responsibility?" Valerie scoffed softly. "He barely knows me, and he certainly doesn't know Landon."

"Maybe he sees something in you," Ellie suggested gently. "Something worth protecting. Or maybe he's just an odd man." Ellie grinned.

Valerie grinned back. "I'd go with the second reason."

Someone tapped at the door, and they both turned to look. Molly was standing there with a big smile on her face.

"Someone sent you some presents, Miss Valerie. And for Landon, too," she said.

Silly Man

Valerie raised an eyebrow. "Presents? From whom?"

Molly shrugged. "They are in the living room."

Valerie and Ellie exchanged glances before heading there. Ellie let out a small gasp as Valerie stared at the grand display in front of them. The room was filled with beautifully wrapped boxes of all shapes and sizes, accompanied by a stunning bouquet of freshly cut flowers.

Among the gifts were a few custom-made plush toys, but the most impressive was a handcrafted wooden crib that showed great skill and care in its creation.

Ellie picked up a card that was nestled among the gifts and read it aloud: "For my new son and the fiery woman who birthed her. - A"

"Antonio," Valerie muttered, shaking her head. "Who else would it be?"

Ellie looked at Valerie with a mix of curiosity and amusement. "Who else, indeed?" Ellie said, setting the card down. "This is... quite the display. He really doesn't hold back, does he?"

Valerie walked over to the handcrafted crib, running her fingers along the smooth wood. It was beautiful, and the attention to detail was astonishing. She could feel the care that had gone into making it. "This must have cost a fortune," she murmured, her mind reeling. "Why would he do this?"

Ellie shrugged, a thoughtful look on her face. "Maybe he thinks this is his way of showing he cares. Or maybe he's trying to prove something to himself—or to you."

Valerie sighed, feeling a mix of gratitude and frustration. "I just don't know what to think."

Lucas bounced into the room right then, his eyes widening at the sight of the gifts. "Wow! Presents!"

Valerie smiled at his excitement. "Yes, Lucas. These are gifts from someone who wants to make sure Landon has everything he needs."

Lucas picked up one of the plush toys and hugged it. "Can I give this to Landon?"

"Of course," Valerie replied, watching him hurry to the nursery. The sight of Lucas caring for his cousin brought a sense of warmth to her heart.

As she continued to look at the gifts, her thoughts turned back to Antonio. His actions were generous, but they also felt like a way to insert himself into their lives. She needed to understand his true intentions.

"Look at this one," Ellie said, holding a box.

Valerie looked at the white box wrapped in a pink lacey bow.

"It has your name. A special present just for you," Ellie

Silly Man

said, her eyes twinkling mischievously. Valerie had a sneaky suspicion she was secretly enjoying this.

"Go on, open it," Ellie urged, her eyes gleaming with curiosity.

Valerie hesitated for a moment, her gaze fixed on the box. It was a gift from Antonio, a man she barely knew, and yet it felt strangely personal and….intimate. The curiosity that had been building inside her won over, and she found herself intrigued, unable to resist the urge to uncover its secrets. Taking a deep breath, she untied the pink bow and carefully removed the wrapping paper.

"Oh," Valerie whispered, lifting a delicate, beautifully crafted dress from the box.

"Wow!" Ellie breathed when Valerie held the dress in front of her to show her.

It was a stunning piece, made of soft, flowing fabric in a deep shade of emerald green that matched Valerie's eyes. The dress was elegant and sophisticated, with intricate lace detailing and a fitted waist that flared out into a graceful skirt. It was the kind of dress that made someone feel special just by looking at it.

"Valerie, it's gorgeous," Ellie said, her voice filled with admiration. "He has great taste."

"Why," Valerie mumbled. "Why did he send me this?"

Ellie's expression shifted, a hint of uncertainty in her eyes. "Maybe he's trying to make an impression, or maybe he wants to show you he cares. Whatever the reason, it's clear he put a lot of thought into this."

Valerie sighed, running her fingers over the delicate lace. "He doesn't care about me. That's just ludicrous. He is doing this to get those codes out of me even though I told him I don't have them."

Ellie looked skeptical. "He is making this grand gesture just for some secret numbers? Seems unlikely."

"I don't know, Ellie. But I am going to find out," Valerie said.

Eleven

Let Me Handle It

River's voice thundered through the room. "Absolutely not!"

"River," Ellie started, placing a hand on his arm, but he glared at her before turning back to Valerie.

"Under no circumstances do you need to be seeing Antonio again," he insisted.

Valerie took a deep breath, trying to remain calm in the face of her brother's anger. "River, I understand your concern, but we need to sort out what Antonio wants from me. We never got to put that whole Julian thing to rest because I went into labor!" she exclaimed.

"You have bigger things to worry about now, Valerie. I will set

The Mafia Boss's Pregnant Bride

things straight with Antonio Costello. All you need to worry about now is being a mother to your son," River argued.

"And what if he won't stop, River? What if ignoring him just makes things worse?" Valerie asked, frustration seeping into her voice. "We can't pretend he doesn't exist. He has already intruded into our lives, and we need to know what he really wants."

"Valerie, you're not dealing with an ordinary man," River said, his tone softening but still firm. "Antonio is dangerous, and I don't want you or my nephew anywhere near him. Let me handle this."

"No, River," Valerie said firmly. "I am used to dealing with men like this, so let me figure this out. If he wanted to hurt me, he would've already, but he didn't," she said.

River's jaw tightened, and for a moment, it seemed like he might continue to argue, but then he took a deep breath, his shoulders relaxing just slightly. "Valerie, I know you're strong. But this isn't just about you anymore. It's about Landon. You have to be careful."

"I will be careful," Valerie promised, her voice steady. "But I can't just ignore this. We need answers, and the only way to get them is to confront Antonio myself."

Ellie, who had been quietly observing, spoke up. "River, maybe we should trust Valerie on this. She knows what she's doing, and we can support her while still keeping Landon safe."

River looked between Ellie and Valerie, his expression a mix of frustration and reluctant acceptance. Finally, he nodded. "Alright, Val. We'll do it your way."

"Thank you, River," Valerie said, feeling a wave of relief.

She quickly left the room, her heart pounding in her chest. As much as she wanted to assure River that everything would be fine, she was scared, not for herself, but for Landon. He was her world now, and the thought of putting him in danger made her blood run cold.

Valerie went inside Landon's room. The room was filled with an array of presents Antonio had sent over. Molly had moved them in here, and Valerie hadn't had the chance to look through them until now. She walked over to Landon's crib and looked down at his peaceful, sleeping face. The sight of his tiny chest rising and falling with each breath filled Valerie with a sense of happiness.

Taking a deep breath, Valerie began to sort through the gifts. There were bags of baby clothes, diapers, and pretty much everything she'd ever need for Landon. Her focus went to the handcrafted crib. It was a beautiful piece of work, meticulously detailed. There was something personal about it, almost as if Antonio was trying to make a statement beyond mere generosity.

As she sifted through the gifts, Valerie found a small, unmarked envelope tucked away under the crib's mattress. Her heart skipped a beat as she opened it and pulled out a neatly folded letter. The handwriting on it was elegant, and she read the words carefully:

Bella, I understand that my actions might seem intrusive, and for that, I apologize. But know this: this is not a game. Antonio.

That was it. That was all he wrote. Valerie thought the man was weird.

Just then, she heard a soft knock on the door. She turned to see her fourteen-year-old niece Tiffany standing there, her eyes wide and curious. "Aunty Val, what are you doing?"

Valerie forced a smile. "I was just thinking."

Tiffany walked over and looked at her. "Thinking about what?"

Valerie quickly folded the letter and put it back in the envelope, setting it aside before turning her full attention to Tiffany. "Just thinking about how lucky I am to have all of you and Landon," she said, reaching out, tugged at her braid.

Tiffany's face lit up with innocence, her eyes sparkling. "Can I help with sorting the presents?" she asked eagerly.

"Of course," Valerie replied, her heart warming at her eagerness. She looked at Tiffany carefully. This girl had grown so

Let Me Handle It

beautiful. River and Ellie needed to make sure they keep a close eye on her. "Let's see what else is in these boxes."

As Tiffany and Valerie explored the gifts together, she couldn't help but marvel at the sheer quantity and quality of the items Antonio had sent. A part of her felt uncomfortable accepting so much from someone she barely knew, especially when that someone was technically her enemy.

Well...not her enemy, per se. More like Julian's enemy, Valerie thought.

Tiffany held up a stuffed bunny. "Look at this one. Doesn't he have a funny face, aunty Val?"

Valerie giggled. "I guess he does."

Valerie turned back to the gifts, and her thoughts returned to the meeting with Antonio. What would she say to him? Should she thank him for the gifts? Or should she yell at him for inserting himself into her life?

And that dress...what was that all about?

Later that evening, after putting Landon to bed, Valerie sat in her living room, the small envelope from Antonio resting on the coffee table in front of her. She couldn't shake the feeling that this was just the beginning of something much more complicated.

River and Ellie joined her, their expressions reflecting their shared concern. River spoke first, his voice gentle but firm. "Val, are you sure about this? Confronting Antonio on your own?"

Valerie nodded, determination in her eyes. "I need to know what he wants, River. I can't live in fear of the unknown. I'll meet with him and get the answers we need."

Ellie reached out and squeezed Valerie's hand. "We'll support you, whatever you decide. Just be careful, okay?"

Valerie smiled gratefully. "I will, Ellie. Thank you."

Twelve

A Family

"I need you to be honest with me, Antonio," Valerie said.

Antonio sat across from Valerie, his eyes filled with warmth and sincerity. "I will always be honest with you, Amore," he said, a playful grin tugging at the corners of his lips.

Valerie's expression twisted into a scowl, her distaste for endearments evident. "Stop it with the nicknames," she barked.

It was clear that she wouldn't tolerate any form of affectionate language from him, but Antonio found it all the more entertaining to push her buttons. He lifted his arms in mock surrender and offered her an apologetic smile. "I'm sorry," he said, meeting her intense gaze. "But I can't seem to help myself."

Her body grew taut with tension as she glared at him, demanding answers. "What is your game, Antonio? Why are you forcing yourself into my life?"

Antonio leaned in closer, his expression grave as he rested his elbows on his knees. "Would you believe me if I told you that all of this was for the chance to win your affection?" The words hung heavy in the air between them, charged with emotion and sincerity.

Valerie's piercing green eyes narrowed as she stared at him, her gaze intense and unwavering. She was dressed in an oversized white T-shirt that hung loosely over her slim frame, paired with worn stone-washed jeans that hid her beautiful curves. Her simple attire did injustice to her beautiful body, and yet Antonio fought against the raging desire to take her upstairs and ravish her.

"No, I don't believe you. You don't know me, Antonio. And I don't know you. Why would you suddenly want my affection?" Valerie barked, her voice laced with suspicion and confusion. Her words were like a slap in the face, bringing Antonio back to reality and reminding him of the barriers between them.

"My feelings for you are complicated. I do not understand them myself," Antonio said earnestly.

Valerie rolled her eyes. "Spare me the dramatics, Antonio. I

A Family

don't have time for your games."

Antonio let out a long sigh. Porca puttana, women are such complicated creatures! A man pours his heart out, and she refuses to acknowledge him! "Bene! Don't believe me then. Why do YOU think I'm doing it?" he asked sheepishly.

Valerie's gaze bore into him, her features hardening like stone. "I see right through you," she accused. "You're only doing this because you crave control. You want to manipulate me, make me feel indebted to you. Showering me with gifts and barging into my life uninvited, all in hopes of getting what you want from me. Like those codes Julian supposedly left with me."

Antonio's jaw clenched as he fought to keep his temper in check. "Is that so?" he asked coolly.

Her eyes narrowed in determination. "Yes," she said firmly.

"If you truly believe that I have ulterior motives, then why not just give me what I want? The codes, I mean," Antonio challenged. The tension crackled between them like a spark waiting to ignite into a blazing fire.

"Because I don't have it, you bastard!" Valerie cried.

Her cheeks turned a fiery red, and her chest heaved with frustration. With a determined bite of her lower lip, she glared at him with her piercing green eyes. Those eyes looked glittery as if tears would fall at any moment now.

Damn, she was gorgeous in her anger. Antonio's mind wandered to all the things he wanted to do to her. Make love to her every night, have more redheaded babies, maybe name them after pasta dishes...

"Antonio!" Valerie's growling voice brought him back to reality.

"Si?" he asked with a raised eyebrow, trying to keep his cool amidst her passionate outburst. "Sorry, what were you saying?"

"I said...I don't have any codes. I don't know where they are. Julian never gave me anything special other than my son," she said, frowning.

"Ah, I see." Antonio's mood brightened at the mention of Landon. "How's my bambino?"

Valerie blinked. "Your...what?"

"Sorry. It means my little boy in Italian," Antonio explained. "How is my little boy?"

"He is not your little boy," Valerie mumbled, but her voice lacked conviction for some reason.

Antonio leaned forward. "Did he like the presents I sent? Your son?" he asked, his tone gentle and curious.

Valerie's response was laced with irritation as she scrunched

A Family

her nose adorably. "No, he didn't. He is a newborn, after all. He is not old enough to have preferences."

Undeterred by her dismissive attitude, Antonio pressed on. "Well then, did you like the presents I sent for you?"

Valerie took a deep breath and exhaled slowly. "I like them very much. Thank you."

Ah...they were finally getting somewhere. Antonio grinned. "I'm glad to hear that," he replied. "Only the best for my future wife."

"I am not your..." Valerie stopped and groaned as if realizing that arguing with him was pointless. "I appreciate the gifts, I really do. But I can't help you, Antonio. I don't know what Julian did with the codes."

Antonio waved his hands dismissively. "Do not worry about those codes, Amore. I will find them on my own eventually. I won't bother you about them anymore."

Valerie's eyes brightened with a glimmer of hope. "Really? So you will leave us alone?"

Antonio smiled sweetly at her. "I didn't mean that."

Valerie's expression fell, her eyebrows knitting together in confusion. "Then what did you mean?"

Antonio leaned forward, his intense gaze fixed on Valerie.

"What I mean is, I won't constantly hound you about the codes anymore. But that doesn't mean I'm going to vanish from your life, sweetheart. I have my own motivations for wanting to stay involved."

Valerie studied him, her sharp eyes piercing his. "And what could those motivations possibly be?"

Antonio took a moment to choose his words carefully. "Let's just say I have a deep-seated interest in your safety and well-being. And, of course, Landon's as well," he said, hoping she would understand and trust him.

"B…but…why?" Valerie asked, her voice tinged with uncertainty.

Antonio stood up and stalked toward her like a predator approaching his prey. "Because, mia cara," he said, dropping to one knee in front of her and grabbing her hand. "I have grown fond of you."

She only stared, her eyes wide and filled with confusion and curiosity.

Antonio's words were slow and deliberate as he spoke, the weight of his feelings heavy on his tongue. "I care about you," he said, looking deep into Valerie's eyes. "And I care about Landon. Though he may not share my blood, he holds a special place in my heart."

As soon as the words left his lips, he saw the confusion and

A Family

disbelief in Valerie's expression.

"Antonio," she whispered. "I don't understand why. Why would you care about any of us."

He shrugged. "I don't know why either. Maybe it's because I find you intriguing. You challenge me because you're stubborn. Or perhaps it's because you're the most beautiful woman I've ever met, and I want you in my bed and…" He paused dramatically before continuing. "My life."

Valerie blinked up at him. "Are you serious?"

"Si," he said simply. "Something about you draws me in. And I can't resist."

She was silent for a moment as she processed his words. "What do you want me to do?" she asked.

"I want you to go back to your brother's house, collect your things, and move in with me," Antonio declared. "With your son, of course, so we can be a family."

"You are insane," Valerie said, but the stubbornness in her voice was gone.

Antonio offered her a devilish smile. "Yes, I am. My Nonna tells me that sometimes too. That's what I call my grandma, and she raised me like she was my mother. You will love her."

Valerie's eyes looked clouded as if she was in a daze. "A family?

You...me...Landon...your grandmother?"

"Yes," Antonio confirmed. Her breath hitched as he leaned in close, his lips almost touching hers.

Her voice quivered as she asked, "And if I refuse?" Her eyes lifted to meet his, and the tension between them grew palpable.

Antonio lightly brushed his lips over hers. "Then I keep trying until you stop refusing me. I'll do whatever it takes until you're mine," he whispered against her lips, a thrill racing through his body at the thought of making her his.

"And you, Valerie Foster," he continued. "Will eventually be mine."

Thirteen

Men are Great Idiots

Valerie's head was spinning when she returned home. Antonio's words played like a broken record in her mind.

A family. With Antonio?

She laughed out loud at the absurdity of it all. Who did he think he was, her knight in shining armor?

River was waiting for her in the living room, shooting out of his chair as soon as he saw her. Meanwhile, Ellie sat on the couch with her eyes wide open, waiting for the drama to unfold.

"What did that asshole say to you?" River demanded with a growl.

Valerie looked at Ellie. "Sometimes I think men are great idiots," she declared, earning a snort from Ellie.

River's face twisted with confusion and concern. "What do you mean by that, Valerie?"

Valerie shook her head, trying to make sense of the chaos in her mind. "Antonio... he said he wants us to move in with him. Me and Landon. He wants to be a family."

River's expression darkened, his fists clenching at his sides. "What?"

"Yup, and what's worse is, I think he is actually serious!" Valerie exclaimed. "That arrogant bastard thinks he can just swoop in and take over our lives? Absolutely not!"

Ellie's eyes widened even further if that were possible. "He really said that? And you didn't... I don't know, punch him in the face or something?"

Valerie couldn't help but laugh. "No, I didn't punch him. But I told him he was insane. I don't know what he's thinking, Ellie. He's delusional if he thinks I'll just pack up and move in with him."

River stepped closer, his voice softening. "Valerie, you know you don't have to do anything he says, right? We're here for you. We can protect you."

Valerie nodded, feeling a bit of the tension ease from her

shoulders. "I know, River. But it's not just about protection. It's about understanding what he really wants. He said he cares about me, about Landon. And part of me wonders if there's some truth to that, twisted as it might be."

Ellie, her gaze intense, leaned forward. "So what are you going to do, Valerie?"

Valerie sighed, running a hand through her hair. "I don't know."

"Why don't you get some rest? I'm sure it's been a long day," Ellie said softly.

Valerie retreated to her bedroom. As soon as she closed the door, she collapsed on her bed, feeling completely drained. Her mind was a jumbled mess of thoughts and emotions, and she couldn't make sense of anything.

Part of her was angry at Antonio for even suggesting the idea of them being a family. It felt like he was trying to manipulate her, using Landon as a way to get what he wanted. But then there was another part of her that couldn't help but wonder if there was any truth to his words. Did he really care about them? And if so, what did that mean for their future?

Despite her initial dislike of him, there was something about Antonio that drew her in. Maybe it was his charm or the way he seemed genuinely interested in Landon's well-being.

Or maybe she had lost her mind.

Valerie lay there, staring at the ceiling, her thoughts a tangled mess of confusion and frustration. Antonio was a dangerous man, and yet there was something undeniably magnetic about him. His presence was overwhelming, his words a strange mix of menace and affection. It made her question everything.

She buried her face in her pillow and screamed into it. Immediately, she heard Landon cry in the next room.

Oh great...now she had done it.

Valerie sprang up and rushed to Landon's room. His wails echoed off the walls. Scooping him up in her arms, Valerie held him close, trying to soothe him back to sleep.

"I'm sorry, sweetheart," she whispered, rocking him gently. "Mommy's just a little overwhelmed right now. I didn't mean to wake you up."

Landon's cries began to soften as Valerie hummed a lullaby, his tiny body gradually relaxing in her arms. The warmth of his body against her, the steady rhythm of his breathing as he calmed down—it grounded Valerie, reminding her of what truly mattered.

Antonio's words might be a confusing mess in her mind, but her priority was clear: her son. He was her world, and nothing and no one, not even Antonio with all his charm and menace, could change that.

Men are Great Idiots

Once Landon was back asleep, Valerie placed him carefully in his crib and stood there for a moment, watching him. He was so small, so innocent. Valerie couldn't trust him around someone like Antonio. But then again, Julian wouldn't have been any better either.

He might've been worse, much worse.

Returning to her room, Valerie tried to clear her mind. She needed to sleep.

~-~

The next morning began with a sense of unease lingering in the air. As Valerie woke up and went to check on Landon, a sickening feeling weighed heavy on her chest.

She couldn't understand why. It was just any other morning, right?

"Morning, Valerie," Ellie greeted her, eyes scanning Valerie's face for any signs of distress. "How did you sleep?"

"Not well," Valerie confessed, trying to mask the fear creeping into her voice. "But I'll manage."

"Pancakes!" Lucas said enthusiastically.

Valerie couldn't help but smile at his excitement. "Your favorite," she said.

"Eat up, everyone," Ellie said, matching Lucas's enthusiasm.

"Can Landon have some too?" Lucas asked.

Tiffany laughed next to him. "Don't be silly, Luke. Landon is a baby. He can only drink milk."

Lucas pouted for a moment, but then his face brightened with determination. "When he is older, I'll share my pancakes with him," he declared, making Valerie smile.

"That's very sweet of you, Lucas," she said, ruffling his hair. "I'm sure Landon will love that."

They sat down for breakfast and fell into their normal routine. But the sense of unease didn't dissipate. Valerie kept glancing at the window, half-expecting something—or someone—to appear. Would Antonio try to call her again today?

She cut a piece of pancake and put it in her mouth. Despite the sickly sweetness of the syrup, her restlessness only grew more intense. Suddenly, the screeching of tires shattered the peaceful morning, sending her heart racing. Instinctively, Valerie moved closer to Landon's baby carrier.

Without warning, the door exploded in a shower of glass shards, as if hit by a wrecking ball. In a split second, their quiet morning had turned into a chaotic action scene ripped from a nightmare.

"Upstairs, now!" River barked through clenched teeth,

Men are Great Idiots

pulling out a gun from his pocket.

It took Valerie mere seconds to realize that they were under attack. Their safe haven was no longer safe, and they were thrust into a fight for survival.

Fourteen

You are Hurt

G lass shattered. Boots thudded.

Instinct kicked in for River. He grabbed his gun and dove behind the cabinet while Ellie scrambled to her feet, grabbing Lucas's hand. She didn't hesitate for a second, and neither did Valerie and Tiffany. Valerie had Landon in her arms. All of them ran upstairs immediately.

Gunfire cracked through the house, bullets splintering wood and punching holes in the walls. River peered around the cabinet and spotted masked men swarming inside, assault rifles blazing.

This wasn't just a break-in. It was an attack.

River squeezed off a shot, dropping one of the bastards. The

You are Hurt

others scattered, ducking behind furniture and returning fire.

He heard his men rushing in, shouting. Bullets zinged by, chewing into the cabinet inches from his face. He leaned out and took aim, squeezing the trigger in a steady rhythm. The intruders fell one by one, their blood pooling on the hardwood.

The gunfire slowed, then ceased. Silence descended, broken only by River's ragged breaths.

He stepped out from behind the cabinet, pistol still gripped tightly in his hands as he scanned the room. Bodies littered the floor, blood and shell casings scattered around them. The metallic tang of gun smoke coated his tongue.

His heart pounded, fueled by a mix of adrenaline and rage.

Who dared attack his family?

Right then, he noticed a tattoo on one of the dead man's forearm.

A red Cobra.

"I think we got them all, Boss," James said, breathing hard.

"Good," River replied, his voice hoarse. The urgency of the moment didn't allow him the luxury of a breather. He had to keep moving.

Suddenly, the front door burst open again. More masked men charged in, their eyes cold and feral beyond those black ski masks.

River pushed James aside and shouted, "More incoming!" Ducking low, he sprinted for the fireplace mantle where he'd hidden an extra gun.

Shouts echoed through the house, and the air turned hot with lead. Bullets buried themselves in plaster and woodwork while River's men fought back fiercely.

"Fall back!" River yelled, grabbing the extra gun. A bullet grazed his shoulder, pain flaring white-hot, but he gritted his teeth and kept moving. There was no way he wold let these cobras win.

Despite their resistance, the attackers kept advancing, an endless wave of black-clad figures. They were outnumbered but not outgunned.

With guns in both hands, River threw himself back into the fray. Shots echoed off the walls, reverberating in his ears as they desperately held their ground.

Suddenly, two men charged him from the side. No time to aim—River swung a fist at one while firing at the other. Blood splattered as his bullet hit home.

The second goon lunged at him, tackling him to the ground.

You are Hurt

Shit, he should've paid more attention.

The man held a gun to his forehead, but suddenly, someone barreled into him.

The impact sent the man sprawling, his gun skittering across the floor. River looked up to see Antonio standing over him, grinning.

"You," River grunted, taking Antonio's hand and getting to his feet. "What are you doing here?"

Antonio's grin widened, but his eyes remained serious. "Saving your ass, apparently."

"Shit," River growled, raising his gun and firing at another intruder who had tried to sneak up on them.

Antonio pulled out his own weapon, his movements swift and precise. Despite River's initial shock and anger at his sudden appearance, he couldn't deny Antonio was an asset in this fight. Antonio moved with a lethal grace, each shot deliberate and deadly.

Together, they pushed back against the attackers, driving them out of the house inch by inch. River's men regrouped, taking advantage of the temporary shift in momentum. The air was thick with smoke and the smell of gunpowder, but they pressed on, determined to protect their home and loved ones.

After what felt like an eternity, the last of the attackers were either down or retreating. The silence that followed was almost deafening, punctuated only by the labored breathing of the survivors.

Antonio lowered his gun, his face streaked with sweat and blood. "Where are Valerie and the kids?"

River glanced around, ensuring the area was secure before responding. "Upstairs. Ellie took them to the safe room."

Antonio nodded, his expression softening for a moment. "Good. Let's check on them."

They moved quickly, adrenaline still coursing through their veins. The house was a war zone, debris and blood staining the once peaceful home. River couldn't let himself think about the damage or the bodies. Not yet.

As they reached the top of the stairs, they could hear Ellie's soothing voice, attempting to calm the kids. River tapped on the hidden panel that concealed the entrance to the safe room.

"It's me," he called out. "It's safe now."

The panel slid open, revealing Ellie with Lucas clinging to her leg and Landon cradled in Valerie's arms. Tiffany's eyes were wide with fear, but she stepped forward as soon as she saw her father, and relief washed over her face.

You are Hurt

"Is everyone okay?" River asked.

"They're okay," Ellie confirmed, her voice trembling slightly. "What about downstairs?"

"It's over, for now," River replied, pulling Lucas into a hug. "The attackers are either dead or gone."

Valerie's gaze shifted to Antonio, standing just behind River. "What are you doing here?" she demanded, her tone full of confusion and frustration.

Antonio stepped forward. "I came to visit you. This was quite the welcome."

"Were they your men?" Valerie snarled.

Antonio lifted his hands in mock surrender. "No, no, Bella. I wouldn't attack you, my future wife. Besides, if I did, I'd do a better job than whoever they are."

"Red Cobras," River said, ignoring Antonio's teasing words. "They were the ones who attacked us."

Ellie's eyes widened. "What do we do now? Do we have to move houses?"

River shook his head. "No. We aren't running away like cowards. I will amp up the security."

Valerie looked uncertain, but Ellie placed a reassuring hand on her shoulder. "It's going to be fine, Valerie."

Valerie sighed, glancing at River and then at Antonio. "It's nothing I haven't seen."

She suddenly noticed the blood dripping down Antonio's shoulder and gasped.

"Y-you...you are hurt!" she said hoarsely.

Fifteen

Live With Me

Antonio wiped a hand over his face, blood smearing across his cheek. "Ah. I guess I was shot. It's probably just a flesh wound. Nothing I can't handle." He grinned at Valerie.

Valerie shook her head. Was this man for real? "I need to see to that," she said, her tone firm.

"Why? Are you worried about me amore mio?" he smiled sheepishly.

Valerie sighed, exasperated by Antonio's flirtatious antics. "Not the nickname, please." She looked at Ellie. "Would you mind watching Landon while I take care of Antonio?"

Ellie nodded. "Of course."

Valerie grabbed his arm. "Come with me," she said.

"Ahem..." River cleared his throat. "I don't think you should be alone with him, Val."

Valerie glared at River. "He just helped us, didn't he?"

River hesitated. "Yes, but..."

"Let Valerie help Antonio," Ellie scolded River and motioned Valerie to carry on.

Valerie looked at Antonio. "Come with me."

Antonio nodded and obediently followed Valerie out of the room.

Valerie led Antonio to the bathroom, where they kept the first aid kit. She motioned for him to sit on the edge of the bathtub while she rummaged through the kit for some antiseptic and bandages.

Valerie's cheeks flushed with warmth and her neck prickled with heat as she mustered the courage to ask, "Um, would you mind taking off your shirt?" She wasn't exactly inexperienced with men, but the thought of seeing Antonio bare-chested made her stomach clench for some reason.

Antonio glanced down at the blood-soaked fabric of his shirt before meeting Valerie's gaze. He hesitated for a moment before slowly lifting his arms, allowing the shirt to pull free from his body. As it fell to the floor, he felt the familiar sting of his wound, but he did his best to maintain a calm demeanor.

"Thank you," Valerie murmured.

Valerie couldn't help but stare as Antonio removed his shirt, revealing his chiseled chest and broad shoulders bared for her to see.

He was a sight to behold, with his dark chest hair that trailed down from his broad chest all the way to his stomach. He was covered in tattoos and scars of different shapes and sizes that seemed to tell stories of their own. His deep olive complexion contrasted beautifully with the darkness of his eyes that seemed to hold a thousand secrets.

Valerie's breath hitched as her eyes wandered down from his hypnotizing chest to his chiseled stomach, tracing the ridges and curves with her gaze. And then she couldn't help but notice the impressive bulge between his pants, causing her cheeks to flush hot with desire.

Oh, sweet baby Jesus. Was that his...

"Valerie?"

His deep, seductive voice snapped her back to reality as she quickly averted her gaze to his face, cheeks flushing with embarrassment. "Wa...what?" she stammered.

"You are staring at me. Is the sight of my wound making you sick?" Antonio sounded worried.

Valerie shook her head. "No, of course not." She finally looked at his wound. It was oozing blood pretty badly now.

"Then is it my scars? I know they can be off-putting to most people." Antonio sounded sad now.

Valerie swallowed hard, trying to regain her composure. She couldn't believe how intensely she was attracted to him. She had to focus on the task at hand. "No, it's not that. I was just… distracted for a moment." She quickly retrieved the antiseptic and bandages from the first aid kit and turned back to him. "Let's get this taken care of."

She gently cleaned the wound with the antiseptic and applied pressure to stop the bleeding. Then she carefully wrapped the bandage around his shoulder, tying it securely to ensure he wouldn't bleed out.

"There," she said, stepping back to admire her handiwork. "I think that should hold for now. We need to get you to a proper doctor as soon as possible, though."

Antonio nodded. "Thank you, Valerie." His eyes locked on her with a new intensity, making her heart race.

"Why did you really come here?" Valerie asked, breaking the tense silence between them.

Live With Me

Antonio smiled. "To see if you changed your mind yet."

"Change my mind?" Val blinked.

"About coming to live with me," Antonio said, his voice steady. "After this attack, I think you really ought to. If not for you, for your son's sake. I have enough guards to call my house a fortress. I can keep you safe."

Valerie gulped. Her heart raced at the mere thought of sharing a roof with this intimidating and imposing man. She instinctively squeezed her thighs together as if to conceal any signs of arousal in his presence.

Oh, dear god. She was in trouble.

~-~

A few minutes later, Valerie and Antonio joined the rest of the family downstairs.

"I'll be damned if I let you take my sister to live with you," River snarled when Antonio brought it up.

Antonio turned to River, and for a moment, they engaged in a staring contest. "I get you don't trust me, Foster, but think about the safety of Valerie and Landon. My house is the most secure place they could be right now."

"I can keep her safe," River barked.

"Your house has been compromised, and it is not safe for a newborn baby," Antonio argued.

"He is not wrong, Dad. I can run and hide, and even Lucas can figure out how to do it, but Landon is helpless," Tiffany chimed in.

Valerie looked at her with admiration. Since when did this girl get so smart and aware?

"But…"

"I will go with him," Valerie said before River had the chance to say anything else.

River turned to Valerie, his eyes wide with surprise. "Valerie, you can't be serious."

Valerie took a deep breath, her expression resolute. "River, I have to think about Landon. If Antonio's place is as secure as he says, then it's the best option right now."

River clenched his jaw, struggling to keep his composure. "You don't have to go with him. I can keep you safe here."

Valerie shook her head. "I have full confidence in your abilities, but if I stay here, not only will you have to worry about Ellie and the kids but also about me. I can't let you take on that much stress. Let me go with Antonio."

Live With Me

Antonio stepped forward. "I promise you, they'll be safe. You can come and check on them whenever you want."

Valerie looked at River, her eyes cold and determined. "I am going with him, River."

Sixteen

Is it to your liking?

River's voice barked out, sharp and urgent, as Valerie packed up her belongings into suitcases to move in with Antonio. Her hands trembled with nervous energy, and her heart raced in her chest. "Don't do this, Valerie. This is insane," he pleaded.

It was two days after the event, and she had told Antonio to prepare for them to live with him. Antonio looked very excited and his excitement had seemed a little too much for her liking. River constantly badgered her about changing her mind but Valerie was firm with her decision.

Valerie turned to face River, trying to stay calm and composed. "River, please. Just let me go. It's going to be okay," she said, though doubt gnawed at her insides.

Is it to your liking?

Desperate for support, River turned to Ellie, who stood beside Valerie with a worried expression on her face. "Ellie, tell Valerie she's making a mistake," he implored.

Ellie let out a heavy sigh, her gaze shifting between the two of them. "Valerie, are you absolutely certain this is what you want?" she asked softly. Doubt clouded her eyes as she spoke, mirroring Valerie's own uncertainty about the decision.

"Yes. I think it's best I live separately from you guys. At least for a while," Valerie replied.

River's eyes turned dark. Valerie could tell she had hurt his feelings, so she quickly added, "It's not because I think you can't protect me, River."

"Then why?" he demanded.

Valerie took a deep breath, steeling her nerves. "I just…I can't keep relying on you guys to protect me all the time. I need to learn how to do it on my own," she explained, hoping he would understand.

"By going to live with my enemy?" River roared.

"Well, he did offer to call it a truce," Ellie reminded him. She looked at Valerie and smiled as if to show she was on her side.

River's expression hardened, but his eyes were filled with concern rather than anger. "Valerie, this is dangerous.

Antonio might have offered a truce, but can we really trust him?"

Valerie paused, searching for the right words. "River, I know this seems reckless. But I need to do this. For myself and for Landon. If Antonio can provide a safe environment, it's worth trying."

River ran a hand through his hair, frustration evident in his stance. "I just can't believe you're willing to go through with this. You're walking into the lion's den."

Valerie turned to Ellie, hoping for some reassurance. "Ellie, you understand, right?"

Ellie sighed, her expression torn. "I really hope you know what you are doing, Valerie. But I thought you hated Antonio. So what changed?"

Valerie looked at Ellie, her thoughts a whirlwind. "I didn't hate him, Ellie. I was just annoyed by him. But after what happened today, I realized something. Antonio showed up, and he helped us. He fought alongside us, and maybe, just maybe, there's more to him than I thought."

River scoffed, his frustration palpable. "So you're willing to trust him because he showed up once? Valerie, this could be a trap."

Valerie shook her head, trying to explain. "It's not just about trust. It's about survival. The Red Cobras are relentless. If

Is it to your liking?

Antonio can provide us with a safe place, even temporarily, we should take it. I need to protect my son, River. And he didn't just show up once. He was there for me at the hospital even though he didn't have to."

Ellie stepped closer, her hand resting on Valerie's arm. "Valerie, if you really believe this is the right choice, then we will support you. But please, be careful."

"I will be," Valerie promised, her voice steady.

River's shoulders sagged in defeat, his voice softening. "Just promise me you'll stay vigilant. Don't let your guard down around him."

"I promise," Valerie said, hugging him tightly. "I'll keep my guard up."

"If you feel like you are in danger..."

"I will call you right away," Valerie said, cutting River off.

River nodded grimly.

Ellie gave Valerie a reassuring squeeze on the shoulder. "Take care of yourself, Valerie. We'll miss you."

"Where are you going, Aunty Val?" Lucas asked, tugging at Valerie's sleeve.

She took his hand in hers and squeezed it. "Landon and I are going to stay somewhere else for a little while."

Lucas's small brow furrowed in confusion. "But why can't you stay here with us?"

Valerie glanced up at River and Ellie, searching for the right words. "It's just for a little bit, sweetheart. I'm sure I can visit you whenever I want."

River's expression softened as he knelt beside him, ruffling Lucas's hair. "I will take you to see Aunty Val and Landon when you miss them, alright?"

Lucas nodded again, this time with a bit more confidence. "Okay, Daddy."

Valerie stood up, taking a deep breath. She hoped she was doing the right thing.

She gathered her things and Landon and headed out. Antonio's car was waiting outside, and he stood by it, watching them approach.

"Ready?" he asked, his tone surprisingly gentle.

Valerie nodded.

"Let's get you settled in," he said.

They climbed into the car after River helped Landon strap into his car carrier. He looked at Antonio and glared. "If you

Is it to your liking?

hurt any of them..."

"I won't," Antonio interrupted swiftly.

The journey was a blur. Valerie barely noticed when they crossed from their territory into Antonio's.

"Here we are," Antonio announced, pulling up in front of his mansion.

Inside, some men rushed to help them with their luggage.

"Lucia will show you to your rooms," Antonio said, motioning toward a young woman who was standing by the door.

Lucia, with kind eyes and a warm smile, stepped forward. "Follow me, please," she said gently.

Valerie gathered her children, and they followed Lucia through the grand hallways of Antonio's mansion. The place was even bigger than she remembered. As they walked, she could sense the watchful eyes of Antonio's men.

"Here's your room, ma'am," Lucia gestured to the large, luxurious suite.

"I put the little one's crib near your bed," she said, gesturing at the big bed. "Is that alright?"

"Of course. Thank you, Lucia," Valerie said and smiled sweetly.

The Mafia Boss's Pregnant Bride

Valerie watched Lucia retreat down the hallway after a moment and sighed. She wondered if this was the right decision for the fiftieth time.

"Is it to your liking?"

Valerie nearly yelped as she heard Antonio's deep voice close to her ear. How the hell did he sneak up on her so fast?

Seventeen

Men Like Him

Suppressing a laugh, Antonio watched as Valerie jumped in surprise. Apparently, she hadn't heard him approaching from behind.

"Hello, beautiful. I'm here to check if you need anything," he said with a smile.

Valerie nervously bit her lip. "That won't be necessary," she responded shortly.

"Nonsense." Antonio waved off her protest. "What can I help you with? Unpacking? Babysitting? I'm a jack of all trades," he said as he eyed Landon in his crib.

Valerie scoffed. "For some reason, I don't see you as a babysitter."

"I will prove you wrong," Antonio challenged, raising an eyebrow.

Valerie looked at him for a moment, then, without another word, turned and walked away. But Antonio knew that was just part of the game, the push and pull they found themselves in. He wasn't going to let her go that easily.

He followed, keeping a few steps behind her.

She went to the room next to hers and looked around. For a moment, her facial expression softened. "You have a library," she stated.

"Yes," Antonio replied, his voice warm with pride. "It's one of my favorite rooms in the house. Feel free to use it anytime you like."

Valerie seemed to relax slightly, her eyes wandering around the room. "It's really nice."

Antonio took a step closer. "How about I show you the rest of the house?"

"That's not necessary," Valerie said a little too quickly, making him smirk.

"Why not?" he asked, quirking up his eyebrow.

Valerie shifted uncomfortably, avoiding his gaze. "I just... I don't want to impose."

Antonio chuckled softly. "You're not imposing, Valerie. I invited you to live here. Besides, it might help you feel more at home."

Valerie hesitated for a moment, then nodded reluctantly. "Okay, but just a quick tour."

Antonio smiled, gesturing for her to follow him. "Of course, just a quick tour. This way."

As they walked through the grand hallways, Antonio pointed out various rooms and features of the mansion. "This is the dining room, where we have meals. And over here is the kitchen. If you need anything, just let the staff know."

Valerie nodded, taking in the opulence of the house. "It's all very impressive," she admitted.

"Thank you," Antonio replied, leading her to a large, sunlit room. "And this is the living room. A good place to relax."

Valerie glanced around, noting the comfortable furniture and large windows. "It's nice."

Antonio watched her carefully, gauging her reactions. "I want you to feel comfortable here, Valerie. This is your home now, too."

She looked at him, her eyes narrowing. "Is that all you are asking for? For me to be comfortable?"

"Are you always this suspicious?" Antonio chuckled.

"Only when it comes to men like you," she snapped.

Antonio cocked his head and grinned. "Men like me? What kind of man do you think I am?"

Valerie glared at him, her eyes sparking with a mix of irritation and defiance. "The kind who thinks he can buy loyalty and trust with grand gestures," she said sharply.

He chuckled, a low, amused sound. "Maybe. Or maybe I'm just trying to make a good impression," he countered, maintaining eye contact.

She crossed her arms, clearly unimpressed. "I know what you want from me, Antonio."

"And what do you think I want from you?" he asked.

"You want to manipulate me and seduce me to get what you want," she said.

"I told you I don't plan on coercing you for the codes at the moment. And seduce you? Well…" he paused and moved closer to her.

Even though she wasn't petite by any means, he still stood head and shoulders above her. From this vantage point, he could catch the faint aroma of jasmine tangled in her luscious red locks. It was a scent that wrapped around him like a warm embrace, intoxicating and alluring.

"Perhaps I do want to seduce you. Are you seducible, cara mia?" he whispered.

Valerie's cheeks flared red, her green eyes widening, taken aback by his words.

"I..." she stammered before taking a step back, breaking their proximity. "No, I am not! You're... you're... crazy!" she finally spat out, her chest heaving.

An amused smirk tugged on Antonio's lips as he watched the fiery tempest before him. He was aware that he was treading dangerous waters, but years of placing bets on uncertainty had made him somewhat of a thrill-seeker. "Crazy, moi?" he echoed with feigned surprise.

Suddenly, a faint cry floated from Valerie's new bedroom. Landon must've woken up.

Valerie rushed to her immediately. Antonio followed but didn't go near, giving them space. She picked up Landon and cradled her close to her chest, murmuring soothing words into her ear.

The sight made Antonio's heart clench. They were outsiders in his world, but he desperately wanted to make them his own. For a moment, the room felt warmer, more like a home than a battleground.

When Landon was finally settled, Valerie looked up at Antonio, her eyes still wary but softened by the maternal love she had just displayed. "Antonio, I don't know what game you're playing, but my child comes first. Always."

"I know," he said, hoping she would hear the sincerity in his voice.

"And I won't sleep with you," she declared.

His lips quirked up at that. "No?" he asked in a teasing tone.

"No," she said more firmly.

She narrowed her eyes at him, a challenge presented without a word being spoken. Valerie was as fierce as she was beautiful, and Antonio found himself drawn to her more and more.

He raised his hands in mock surrender, a teasing smile on his lips. "Understood, Valerie. No funny business."

She narrowed her eyes at him, clearly not entirely convinced, but a hint of a smile tugged at the corner of her mouth. It was a small victory, but he would take it.

"Good," she replied, her tone softening slightly. "Now, if you don't mind, I need to get Landon settled."

"Of course," Antonio said, stepping back further. "If you won't sleep with me, could you at least do me the honor of having dinner with me tonight?"

Valerie paused, her eyes narrowing slightly as she considered his request. The suspicion was still there, but he could see a flicker of curiosity in her gaze.

"Dinner?" she repeated, her tone cautious.

"Yes, dinner. Nothing more, nothing less," he said, keeping his voice light and nonchalant.

She studied him for a moment, then sighed. "Fine. Dinner. But just dinner," she agreed.

A genuine smile spread across Antonio's face. "Perfect. I'll have it arranged."

Valerie gave him a wary nod before turning her attention back to Landon, who had settled comfortably in her arms. As she rocked her son gently, Antonio slipped out of the room.

Eighteen

Dinner Date

~~~~~~

Valerie stared at herself in the mirror.

Dinner with Antonio.

It was such a simple thing, and yet, she felt nervous, though she had no idea why.

Taking a deep breath, she smoothed out the fabric of her dress, trying to steady the flurry of emotions swirling inside her. This was just dinner, nothing more. Still, there was something about Antonio that made her feel both on edge and oddly intrigued.

Landon had finally settled, her tiny breaths even and calm. Lucas was taking a nap in the other room, seemingly at ease in this new environment. Valerie had to admit that Antonio

Dinner Date

had done everything possible to make them feel comfortable here. But was it a genuine concern or part of a larger scheme?

"You are thinking too much," Valerie whispered to herself.

Valerie shook her head, trying to clear her doubts. Tonight, she needed to stay focused, be present, and be watchful. This was an opportunity to learn more about Antonio, to understand his motives, and to figure out if he could be trusted.

With one last look in the mirror, she squared her shoulders and left the room. The hallway was dimly lit, creating an ambiance that was both intimate and mysterious. She walked down the corridor, her footsteps echoing softly on the polished wooden floor.

When she reached the dining room, Antonio was already there.

Even with his scarred face, he looked effortlessly handsome in his tailored suit, Valerie thought.

The table was set beautifully, with candles casting a warm glow over the elegant place settings. Soft music played in the background, adding to the inviting atmosphere.

He was leaning against his chair, his face resting on his fist as if he was deep in thought. He looked like a king, Valerie thought to herself.

He looked up as she stepped inside the room, his dark eyes lighting up. "Ah, I am so happy you didn't change your mind, Amore," he commented. His voice was deep and husky as he added, "You look beautiful."

Valerie blushed in spite of herself. "Thank you," she managed to say, trying to keep her voice steady as she walked toward the table. "This looks... great."

Antonio stood and pulled out a chair for her. "All for you, darling."

As she sat down, she couldn't help but feel a mix of emotions—caution, curiosity, and an unexpected hint of excitement. Antonio took his seat across from her, his gaze never wavering.

The first course was served, and they began to eat in a comfortable silence. Valerie could feel Antonio's eyes on her, making her heart beat just a little faster. This was new territory for her, and she wasn't what do to with it yet.

As dinner progressed, so did the intensity of his stares. Uncomfortably, she looked down at her plate, poking at the food that suddenly had lost its flavor. "Antonio, why are you doing this?"

He put down his utensils and cleared his throat. His eyes bore into hers, the look in them unreadable. "Doing what, exactly?"

"All this." She gestured towards the extravagant dinner spread,

Dinner Date

the glow of the candle lights flickering in his eyes. "Why make all this effort?"

He drew in a deep breath and leaned back in his chair. For a moment, he was silent. Then he chuckled softly, a wry smile touching his lips. "Because, Valerie, I want to win you over," he confessed. "Because I want to prove to you I'm not some monster."

"You killed Julian," she whispered.

"I didn't kill him," he corrected her.

"Okay. Your men did. Not much different, is it?" she pointed out.

He took a bite of his steak and chewed it slowly before replying. "No, I suppose not."

"Whether he was a shitty person or not, he was still the father of my child," she said.

"Unfortunately," he said flatly.

His tone made her look him in the eyes. "What?"

"It's unfortunate that Julian is the father and not me," Antonio said casually.

His statement caught her off guard, her fork clattering onto her plate. Antonio's gaze was unyielding.

"Do you just say whatever you feel like?" she snapped

Antonio grinned. "I guess I do."

She took a deep breath, trying to steady herself. This man was already driving her crazy. How was she supposed to survive living with him?

"Alright," Antonio said, his tone softening as he leaned back in his chair.

Her heart pounded louder in her chest as she gathered her thoughts before speaking again. "And what if all of this effort doesn't change my mind about you?" she asked, matching his direct gaze with a challenging stare.

The corners of his mouth upturned further into a grin as if he liked her defiance. "Then, cara mia," he leaned forward, placing his hands flat on the table, "I'll keep trying until you do."

"And what if I'm not worth the effort?" Valerie challenged, her voice barely rising above a whisper as she stared into Antonio's confident, dark eyes.

"You can't decide that for me," he shot back immediately, his gaze never wavering. "You're worth it to me."

Valerie scoffed, pushing her plate away. "You've made a mistake then."

Dinner Date

"I don't think so," he replied stubbornly, crossing his arms over his chest. "But only time will decide."

"Time?" she echoed, feeling her heart tighten in her chest. "On whose clock, Antonio? Mine or yours?"

His smirk widened at her words. "On ours, Valerie," he said, his fingers absently tracing the rim of his wine glass.

Valerie blinked twice, processing that. Then she rose abruptly from the table. "I should go to bed."

"Of course," Antonio said, standing up too. "I shall walk you to your room."

"That's not necessary," she protested.

"I insist," he said in a tone that suggested he was not going to take no for an answer.

Valerie sighed and went to check on Landon. He was still sleeping in his crib, peacefully.

She turned to face him. "Thank you for dinner, but you can leave now."

His lips twitched upward in a lopsided grin. "Of course, Valerie," he replied, running his fingers through his dark hair with an air of nonchalance that didn't fool her for a second.

She was about to close the door when he stopped it with

his hand. "Valerie," he began, his voice uncharacteristically serious. "I just want you to know that you will be mine eventually."

Valerie rolled her eyes. "Good night, Antonio."

"Good night, amore," he said and finally let go of the door.

With that, she quickly shut the door behind her and leaned her back against it. Despite herself, she felt her heart pounding in her chest—a deafening sound in the otherwise quiet room.

Perhaps it was the lingering smell of his cologne or the disturbing sincerity in his voice, but she couldn't shake off a feeling of unease as she slipped under the covers.

Outside her bedroom window, she heard Antonio's footsteps echoing in the hallway before they gradually faded into silence. And then there was nothing but the sound of her beating heart and the distant howling of a wolf in the night.

As Valerie lay there alone in the darkness, thoughts of Antonio clouded her mind. His confidence. His persistence. His relentlessness.

God... what have I gotten myself into? she thought to herself.

Nineteen

Sweet Old Lady

Valerie's heart skipped a beat as she saw the imposing figure of a large man standing in her bedroom doorway. It wasn't unusual to be surrounded by Antonio's henchmen, but it still put her on edge. "Can I help you with something?" she asked, trying to hide her nerves.

The man cleared his throat and spoke in a gruff voice. "Signora Costello requests your presence, Miss Valerie."

Valerie furrowed her brows in confusion. The first thought that came to mind was that he must be talking about Antonio's wife. Who else would have the same last name as him?

But then she realized that couldn't be possible. After all, why would Antonio make her live with him if he had a wife? And he also threatened to make her his!?

Unless...

Unless he was planning on making her his mistress and keeping her under the same roof as his unsuspecting wife.

No, that's ludicrous.

It sounded like something out of a soap opera, but knowing Antonio, it could very well be true.

Valerie's head spun with these thoughts as she followed the henchman down the hallway. This was the crazy life she had chosen.

They stopped in front of an ornate door, and the henchman knocked softly before opening it. "Signora, I have brought Miss Ellie."

Valerie stepped inside hesitantly, her eyes widening as she took in the room. It was elegantly decorated with rich fabrics and antique furniture. Sitting in an armchair near the window was an elderly woman with a kind yet sharp expression. Her eyes were dark like Antonio's, filled with both wisdom and an undeniable strength.

"Come in, dear," the woman said, her voice warm but authoritative. "I've been wanting to meet you."

Valerie swallowed hard and stepped further into the room.

Sweet Old Lady

"Hello," she said, trying to keep her voice steady.

The woman smiled slightly. "I am Antonio's Nonna, Lizbeth Costello. And I wanted to meet the woman who has stirred such emotions in my grandson."

Valerie blinked in surprise. This sweet old lady was Antonio's grandmother? "It's an honor to meet you, Signora Costello," she said politely.

Lizbeth waved a hand dismissively. "Call me Nonna like Toni does. Now, sit with me. Let's talk."

Valerie sat down in a chair opposite her, feeling both curious and apprehensive. "What would you like to talk about?" she asked.

Lizbeth leaned forward slightly, her eyes studying Valerie intently. "I know my grandson can be difficult. He has his… ways. But I want you to understand something, Valerie. He is not heartless. And I do believe he cares for you."

Valerie took a deep breath, considering her words carefully. "He doesn't know me enough to care for me."

Lizbeth nodded thoughtfully. "Perhaps you are right. And how do you feel about Antonio? Be honest with me, child."

Her directness caught Valerie off guard, but she appreciated it. "I don't know," Valerie admitted. "I don't trust him completely, but I'm trying to find a way to coexist."

Lizbeth smiled softly. "I know you are afraid, but I can feel the strength in you, my child. If anyone can handle my grandson, it's you."

Valerie's cheeks warmed at that. "Th...thank you."

Lizbeth's smile widened, her dark eyes twinkling. "And I see the appeal. You, my dear, are gorgeous. And my Toni always had a weakness for true beauty."

Valerie blushed, feeling a mix of embarrassment and gratitude. "I don't know about that," she murmured.

"Believe it," Lizbeth said firmly. "And you needn't worry about my Toni. He can be overwhelming, but he means well. He is fiercely protective of those he cares about."

Valerie thought about her words, trying to reconcile the ruthless man she had come to know with the one Lizbeth was describing. "I hope you're right," she said softly. "For my baby's sake, if nothing else."

Lizbeth's eyes lit up. "Ah, the baby. Where is he? I must see him. Oh, this house has been missing the warmth and laughter of a child."

A small smile tugged at Valerie's lips. "Landon is still sleeping, but I can bring him to you when he is awake."

Lizbeth's smile widened. "Could you? Oh, please do."

Sweet Old Lady

"Of course," Valerie replied warmly.

Lizbeth's face suddenly turned serious again. "This may be hard for you now, but try to take it easy on my grandson. He may seem like a tough man, but I know better. The things he had been through as a boy..." She stopped and shook her head as if to shake away a bad thought.

"What is it?" Valerie asked quietly.

Lizbeth looked at her and smiled. "Not my story to tell, dear."

Valerie stared at her curiously. What did she almost tell her?

The sound of footsteps made them both turn to the door.

Antonio was standing there, looking at them sheepishly. "Nonna," he rumbled, his eyes darting between them uneasily.

"Toni," Lizbeth greeted with a soft smile. "Come in. Valerie and I were just discussing her baby."

He walked inside, shooting Valerie a sidelong glance before turning to his grandmother. "I hope you haven't been giving her the third degree, Nonna."

Lizbeth waved Antonio off dismissively. "Nonsense, she is a strong woman. She can handle a chat with an old lady."

Antonio sauntered over to them. "An old lady? But you, Nonna, are no ordinary old lady."

Lizbeth waved her hand dismissively again. "No matter. We are just about finished so that you may steal your woman back."

Heat spread through Valerie's neck and ears as she heard the term "his woman." Oh god, was his grandma also scheming to make her be with Antonio too? She thought Lizbeth was a sweet old lady!

"I am glad to hear that, Nonna," Antonio said, giving Valerie another sly smile as he held out his hand.

Valerie took his hand without thinking and let him pull her out of the room.

"Where are you taking me?" she breathed as he led her down the hallway.

"Don't worry, mia cara. I am not kidnapping you. You have visitors," he said, chuckling.

"Oh? Who..." Valerie stopped as they stepped inside the living room. Her mood brightened. "River! Ellie!"

Ellie flashed her a smile and walked over to hug her. "Oh, Valerie. I am so glad you are okay."

"Of course she is okay," River barked. "I would cut Antonio's heart out if she wasn't."

"Ah, Foster. Always so pleasant," Antonio commented.

Sweet Old Lady

Valerie ignored them both and hugged Ellie back. "Thank you for visiting me," she said through tears.

Twenty

A Kiss

Valerie's heart leaped with joy as she watched Lucas and Tiffany behind her brother. "Aunty Val!" he squealed, running up to her with his arms outstretched for a hug.

"Hey! I want a hug too," Tiffany giggled, rushing toward Valerie.

Valerie couldn't help but smile widely. Seeing them here felt like a small piece of normalcy returning to her life.

River pulled Valerie into a tight, protective hug after the kids let her go. "Are you really okay?" he whispered, concern lacing his voice.

Valerie nodded, pulling back to look at him. "I'm fine.

A Kiss

Antonio has been... considerate."

River's eyes flicked to Antonio, who was watching them with a guarded expression. "Good," he said, his tone clipped. "We're here to make sure it stays that way."

"Where is Landon? Is he in her crib?" Ellie asked. "I want to hold him."

Valerie laughed. "I will grab him for you," she said.

The anticipation in Ellie's eyes sparkled like stars. "I can't wait. I miss cuddling my nephew."

With a smile, Valerie made her way to her room, feeling a sense of warmth and contentment settle over her.

As she entered her room, she found Landon awake and cooing in his crib. Valerie gently lifted him into her arms, relishing the weight of his tiny body and the softness of his baby skin.

"You are so loved," Valerie whispered. "You will have everything mommy never had," she said, suddenly feeling sad.

With a tender smile, she kissed Landon's forehead, feeling the warmth of his little body against hers.

As Valerie made her way back to the living room, Landon cradled in her arms, she found River and Ellie chatting among themselves. Antonio sat on the couch, keeping his distance.

Ellie's eyes lit up when she saw Valerie with Landon. "There he is!" Ellie exclaimed, reaching out to take him from Valerie's arms.

Valerie handed Landon over to Ellie, watching as she held him close, a look of pure love and adoration on her face. It filled Valerie with a sense of hope for the future, knowing that despite the challenges they faced, they were surrounded by love and family.

But all good things had to end eventually and soon, it was time for them to leave. Valerie placed Landon back inside his crib and came back to the living room to say her goodbyes.

"Take care of yourselves," Ellie whispered as she hugged Valerie goodbye. "If you need anything. Anything at all, River will do it. You know that, right?"

"Yes," Valerie said, trying not to cry.

As she watched them leave, a pang of sadness tugged at her heart. She felt Antonio's presence behind her and her body tensed.

"Family is so important, isn't it, Amore?" he said raspily.

Valerie turned around to face him.

His black eyes were sad, and he had a dark shadow over his face. Something inside her twitched. What was up with his expression? "Yes," she said.

A Kiss

"Which is why I can't let you go," he said grimly.

"You can't force me," Valerie snapped, instantly getting angry. "I don't want to be part of your sick, twisted idea of a family."

Antonio's expression hardened, his jaw set in a tight line. "You misunderstand, Valerie. I'm not talking about forcing you to stay. I'm talking about convincing you to be mine."

Valerie stared at him. "No, you are right," she said slowly. "You didn't force me to stay here. I came of my own accord, but it doesn't mean I agreed to be yours."

He took a step closer, his gaze piercing into hers. "You will change your mind."

She held his intense gaze, refusing to let him break her with his words. "I won't," she stated boldly. "I'll never be yours, Antonio. I won't let you manipulate me into thinking otherwise."

His lips curved into a devious smirk, his eyes dark. "You're testing my patience, Valerie," he purred, his voice low and dangerous.

"I don't care," she shot back, her heart racing as their bodies were mere inches apart. "I won't succumb to your threats or your empty promises. I know exactly what kind of man you are, and I won't let myself be fooled."

His eyebrow quirked up at that. "And what kind of a man do

you think I am?"

Valerie held his gaze unwaveringly, her voice steady despite the turmoil inside her. "You are a man consumed by power and control. And I suspect you are a..." Valerie hesitated as she tried to find the right word."

"You suspect what, Val?" he asked.

"A man whore!" she blurted out.

Antonio's smirk faltered, his eyes narrowing as he processed her words. Valerie held her breath, unsure of how he would react to her boldness. But instead of anger or retaliation, a deep chuckle rumbled in his chest, catching her off guard.

"Well, that's a new one," Antonio said, amusement dancing in his dark eyes. "I've been called many things, but 'man whore' is definitely a first."

Valerie blinked in surprise at his unexpected reaction. Was he mocking her? Playing games?

Before she could gather her thoughts, Antonio closed the distance between them in a swift stride, his hand reaching out to cup her cheek gently. The touch sent a jolt of electricity through Valerie's body, betraying the defiance in her eyes with a flicker of vulnerability.

"You have fire in you, Valerie," Antonio murmured, his thumb brushing lightly against her skin. "I find it... intriguing."

A Kiss

Her heart pounded erratically in her chest as she struggled to maintain her composure under his intense gaze.

"I won't deny that I'm a man who enjoys the finer things in life," Antonio continued softly, his voice a mere whisper against her lips. "But I can assure you, my interest in you goes beyond mere indulgence."

Valerie's breath caught.

"I don't trust easily, Antonio," Valerie confessed quietly.

A ghost of a smile tugged at the corner of Antonio's lips as he leaned closer, his gaze flickering between her eyes and her parted lips.

"Sometimes, Valerie," he whispered huskily, "the best things in life come from taking risks."

"I don't want to take any risks," she whispered.

Their gazes locked in a fierce battle of wills, neither one willing to give in.

Antonio's gaze did not waver, dark and predatory. "Your words say no, Valerie," he murmured. "But your eyes tell a different story."

Valerie tried to back away, but he grabbed her tightly. His hand slowly slid down, then stopped to intertwine his fingers with hers.

His lips twitched into a smirk, like he found her resistance amusing. She could feel his breath against her skin, sending an unfamiliar thrill up her spine. "Why do you resist me, my love?" he challenged.

"I'm not your love," she shot back, defiant despite the pounding in her chest. "I'm not something you can just claim."

His laughter echoed in the room, low and ominous. "Oh Valerie," he whispered against her ear, sending shivers down her spine. "You're not just something to me. You're everything."

His words struck her, leaving her bewildered. How could he utter such words with such ease? He was lying to her, obviously, but...why was he so good at it!?

"Let go of me," she said weakly.

"I will on one condition," he said, smiling devilishly.

"What's that?" she asked as she swallowed.

He leaned over and whispered in her ear. "You must pay a toll."

"Wha...what?" she asked lamely.

"A toll, Valerie. A small price," he said easily.

"What do you want?" she asked. Something inside her told her that this wasn't going to be good.

A Kiss

Antonio smirked. "A kiss."

Twenty-One

Lying to Herself

Heat pooled in Valerie's stomach and then spread through her entire body. Antonio's eyes, his words, and even his simple request were affecting her deeply, whether she wanted to admit it or not.

"What?" she whispered, even though she knew exactly what he was asking for.

"Kiss me, and I'll let you go," he promised.

Valerie tried to retort, her voice betraying her inner turmoil. "You can't make me kiss you."

Antonio shrugged casually. "I'm not making you. I'm requesting you to pay up."

Lying to Herself

"How is that not a blackmail?" she exclaimed.

Antonio grinned. "I suppose it is. I am a terrible man, so what else do you expect?"

Valerie was torn, her thoughts a whirlwind. There was something about Antonio that piqued her curiosity, and for some reason, she found it hard to refuse him outright.

And it didn't help that she found him insanely attractive too.

Antonio took a lock of her hair and twisted it around his finger. "It's a simple kiss, Valerie. Nothing more, nothing less."

"Just a kiss?" she asked hoarsely.

"Just a kiss."

His nearness was overwhelming, a sensory overload that clouded her thoughts. She could feel his breath on her skin, and the heat radiating from his body was a gravitational force pulling her closer. She was caught between the urge to run and an unexplainable compulsion to let him kiss her.

Before she could fully process her actions, Valerie found herself leaning in, closing the distance between them. Antonio's eyes flickered with a mix of triumph and something else she couldn't quite identify.

When their lips met, a rush of heat surged through her, and

for a moment, everything else faded away.

It started out as a mere brush of their lips, but it felt electric, sending a blaze of fire through her. His hand gently caressed her cheek, his touch tender yet possessive. He angled his head and softly parted her mouth to deepen the kiss and the raw intensity of the moment consumed her, pulling her deeper into its passionate embrace.

It had been so long—too long—since she'd been kissed like this.

This wasn't fair. Why did he have to be such a good kisser? Why did he, of all people, have to make her body feel like this?

She felt herself melting into him as their lips moved in perfect harmony, every nerve ending alive with desire. It left her breathless and yearning for more. And she actually moaned!

Antonio pulled away first, a devious grin on his face as his eyes remained locked on hers. "Goodnight, my love," he said softly, then turned on his heel and left the room.

Damn him.

Damn him to hell!

Valerie stood there for a moment, trying to catch her breath. And then…her stomach rumbled.

Lying to Herself

She groaned. Ever since she had been breastfeeding Landon, she was always hungrier than usual. It was irritating.

She strode toward the kitchen. Maybe she could ransack the fridge and find a snack or something.

In the kitchen, Valerie found an elderly woman by the stove. The woman looked at her questioningly.

Valerie smiled nervously. "Um…sorry. I was wondering if I could get something to eat?" she asked.

The woman's expression softened as she glanced at her. "Of course, dear. I'm Donna, the cook. What would you like to eat?"

"Anything is fine," Valerie said quickly.

Donna nodded and gestured for Valerie to take a seat at the small table in the corner.

As she bustled around the kitchen, Valerie couldn't shake off the lingering sensation of Antonio's kiss. It had stirred emotions she hadn't felt in a long time, igniting a spark that she didn't know existed. She tried to push those thoughts aside.

This was silly. It was just a kiss.

"Ah! I could make you some sandwiches. How does that sound?" Donna asked.

Donna sat down across from Valerie after serving her, her gaze gentle. "Signorina Valerie, isn't it?" she asked. "Signor Costello mentioned you."

Valerie nodded, a slight blush creeping up her cheeks. "Yes, that's me. Please just call me by my first name."

Donna smiled kindly. "It's good to see more people in the house again. It brings a special kind of warmth."

Valerie returned her smile. "Thank you, Donna. Your kindness means a lot."

As she finished her sandwich, Valerie felt a sense of comfort knowing there were caring people like Donna around. It made the complicated feelings about Antonio and their situation a little easier to bear.

She looked at her phone to check the baby monitor and saw that Landon was still sleeping peacefully in his crib. "How long have you been working here, Donna?" she asked, curiosity getting the better of her.

Donna's smile widened as she reminisced. "Oh, I've been with the Costello family for nearly thirty years now. I started when Antonio was just a little boy himself. It's been quite a journey."

Valerie listened intently, intrigued by the glimpse into Antonio's past. "That must have been quite an experience. Was he always…the way he is now?"

Lying to Herself

Donna chuckled softly, her eyes glinting with fond memories. "Antonio has always had a strong will and a fierce sense of loyalty. He can be tough, but there's a heart underneath all that strength. He cares deeply for those he loves, even if he doesn't always show it in the gentlest of ways."

Valerie nodded slowly, trying to piece together what she knew about Antonio. "So he's always been surrounded by this life?"

Donna sighed thoughtfully. "Yes, from a very young age."

Valerie was no stranger to this kind of life, having lived with Julian and with her own brother involved in the Mafia. But for some reason, Antonio seemed different from them.

She looked back at Donna, curiosity getting the better of her. "What was he like as a child?"

Donna's face lit up with a nostalgic smile. "Oh, he was a spirited boy. Always getting into some kind of trouble, but his heart was always in the right place. He was fiercely protective even back then, especially of his family."

Valerie listened intently, even though she knew she should be focusing on her situation. She wasn't sure why she was so eager to learn more about Antonio, despite wanting nothing to do with him.

Or maybe she was lying to herself, and she did want to know more about him.

Twenty-Two

You are Crazy

The moment their lips touched, electricity sparked through Antonio's veins. Hours later, he couldn't stop thinking about her. About Valerie.

His sheets were tangled around his legs as he tossed and turned, craving the feel of her in his arms. He could still taste her on his tongue. The memory of her soft curves pressed against him made his blood burn.

He groaned. This was madness.

He'd never lost control like this, never wanted a woman with such relentless desperation. His body burned for her, but it was more than that. He wanted to know her, all of her—her secrets, her dreams, her fears. He wanted to share his life with her, protect her, and please her.

You are Crazy

Valerie had gotten under his skin, into his soul, in a way no one else ever had. He was drowning in her, consumed by her, and he didn't want to surface for air.

What the fuck was wrong with him?

The familiar urge rose, an itch he'd always scratched without a second thought. His body cried out for release as he thought about touching her again.

Faceless, nameless women paraded through his mind, a succession of willing bodies he'd taken his pleasure from without care or consequence before. It was simple, a straightforward transaction to sate his lust and little more. He treated them well enough, paid them handsomely for their time, but he never saw them as anything other than a means to an end.

But now, he couldn't imagine touching another woman.

He only wanted Valerie.

His hand drifted down to his hard cock, but he jerked his hand away as if burned.

No. He wouldn't sully his thoughts of Valerie in such a way. She deserved better from him, and he found he wanted to give her better.

And her son…he would give him the world, too, even though Valerie wanted nothing to do with him.

The Mafia Boss's Pregnant Bride

He wanted her love, her trust.

His manhood strained against his pajama bottoms.

Goddammit. He couldn't survive this.

Maybe this was a mistake. Perhaps he should go back to the way things were before Valerie happened. Before he found himself craving a simple life, a family of his own…things he'd never wanted before.

But that would mean sending Valerie and Landon back. He didn't want to do that either.

He groaned again, the frustration building inside him. Sleep was elusive, taunting him with visions of Valerie and the life he was beginning to imagine with her. This desire was unlike anything he had ever felt. It was raw, consuming, and undeniable.

Valerie had disrupted the careful balance he had maintained for so long, and he couldn't decide if he was grateful or furious.

A gentle, almost hesitant knock pulled him out of his deep thoughts. His door stood firmly closed, its paint chipped and worn from years of use. Though he couldn't see who was on the other side, a strange intuition told him it was Valerie.

His heart skipped a beat in anticipation, even though he knew he shouldn't feel that way. After all, Valerie didn't exactly

You are Crazy

like him. She was probably here out of practical necessity, needing something from him. Yet still, he couldn't help but hope for some small glimpse of connection with her.

He took a deep breath and forced himself to remain calm. "Come in," he called out, trying to keep his voice steady.

The door opened slowly, and there she was, standing in the dim light of the hallway. Valerie stood by the door, her gaze meeting his with a vulnerability that tugged at his heart.

"Antonio," she began softly, her voice wavering slightly. "I... I need to talk to you."

He sat up, the tension in his body easing slightly. "Come inside."

Valerie hesitated. "I am fine right here."

He grinned. "Why won't you come inside the bedroom? Don't tell me you are scared of me."

"I am not scared of you," she barked.

"Then come inside and walk closer to me," he said in a light tone.

Valerie took a deep breath and stepped into the room, the door closing softly behind her. She walked toward him, stopping a few feet away, her arms crossed defensively over her chest.

"I came to ask you something," she said, her voice firm but edged with uncertainty.

"Yeah?" He cocked his head and asked.

"H-how long do you expect me to stay with you?" she asked.

"Why...as long as you want, of course," he said.

"Okay, but I don't plan on staying here forever. I...I will find a job, and then once I save enough money, I will get my own place to move in with my son," she said. "It will take some time. Maybe a few months or a year, but I will get out of your hair. But don't try to stop me because it won't work. You, yourself, said you are not forcing me to stay here and..."

She rambled on and on about her future escape from him as he stared at her, completely mesmerized. Not only was this woman beautiful to look at, but she also had the most beautiful voice. He could listen to her talk all night.

Fuck...it made his cock so hard it was straining against his underwear, practically throbbing in pain.

"Antonio, are you even listening to me?" Valerie snapped.

He blinked. "Ehh? Of course I am, Bella."

"No, you are not. You had this spaced-out look on your face just now," Valerie complained.

You are Crazy

"I assure you. I listened to every word you said," he protested.

She crossed her arms. "Oh, yeah? What was the last thing I said?" she challenged.

"The last thing you said..." he repeated slowly, mentally retracing the flow of her words. "...You said, marry me, Antonio, and have more babies with me."

Valerie glared at him, her face turning red. "I said no such thing, you...you...idiot!" she spluttered, clearly flustered.

He chuckled, amused by the fierce expression on her face. "Then what did you say?" he asked, knowing very well what she had said.

"I said..."

She yelped as he suddenly grabbed her arm and pulled her toward him.

She gasped as she landed on top of him, her body trembling slightly. He could feel her heart pounding against his chest. "Antonio," she warned, but there was a hint of excitement in her voice that she couldn't hide. She propped herself up as much as she could to look at him.

"What were you saying, Valerie?" he asked.

She gulped audibly, her cheeks flushing a deep shade of pink. "I... I said that I will eventually leave and you can't stop me."

"Is that right?" His voice was barely a whisper now, drowned out by the beating of their hearts.

"Yes," she muttered, trying to look away. But he didn't let her; his fingers softly tilted her chin up to meet his gaze.

"Then I guess I don't have much time to woo you," he said softly. "I better give it my all."

Valerie tried to sit up but didn't get far before he pulled her back into his arms.

"You're crazy," she said. He could tell she was struggling to look angry but failing. Was his little redhead enjoying his company?

Twenty-Three

I Am No Gentleman

Valerie didn't know what possessed her to walk into Antonio's room at this ungodly hour.

Maybe she'd finally lost her marbles, but here she was, face-to-face with him…or rather, nose-to-nose since she was currently half sprawled on top of him.

"Let go of me," she said, struggling against his grip. The words tumbled weakly from her lips as she felt his hand gently caress her back. A tingling warmth spread through her body, radiating from where his fingers touched her.

Their faces were dangerously close, their breath mingling in the small space between them. Her heart thrummed against her chest, matching the intensity of the moment.

"Are you sure you want me to let you go, amore mio?" he rumbled, brushing his lips on top of hers.

Valerie could feel his warm breath on her face, sending shivers down her spine. His gaze was intense, holding her captive in the moment. Her mind raced, trying to make sense of what was happening.

"Let go of me," she repeated, trying to sound more confident this time. But her body seemed to have a mind of its own, responding positively to Antonio's touch.

She clenched her thighs together and felt her nipples tighten under her nightgown.

Oh, god. What if he noticed!?

"Tell me, cara mia. Why are you really here?" he asked, his deep voice searching her eyes.

"I-I don't know," she stammered, feeling completely flustered under his intense gaze.

He raised an eyebrow at her, a hint of amusement in his expression. "You don't know? You just walked into my room in the middle of the night to just talk?"

Valerie swallowed nervously, feeling like a fool. "Yes," she said.

Antonio's lips curled into a small smile. "It's dangerous

I Am No Gentleman

to walk into my room like this, cara mia. I am not some gentleman."

"I know you're not," she fired back, her voice a little shaky but sounding far braver than she felt.

He flipped her over, so now she was under him. She swallowed thickly as she looked into his black eyes.

"You're scared," he laughed, his hands gripping her wrists above her head. His face was inches away from hers, so close she could see the hideous scar on his cheek. It made him look like the devil.

"I'm not scared of you!" she retorted, trying to break free from his grip, but he held her firmly in place.

"Oh, really?" he smirked, his eyes sparkling with mischief and something else—desire, maybe?

Trying to gain some control over the situation, Valerie glared at him and snapped, "Yes...really!"

He laughed again, richer this time. "God, you're a feisty one. I like that."

Valerie rolled her eyes. "I'm not here to entertain you."

"Then perhaps you want me," he said matter-of-factly.

The breath hitched in her throat. "What?"

His eyes didn't leave hers, inspecting her, testing her. "You want me, don't you?" His voice was a low growl, filled with arrogance and amusement.

She wriggled under him, her cheeks burning red. "Yeah, right. You wish," she retorted.

"But why else would you be here, Valerie, all alone in the devil's den?" Antonio teased as he moved closer to her face.

"Like I said, to tell you about my plans," she said without missing a beat.

He stopped for a moment and then laughed, releasing her hands. His laugh was rich and intoxicating. It made the hairs on the back of her neck stand up.

Catching her breath, Valerie pushed him off forcefully and sprang up from the bed.

"No need to get violent, cara mia," Antonio grinned, his dark eyes scanning her from head to toe.

She crossed her arms over her chest defensively. "I'm not violent," she replied sternly.

"But you are a liar," he said quietly, his gaze locked on hers. He was right. She did desire him. She wasn't sure how it happened or when, but it did.

She stayed silent; there was nothing more to say.

Antonio's gaze softened as he reached out to stroke her cheek gently. "It's okay to want something…someone."

"But…but you're not someone to be wanted," she protested weakly but didn't move away from his touch. "And I definitely do not want you."

A slight grin played at the corners of his mouth as he drew her in again, his hand gently resting on the small of her back. Her body tingled with anticipation.

"I see," he whispered, his breath warm against her ear. "Then why did you come here and tempt me?"

"I-I didn't come here to tempt you," she managed to stammer out, though even she could hear the unconvincing tone in her voice.

He grabbed her waist and pulled her to his lap again, making her straddle him. His breath was hot against her skin as he chuckled, his finger tracing a tantalizing path along the curve of her breast.

The thin, silky nightgown clung to her body, revealing every curve and eliciting a low growl from his throat. His lips brushed against her earlobe, and she gasped as she felt his tongue on her skin.

He whispered, "Liar…you knew exactly what you were doing when you came in here dressed like this."

The Mafia Boss's Pregnant Bride

The heat between them was palpable, his desire evident as she felt his erection pressed against her sex. It felt hot and…big.

Her heart raced as she waited for his next move.

"So, what will it be, Valerie?" he murmured, his hands gripping her hips tightly. There was a hunger in his eyes that mirrored her own. 'Will you keep denying me all night? Pretend that you don't want me?"

"Why should I want you?" she shot back, trying to sound bolder than she actually felt.

His smirk only deepened. "You shouldn't. But you do."

Valerie shivered as his fingers traced the contours of her body, and she leaned into his touch.

"Stop playing games," she snapped, though the hint of desperation in her voice betrayed her.

"Am I?" he chuckled, leaning in to kiss her collarbone. His lips felt like fire against her skin. The thin silk of her nightgown did nothing to shield her from his searing heat.

He moved his hands to the hem of her nightgown, pulling it up, but she stopped him.

"No, don't!" she said breathlessly.

He grinned, the predator at the end of the hunt. "Give me

I Am No Gentleman

a reason not to," he challenged. His fingers, sinful and soft against her heated skin, curled against the hem of her dress, ready to pull it up.

"I—" she stuttered, the room suddenly feeling too hot.

His fingers stilled. "Yes, Valerie?"

"I just gave birth not that long ago and my body…" she hesitated.

He snorted. "You think I care about that?"

Her eyes widened. "You should. It's… it's different."

His eyes roved over her body as if he could see through her nightgown.

"I have stretch marks lining my stomach, and my breasts… they are saggy from breastfeeding," she said. God, she hated how insecure she sounded, but it was the truth.

He stared at her for a moment, his face unreadable. "So?" he said finally, looking up at her. His eyes were soft, not mocking.

Valerie blinked at him. "So… so it's not attractive," she said. She could hear the bitterness in her own voice and felt a lump in her throat.

He frowned slightly. "Who said that?" he asked quietly.

"I..." she hesitated, biting her lip. "I did. I do. And besides, the doctor said I can't have sex for another six weeks. So if you want to fuck me..."

"Make love," he corrected her with a growl.

"What?" she frowned, looking down at him.

"I want to make love to you, Valerie. I don't just want to fuck you." His voice was stern, but there was a softness in his eyes that melted her insides.

"Oh," was all she could manage to say.

"I will wait then. Six weeks, you say?" He asked, looking straight into her eyes as if challenging her to change her mind.

"Yes," she nodded, feeling heat consuming her again. Was she really making plans to have sex with Antonio, of all people?

No, she was just stalling for time, Valerie told herself.

He let go of the hem of her gown, his hands instead falling onto her thighs, holding her still on his lap. His touch was warm, and the heat radiated through the fabric of her nightgown into her skin.

"Well," he said finally, breaking the silence that had fallen between them. "At least we can do this," he said and kissed her.

Twenty-Four

Breakfast With the Mafia Boss

Valerie felt Antonio's lips against hers, the kiss both demanding and soft. His hands moved to her waist, holding her still as he deepened the kiss. His tongue traced her lower lip, seeking entrance, and when she parted her lips to allow him in, a low growl escaped his throat.

His hands traveled upward, skimming over the fabric of her gown until they cupped her breasts. The touch was electrifying, making her gasp against his mouth.

Suddenly, Antonio pulled away, breaking the kiss abruptly. A different look was in his eyes now, a fierce determination that made Valerie's insides flutter.

"I won't touch you until you're ready," he said, his voice hoarse with desire. "But I can't promise I won't kiss you."

"Like I would let you again. This was a mistake," Valerie said breathlessly.

"Was it?" Antonio's eyes were darker than ever before. Valerie swallowed, feeling a lump in her throat.

"I think so," she said, her voice weak.

"Prove it," he challenged, his fingers resting lightly on her hips.

"What?" Her heart pounded in her chest as he looked up at her, waiting for her answer.

"I don't believe you," he said simply. "I think you like this just as much as I do."

Valerie blinked, taken aback by his words. But there was no denying the truth of them. The way he touched her, kissed her…it was unlike anything she had ever experienced before.

And she wanted more. She wanted him.

"I-" she started to say, but he was already pulling her close again, pressing his lips to hers in another searing kiss. His hands went to her waist, pulling her closer as he deepened the kiss.

"Just admit it," he murmured against her lips. "You want me as much as I want you."

Valerie pulled away, breathing hard. "Fine," she admitted, unable to keep the desire out of her voice. "But that doesn't change anything."

"Doesn't it, Valerie?" Antonio looked at her with an intense gaze that sent shivers down her spine.

"No, Antonio." Even though the way he said her name made her heart flutter, she tried to sound stern. "We can't do this."

"Why not?" There was a note of frustration in his voice.

"Because... because it's not right!" It sounded weak even to her own ears.

He raised an eyebrow at that. "And who says what's right and what's not?"

"I do." Valerie met his gaze head-on, refusing to back down.

He stared at her for a moment before a slow smile spread across his face. "Alright then," he said finally. "I suppose we'll have to see about that."

And with that, he let her go, his hands falling away from her body. She felt a sudden chill without his touch but ignored it.

As she stumbled out of his room and back to her own, Valerie knew one thing for sure: she was in deep trouble. And the worst part was, she wasn't sure if she wanted to get out of it.

The Mafia Boss's Pregnant Bride

~-~

The next morning, Valerie woke up early but didn't want to get out of bed. Landon, who had woken her up three times throughout the night, was now sleeping peacefully in his crib.

She suddenly heard footsteps coming into her room and opened her eyes fully in alarm.

"Who is it?" she asked when she heard someone knock.

"It's me," Antonio's smooth voice floated from outside.

Her heart pounded. She had nearly run to her room after their encounter yesterday, and now she had to face him first thing in the morning?

"Come in," she said, pulling the blanket up to her chin.

"Antonio," she murmured, alarmed as he came inside. His dark eyes met hers, a hint of amusement flickering in them.

"Valerie," he said smoothly, moving to stand by the edge of the bed. "Good morning."

"What are you doing here?" she asked.

"I came to invite you to breakfast," he said.

Landon's faint crying interrupted her response, and she quickly got out of bed. She hurried to her crib and saw him flailing his arms around, his red face streaked with tears.

"Aww, sweetheart. Are you hungry?" Valerie cooed and snuggled Landon to her chest.

She looked at Antonio. "I will be there after I feed her."

"I will wait for you," Antonio said and walked out of the room.

As soon as Valerie took a seat on the rocking chair, she started to feed Landon. Watching her little mouth latching onto her brought a feeling of warmth to Valerie's heart. All the fears and doubts seemed to fade away in that moment, replaced only by the love she had for him.

After she was done, Valerie walked to the dining room with Landon in her arms.

The fresh scent of pancakes filled the air and warmed Valerie up.

Valerie looked at the breakfast table. There was a stack of pancakes sitting right in the middle. There were also eggs, bacon, bread, and fruits. A breakfast fit for a king and a queen.

"Sit and eat, Valerie. I can have Lucia take Landon until you are done," Antonio said, his eyes impossibly gentle.

Valerie hesitated for a moment, glancing down at Landon, who was now peacefully asleep in her arms. The idea of sitting down to breakfast with Antonio was both tempting and terrifying for some reason.

"Alright," she finally agreed, her voice soft.

Antonio nodded. "Lucia!" he called.

Lucia hurried in as if she was on standby and took Landon off Valerie's hands.

Valerie took a seat at the table. "Thank you," she said, feeling a bit overwhelmed by the gesture. It had been so long since someone had taken care of her like this. She was always the one doing all the cooking and cleaning when she lived with Julian.

"You're welcome," Antonio replied, his eyes meeting hers with a warmth that made her heart flutter.

"Your grandmother...will she not join us?" Valerie asked.

Antonio wrinkled his forehead at that. "Nonna isn't feeling well this morning."

Valerie's heart sank a bit. "I'm sorry to hear that. I hope she feels better soon," she said.

Antonio nodded, a faint shadow crossing his features. "Grazi, Valerie. She'll be alright. Just needs some rest."

They continued their breakfast in comfortable silence for a

while.

"I…" Valerie hesitated.

Antonio narrowed his eyes. "Yes?"

"I was wondering… what are your plans for the day?" Valerie asked tentatively.

Antonio set down his fork and regarded her thoughtfully. "I have some work to attend to at the vineyard. Would you be interested in joining me?"

"What will a Mafia boss do at a Vineyard?" she blurted out.

Antonio's lips quirked up in a small smile at her question. "Contrary to popular belief, I am more than just some criminal. I have several business, including a vineyard. And I tend to the grapevines and oversee the production of our wine. It helps me relax and stay connected to my family's roots."

Valerie cocked her head, intrigued by this unexpected side of Antonio. "I would love to see that," she said, her curiosity piqued.

He raised an eyebrow. "Will you?"

Valerie wondered if she should retract her statement. Maybe she should hold back and not show so much interest in him.

But her curiosity won in the end.

"Yes," she said.

Twenty-Five

Sweet Wine

Valerie felt a mix of nervousness and excitement churning in her stomach as she finished her breakfast. She followed Antonio outside, where a sleek black car was waiting for them. The drive to the vineyard was surprisingly peaceful, the scenery changing from the bustling city to rolling hills and lush vineyards.

"I've never been to a Vineyard before," she said to Antonio after a moment.

Antonio glanced at her with a small smile, his eyes reflecting the sunlight filtering through the leaves of the passing trees. "Is that right?"

Valerie nodded.

"What places did your man take you then?" he asked.

Valerie blinked. "What do you mean?"

"Julian. He was your boyfriend, wasn't he? Didn't he take you out?" Antonio asked.

Valerie looked away, avoiding his gaze. "No," she said, her voice barely audible.

Antonio sensed the discomfort in Valerie's response and chose to remain silent, much to her relief. The car glided through the winding roads leading to the vineyard, surrounded by rows of lush grapevines basking in the golden sunlight.

"Wow..." Valerie mused. "It's beautiful out here."

Antonio grinned widely. "Wait until you see everything inside and taste the wine. We create the finest wine around here."

"I bet all the Vineyard owners say that about their wine," Valerie retorted.

Antonio chuckled, the sound deep and rich.

Valerie shivered. Even the sound of his laughter affected her physically. This was too dangerous being so close to him.

"Perhaps they do, but I can assure you, our wine truly speaks

Sweet Wine

for itself," he said, unaware of her strange reaction to him.

They stepped out, the sweet scent of ripening grapes hitting her nostrils. Valerie took in the picturesque scene, feeling a sense of peace settle over her that she hadn't experienced in a long time.

Antonio led her through the vineyard, his stride confident and purposeful as he explained the process of winemaking, his passion for it evident in every word.

Valerie listened intently, hanging on his every detail as they moved from the rows of grapevines to the production area where large barrels stood like silent sentinels, guarding the secrets of fermentation.

"This is amazing," Valerie murmured, her eyes meeting Antonio's with newfound respect. "I had no idea how much goes into making wine."

"It's a labor of love," Antonio said as he poured two glasses of wine. He pushed one of them toward Valerie. "Go ahead, taste it."

Valerie hesitated, her fingers wrapping around the delicate stem of the glass. She brought it to her lips, taking a small sip. The rich flavors exploded on her tongue.

Antonio watched her with a knowing smile, his eyes twinkling with amusement at her reaction. "Impressive, isn't it?" he remarked.

Valerie nodded, unable to tear her gaze away from him. There was something magnetic about him, something that drew her in despite the danger she sensed lurking beneath his charming façade.

As they stood there in the dimly lit production area, surrounded by the heady scent of fermenting grapes and aging oak barrels, Valerie felt a strange sense of intimacy settle between them.

Before she could overthink it, Valerie took a step closer to Antonio, the distance between them narrowing until she could feel the heat radiating off his body. His gaze locked with hers, dark and intense as if trying to decipher the thoughts swirling in her mind.

Without a word, Antonio set his glass aside and reached out to gently tilt Valerie's chin up, his touch feather-light against her skin. And then, before she could fully comprehend what was happening, his lips descended on hers in a soft, lingering kiss.

Valerie melted into the kiss, her senses overwhelmed by the taste of wine on his lips and the intoxicating scent of him surrounding her.

When they finally broke apart, Valerie's heart was pounding in her chest, her breath coming in short gasps.

"Mmmm…you taste better than any wine we make here," Antonio said in a teasing tone.

Sweet Wine

Valerie rolled her eyes and pushed him. "You can't just kiss me whenever you feel like it."

"Can't I?" he asked sheepishly.

"No, you can't," Valerie snapped.

"Well, then. My apologies to you, my love. How about we get something to eat now? It's almost lunchtime," Antonio said.

Valerie looked at her phone and gasped. "We should go home. Landon is alone and…"

Antonio grabbed her hand. "Baby is fine, mi amore. Lucia is more than capable of babysitting her."

"But…what if he gets hungry?" Valerie argued.

"Si? You have left her with some milk, no?" Antonio tilted his head.

"Yes. But I didn't mean to leave him alone this long," Valerie said, shaking her head.

Antonio tightened his fingers around Valerie's, his gaze soft. "He will be fine, trust me."

Valerie hesitated. "Okay. But we have to go back as soon as we are done with lunch."

Antonio smiled. "Of course."

As they settled back into their seats, enjoying the warm afternoon sun filtering through the vineyard's leaves, Antonio signaled to one of his employees. In a matter of moments, the man returned with a giant charcuterie board, an array of cheeses, meats, fruits, and nuts laid out in a mouthwatering display.

Valerie's eyes widened in delight at the sight before her. "Oh, this looks amazing," she exclaimed, reaching eagerly for a slice of prosciutto.

Antonio poured them both more wine before taking a seat next to Valerie.

"I am glad you approve," he said.

"What do you care whether I approve or not?" Valerie asked curtly.

Antonio chuckled softly, his eyes dancing with mischief. "My dear Valerie, your approval means everything to me. I live to see that beautiful smile on your face and to hear your laughter."

Valerie blushed, feeling a warmth spread through her at his words. "You are so full of shit, Antonio. Is this how you get women to sleep with you?"

He took her hand and brought it to his lips, planting a soft kiss on her knuckles. "There are no other women. My heart speaks the truth when it comes to you, mi amore."

Sweet Wine

"Lies," she murmured, then decided to change the subject. "Do you ever think about quitting the Mafia?" she asked quietly, her gaze searching his face.

Antonio paused, setting down her hand thoughtfully. "I have thought about it," he admitted slowly. "But it is not so simple."

Valerie nodded understandingly, her fingers tracing patterns on the wooden table.

"If you are worried about your and the boy's safety, you needn't. I will protect you with my life, I swear it," Antonio said determinedly as he placed his hand on his heart.

Valerie wanted to believe him, but part of her still wondered how genuine he was. She had heard promises like this before and got burned for it. She couldn't let that happen again.

Twenty-Six

Wash My Hair

Later that night, Valerie tucked Landon in and watched him sleep. He looked peaceful, and Valerie smiled to herself.

She felt a need to thank Antonio, to let him know how much his gesture meant to her. He wasn't as bad as she had thought. He didn't have to take her out, but he did.

She checked on Landon once more before stepping out, closing the door gently behind her.

The hallway was quiet; the plush carpet muffled Valerie's footsteps as she made her way toward where she knew Antonio would be. Her pulse quickened with each step, the excitement of their earlier escapades mingling with an unfamiliar flutter in her stomach.

Wash My Hair

What was this feeling? Nervousness? Anticipation? She shook her head, dismissing the thoughts.

"Relax, Valerie," she muttered under her breath. "Just say thank you and move on."

She paused at the threshold of Antonio's room, her gaze sweeping over the neatly made bed. Empty. No sign of him. She frowned.

Maybe he was in the bathroom. He did say he was going to take a shower.

But he wasn't in the bathroom either.

Valerie turned on her heel, her mind racing as she retraced her steps down the hallway. Then, there it was—a faint thrum of music vibrating through one of the doors further along the hall.

Maybe he was in the room.

The door loomed closed. She reached for the handle, her heart hammering against her ribs. What was she doing? She should just go back to her room.

But something inside her made her want to see him.

"Here goes nothing," Valerie breathed out, her fingers closing around the cool metal. With a decisive push, she opened the door.

The air seemed to shift as she stepped inside, and the scent of lavender hit her nostrils. Her eyes widened, and a sharp intake of breath was her only response.

There he was, Antonio, sprawled in a giant tub that dominated the room. The water caressed every inch of his skin, glistening in the light as it cascaded down his chiseled chest.

His eyes, usually so intense and mysterious, softened as they met hers. Antonio's lips curved into a small smile.

As her gaze roamed over his form, she noticed a particularly jagged scar running along his shoulder, the puckered tissue standing out starkly against the smooth expanse of his chest.

"Valerie?" His voice broke through her trance.

"Um...sorry," she mumbled.

"Didn't expect company," he added, a corner of his mouth lifting as if challenging her to look away.

His shoulders relaxed against the porcelain, unbothered by the intrusion—or perhaps amused by it.

The silence shattered, Valerie's heart pounded a wild rhythm against her ribs. Heat crept up her neck, staining her cheeks with the unmistakable hue of embarrassment. She had barged into his privacy, his sanctuary.

"Sorry, Antonio, I—I should've knocked," she stuttered out.

Wash My Hair

Her eyes darted away from his relaxed form.

She spun on her heel, the motion abrupt, almost desperate. The room seemed to spin with her, her senses tangled in the scent of lavender and the sound of water rippling with the ghost of her intrusion. She needed to flee, to escape the thick air of awkwardness that pressed down on her.

"Stop."

Valerie halted as she heard his command.

"Valerie," he called again, firm but not harsh. It was an invitation, a challenge, daring her to face what she had stumbled upon.

"Stay." It wasn't just a word. It was a command disguised as a request, and she couldn't ignore it.

She slowly turned around to face him.

Antonio laughed. "Valerie, come closer," he said, his tone light but firm. "There's no need for embarrassment."

Taking a deep breath, she moved towards him.

"Okay, then." She stopped at the edge of the tub, maintaining a careful distance while her gaze flicked over the absurdity of the giant bathtub occupying the center of the room like some sort of ceramic throne. "Why here, Antonio? Why in the middle of the room?"

He leaned back, resting against the rim of the tub, his eyes never leaving hers. Water lapped at his chest, and her eyes wandered down his lower half.

"My eyes are up here, mia cara," Antonio said casually.

Valerie quickly looked at his face and glared.

Antonio's chuckle bounced off the tiled walls, a deep, resonant sound that seemed at odds with the silence that had preceded it. "I take baths to relax," he explained, shifting slightly in the water. "It's therapeutic, helps me unwind."

Valerie bit her lip, looking away from the steam that curled up toward the ceiling. The heat from the bath had turned his skin a shade pinker, making him appear more vulnerable, less like the mystery he usually was. "Therapeutic, huh?" she managed to quip despite the lingering fluster that clung to her like a second skin. "Most people have a tub in their bathroom. Yours is in the middle of a room."

"Conventional methods don't always cut it," he replied, raising an eyebrow as he met her gaze again. His voice held an edge, a challenge.

Valerie crossed her arms, trying to match his coolness, though her heart raced. "Yeah, because nothing says 'rebel' quite like pruney fingers and bubble bath mohawks."

"Exactly." He smirked, the corner of his mouth ticking upward as if he were sharing a secret. "You get it."

Wash My Hair

"Sure." Valerie shrugged. "As long as you don't start hosting meetings in here, I guess you're free to bathe wherever you please."

He chuckled. "You should join me sometimes," Antonio said, his amusement still hanging in the air between them. "Might help you cool off."

"Join you?" Valerie's words came out sharper than she intended, a knee-jerk reaction to the ridiculousness of the suggestion. Yet, behind the sharpness, curiosity flickered.

"Unless you're scared," he taunted, leaning back against the rim of the tub, the water lapping at his shoulders. His eyes danced with a challenge, that same edge from before lingering in his tone.

"Scared?" Valerie repeated, her voice rising. She stepped closer, feeling the warmth radiating from the bath. The idea was absurd, but the heat wasn't just from the steam—it was from his gaze, his presence.

"Of getting a little wet?" He spread his arms along the edges, presenting himself like a king on a throne. "Or is it me you're afraid of?"

"Neither," Valerie shot back.

"Good," he said, a single word that held weight.

Valerie didn't speak for a few moments. "Want me to wash

your hair?" she asked, the words slipping out of her lips before she could stop them.

Antonio's eyes lit up with surprise, a flicker of something unreadable crossing his features before he masked it behind a smirk. "Oh, so now you're offering to wash my hair, Miss Valerie?" His voice was teasing but held a hint of something deeper, a challenge.

Valerie rolled her eyes, feeling the heat in her cheeks intensify. "I just thought... I mean, it's hard to reach the back by yourself," she mumbled, flustered by his gaze that seemed to see right through her.

He chuckled softly, the sound sending shivers down her spine. "I suppose I can't argue with that logic." Antonio leaned forward slightly, his dark hair sticking out in wet tendrils. "But only if you promise not to drown me."

The corner of Valerie's mouth twitched upwards despite herself. "Can't make any promises," she shot back, the banter coming more quickly now that the initial tension had ebbed away.

He leaned back and closed his eyes. "Alright then, mia cara. I am at your mercy."

Valerie exhaled softly and stepped toward him, her pulse speeding. What the hell am I doing? she thought to herself.

Twenty-Seven

In Control

Valerie tentatively reached for the shampoo bottle resting on the tub's edge and poured a small amount into her palm. Valerie began massaging it into Antonio's hair, her fingers moving through the strands with gentle expertise.

Antonio kept his eyes closed, a contented sigh escaping his lips at the soothing sensation.

"You've got gentle hands," he murmured, his voice low and intimate.

Valerie's heart skipped a beat at his words, and she bit her lip, trying to suppress a smile. "I try," she replied softly.

They fell into a companionable silence as Valerie continued

to massage his scalp, the warm water creating a tranquil backdrop. Despite the unusual setting, a sense of peace settled over her in that moment.

The intimacy of the situation felt almost surreal, as though it belonged in a dream. Antonio's damp hair slid smoothly between Valerie's fingers, and she marveled at the trust he was placing in her.

After a few more moments of careful massaging, Valerie dipped her hand into the water and began rinsing the suds from his hair, watching as the bubbles swirled away down the drain. Antonio let out another sigh, barely audible, yet Valerie felt it resonate deeply within her.

"All done," she said quietly.

"That's a shame," he murmured.

She reached down and traced her finger over one of the scars on Antonio's chest. His hand closed around hers, fingers enveloping hers gently against his scarred skin.

Their eyes met in a silent exchange, a question lingering between them. Without breaking their gaze, Antonio brought her hand to his lips and pressed a tender kiss to her knuckles. Valerie felt a sudden surge of warmth engulf her, her heart pounding in her chest.

She swallowed hard, the air thick with unspoken words and unacknowledged feelings. "How did you get these scars?"

In Control

Antonio's lips curved as he held her hand against his chest, the warmth of his touch seeping into her skin. "Just reminders of my line of work," he replied softly. "They are now a part of who I am."

Valerie nodded, understanding flickering in her eyes as she traced the outline of another scar with her fingertip. Each mark seemed to tell a story of its own, tales of battles fought and wounds healed. "And your tattoos? Do they mean something?" she asked softly.

Antonio's gaze softened as he looked at the ink decorating his skin. "Each one tells a story," he began. "They are reminders of my past, but also symbols of my present." He turned his hand slightly, revealing a tattoo of a compass on his wrist. "This one, for instance, is a reminder to always find my way back home, no matter what."

Valerie listened intently, captivated by the vulnerability in his words.

"And this one," he continued, pointing to a design on his shoulder, "represents strength and resilience. In this line of work, you need both in abundance." His eyes bore into hers with an intensity that made her breath catch.

She traced the lines of the tattoo with gentle fingers, feeling the warmth of his skin beneath her touch. The room seemed to shrink around them, leaving only the two of them in a bubble of intimate silence.

Her heart raced with a mixture of emotions—curiosity, desire, and an inexplicable longing for something she couldn't quite define.

"You have your grandma's name tattooed on your heart. You love her a lot, don't you?" Valerie whispered, almost to herself.

Antonio smiled softly. "More than anything in the world. My nonna raised me, you know."

Valerie nodded, a lump forming in her throat as she tried to suppress the surge of emotion threatening to overwhelm her. Antonio's grandmother had played such a significant role in shaping the man before her, revealing layers of him she had never known existed.

"Family means everything to you, doesn't it?" she whispered, the words breaking through the heavy silence.

Antonio's eyes softened further, a faint smile playing on his lips. "Always has been and always will be."

As he spoke, Valerie felt a deep pang within her, a yearning for that kind of unwavering love and acceptance. Antonio's vulnerability was both disarming and captivating, drawing her in like a moth to a flame.

Without another word, he reached out and gently tucked a loose strand of hair behind her ear, his touch light against her skin. His fingers lingered there for a moment longer than

In Control

necessary, sending a shiver down her spine.

In that charged moment, with nothing but the sound of their breathing filling the space between them, Valerie felt something shift irrevocably within her. Antonio had laid bare parts of himself that few had ever seen, inviting her into the depths of his world with an openness that both terrified and thrilled her.

She leaned in, pressing her lips against his.

Antonio's lips met Valerie's with a hunger that mirrored her own. The kiss was electric, a storm of emotions brewing beneath the surface as their bodies drew closer. His tongue gently pushed through her parted lips, deepening the intimacy of their embrace.

Water sloshed out of the tub at his movement, soaking the front of Valerie's shirt, but she didn't care.

"Touch me more," he murmured against her lips, guiding her hand down to his stomach.

Valerie could feel the warmth radiating off his skin, the water droplets clinging to his chest like liquid diamonds. Antonio's body tensed under her touch, a mixture of desire and restraint swirling in the air between them. His scars felt rough beneath her fingertips, each one a testament to battles fought and victories won.

Antonio's eyes bore into hers with an intensity that made

The Mafia Boss's Pregnant Bride

Valerie's breath catch in her throat.

Their lips sought each other again in a fervent kiss, a storm of passion brewing between them. The room seemed to fade away, leaving only Antonio and Valerie in their intimate embrace.

"Per favore, mio amore," Antonio husked when they broke apart, his dark eyes intense. "I need you to touch me."

Valerie hesitated for a moment, her heart pounding in her chest. But then she let her hand drift lower, tracing the lines of his abs before wrapping her fingers around him, feeling his length and girth against her palm.

Antonio hissed in pleasure, his head falling back against the edge of the tub. Valerie started to move her hand up and down, watching as his face contorted with pleasure.

The water in the tub rippled with each movement, splashing against the sides. She could feel the heat radiating off Antonio's skin, the scent of his arousal filling the air.

"Yes, just like that," he murmured, his eyes closed.

As Valerie watched him drown in ecstasy, a strange sense of power surged through her.

In control.

She had done this with another man before, but the experience had never left her feeling in control or fulfilled. There were days when she felt disgusted by it, a reluctance that weighed heavily on her mind.

But with Antonio, everything felt different. As she watched him writhing in pleasure, she found herself drawn to the power she held over him—the pleasure she was able to bring him.

Leaning down, Valerie brushed her lips against Antonio's ear, eliciting a deep groan from him. "Oh, Valerie…my sweet girl. Don't stop," he pleaded, his voice thick with desire.

She had no intention of stopping.

Maintaining her rhythmic hand movements, Valerie kept her gaze fixed on Antonio's face. His eyes were closed, lashes fluttering with each surge of pleasure. His lips parted slightly, teeth gleaming as his chest rose and fell with each ragged breath. His muscles tensed and flexed as he gripped the edges of the tub.

Antonio's moans filled the room, intensifying the sensations that enveloped them both. It felt like she was in a trance, completely immersed in the moment. The power of her touch, the urgency of his responses, and the symphony of their shared pleasure created an electric atmosphere.

Pressing her lips to his ear once more, Valerie felt the warmth of his skin against her mouth. "Valerie…" His voice was a hoarse whisper, a plea for more.

Despite the intensity of the situation, Valerie felt an unexpected calmness settle over her. She knew she wielded the power to bring a man like Antonio to the brink of ecstasy, and she embraced it fully. This new experience was thrilling, erotic, and empowering—a side of herself she had never explored but now reveled in.

And so, Valerie continued, her hand moving with increasing enthusiasm, matching the rhythm of Antonio's ragged breathing. She watched intently as his face contorted with pleasure, brow furrowed and jaw tense. At this moment, he was hers to control, his pleasure, her focus, and responsibility.

As she persisted, excitement surged within Valerie. Her heart pounded in her chest, breaths shallow and rapid with anticipation. Part of her yearned to share in the intense sensations she was evoking in Antonio, to experience the pleasure alongside him.

But for now, she found satisfaction in watching, in feeling the power of her touch bringing Antonio closer and closer to the edge.

With a final groan, Antonio reached his peak and released into her palm. Valerie felt a thrill shoot through her body, imagining the warmth of him spilling into her. The thought stirred a mix of emotions within her, questioning herself and the intensity of the encounter.

"Valerie?" Antonio's voice broke through her reverie, his tone hoarse with lingering desire.

In Control

Caught off guard by her own actions, Valerie hesitated, uncertain of what to say. She had ventured into new territory, and the aftermath left her momentarily speechless.

"I...," she whispered, her voice trailing off as she struggled to articulate her thoughts. "I don't know... I just...felt...I needed..." Her words faltered, a jumble of emotions clouding her mind. Abruptly, she stood up.

"Wait..." Antonio began, but Valerie swiftly turned on her heels and hurried out of the room before he could finish his sentence.

Twenty-Eight

Lovely Sight

Antonio emerged from the bath, feeling the cool air brush against his damp skin, causing droplets of water to shiver along his arms. He wrapped himself in a towel, the fabric absorbing the warmth of the bathwater, and a sense of relaxation replaced the tension in his muscles.

Reflecting on Valerie's actions, Antonio couldn't deny their significance. Her touch had been more than physical; it was a gesture of surrender, a silent acknowledgment of trust. He could still feel the ghost of her touch, stirring joy and satisfaction deep within him.

Drying himself, Antonio paused, contemplating the shift he sensed in Valerie—walls crumbling, defenses yielding.

"Opening up," he muttered to himself with a faint smile.

Lovely Sight

Determination hardened within him.

Valerie's act wasn't merely intimate; it was a declaration, intentional or not. Antonio Leones was not one to shy away from challenges; he intended to claim her heart just as surely as she had claimed his, unwittingly.

Pulling on his pajama pants, still warm from the bath, Antonio caught his reflection in the mirror. A grin lingered on his lips, Valerie's image dancing in his mind—flushed cheeks, wide eyes filled with wonder and perhaps a hint of embarrassment.

Making his way to the bedroom, Antonio replayed their recent encounter in his thoughts. Exhaustion tugged at him, and he murmured into the darkness, "Goodnight, Valerie," allowing her name to settle around him as he drifted into sleep.

Sometime later, a faint cry pierced the night, jolting Antonio awake. Concern gripped his heart—a worry he couldn't ignore. Had their intimacy pushed Valerie too far? Was she overwhelmed with regret?

"Damn," he muttered, throwing off the sheets and swinging his feet to the cold floor. Urgency fueled his movements; there was no time for slippers, no patience for hesitation. He needed to reach her, to assure her that whatever happened, it wasn't a mistake.

Quickly reaching her door, Antonio turned the knob with

care. The hinges gave a soft creak as he entered, finding Valerie tossing and turning in her sleep, clearly caught in the throes of a nightmare.

"Valerie," he called out, his voice sharper than intended.

"No… Please don't. I don't want to," she whimpered, her voice tormented.

In swift strides, Antonio reached her bedside. His hand hovered for a moment before gently resting on her shoulder. Valerie's skin was warm under his touch, trembling with the remnants of her distress.

Her body twitched at his contact, and her deep green eyes fluttered open, glazed with fear. They searched the shadows until they met his, locking in a silent battle between dread and reality.

"Shh, it's just a dream," Antonio murmured, his voice steady despite his racing heart. "You're safe, Valerie. I'm here."

Tears streaked her cheeks, vulnerability etched in every line of her face—a sight that tugged at Antonio's core.

"Stay back," she rasped weakly, a feeble attempt at defiance.

"I won't let anyone hurt you," Antonio countered firmly, his resolve a silent promise. "Not now, not ever."

He held her gaze, a moment of connection filled with an

emotion deeper than fleeting desire.

"What... What are you doing here?" she whispered.

"It's okay, Valerie. I heard you crying, and I had to make sure you were alright," he said softly, trying to reassure her.

Reaching out, Antonio gently wiped away a tear from her cheek, feeling her tremble beneath his touch.

"I'm fine. You can leave now. I don't need your pity," Valerie said curtly.

Instead of retreating, Antonio lay down beside her, pulling her close against his chest, ignoring her protests. "Do I seem like the kind of man who pities anyone?" he asked gently.

She struggled initially, trying to push away from his embrace. "Let me go," she insisted.

Antonio tightened his hold, unable to resist the urge to comfort her. "Valerie, listen to me. You're not alone. I'm here for you, and I won't let anyone hurt you."

Gradually, her body relaxed, sobs fading into quiet whimpers against his chest. He felt her heartbeat slow, matching his own steady rhythm.

"I had a nightmare," she whispered eventually, her voice barely audible.

The Mafia Boss's Pregnant Bride

Antonio stroked her hair soothingly. "I know, sweetheart."

As the night grew quieter, Valerie's breathing steadied, and she drifted back to sleep, her body still trembling slightly. Antonio continued to hold her close, every ounce of her warmth seeping into his skin.

As Valerie's breathing deepened, Antonio allowed sleep to claim him, his arms wrapped protectively around her, a silent sentinel in the night.

~-~

Antonio woke to the soft sound of cooing beside him. Slowly opening his eyes, he saw Valerie playing with baby Landon nearby. The sight warmed his heart—Valerie, embracing motherhood with evident joy, and Landon, reaching out with chubby hands to touch his mother's face.

"Good morning," Antonio greeted softly, careful not to startle Valerie.

She turned towards him with a slight smile. "Sorry. Did we disturb you?" she asked.

Antonio shook his head, his eyes still fixed on the tender scene before him. "Not at all. It's a lovely sight to wake up to," he replied, his grin reflecting his genuine pleasure.

Valerie's gaze met his, a small smile playing on her lips as she cradled Landon protectively. "Don't get used to it," she

Lovely Sight

teased lightly.

Raising an eyebrow, Antonio leaned on his elbow, his attention focused on Valerie. "Oh no? What if I'm already used to it?"

Valerie rolled her eyes playfully, adjusting Landon in her arms as the baby cooed happily, unaware of the unspoken tension between them.

"I mean it, Antonio. Don't start thinking this is some kind of routine," Valerie said firmly, though her tone softened in the early morning light streaming through the window.

Propping himself up, Antonio regarded her thoughtfully. "Why not? I like waking up to you and Landon. It feels... right."

Valerie sighed, her gaze shifting between Landon and Antonio with a mix of affection and concern. "Because things aren't that simple," she explained gently. "You can't just come into our lives and expect everything to fall into place."

Antonio didn't immediately respond. Instead, he reached out, brushing a stray strand of hair away from Valerie's face with a tender gesture.

"Thank you for last night," Valerie said suddenly, her voice filled with gratitude. "For comforting me."

Feeling the warmth of her skin under his fingertips, Antonio traced the line of her cheek gently. "Don't thank me. I wasn't doing you any favors. Everything I do for you is for selfish reasons," he admitted, his voice husky with emotion.

Valerie bit her lip, her eyes meeting his with a mixture of curiosity and concern. "Selfish reasons?"

"Most definitely," Antonio replied, his gaze unwavering. "I am trying to win your heart."

Valerie's eyes widened slightly, a flicker of uncertainty crossing her features. "Is that all this is to you? A game?"

Shaking his head, Antonio kept his eyes locked on hers. "I want you to be mine, that's all."

She sighed, holding Landon closer against her chest. "And what if I don't want you?"

Antonio's expression remained steady, his resolve firm. "You will."

A small, hesitant smile appeared on Valerie's lips. "You know, you're stubborn."

"And you're beautiful," Antonio replied smoothly. "But I'll be the first to admit, I can't win this game without your help."

There was a moment of quiet between them before Valerie spoke again. "I have them."

Lovely Sight

Antonio blinked, momentarily confused. "Have what?"

"What you were looking for," Valerie clarified softly. "I have the codes."

Twenty-Nine

The Necklace

Antonio's dark gaze drilled into Valerie with an accusatory intensity. "You have the codes," he said, his voice flat and devoid of emotion.

Valerie couldn't tell whether he was angry or not, as his face remained stoic and unreadable. She didn't want him to misinterpret her actions. It wasn't that she was intentionally keeping the codes from him! Her heart raced as she tried to find the right words to explain herself, the tension between them palpable.

"I…I can explain," she said hesitantly.

Antonio leaned back against the headboard, his eyes never leaving hers. "Then explain."

The Necklace

"I found it yesterday. I was telling Lucas a story and he was fiddling with my necklace…"

"Necklace?" Antonio stopped her.

"Yeah. This necklace," Valerie said, holding up the pendant to show him. "Julian gave this to me a while back."

She had been meaning to get rid of it ever since he died, but for some reason, something held her back. Now she was glad she didn't.

"I see. Continue," he said.

"Well, Landon grabbed it from my neck and was fiddling with it earlier. It must have triggered something. A switch of some sort and a small compartment opened in the pendant. There was a small piece of paper rolled inside it. With some numbers written on it," she said, releasing a sigh of relief as she finally told him.

Antonio's eyes narrowed as he processed Valerie's explanation. He reached out a hand, signaling for her to hand over the pendant. She hesitated for a moment, unsure of how he would react, but finally placed it in his outstretched palm.

Silence settled between them like a heavy fog, and Valerie could feel the weight of his gaze on her as he unrolled the tiny piece of paper. His expression shifted as he read the numbers inscribed on it. Without a word, he stood up and walked to the window, his back to her.

Valerie held her breath, waiting for him to speak, her heart pounding in her chest. "Well?"

"This is it," he said. "These are the codes I was looking for." His lips curled into a small smile.

"What are they?" she asked.

"I can't believe it. That bastard Julian is smarter than I thought," Antonio said, ignoring her question.

"What are they for?" she asked again.

Antonio turned to face her, his eyes now holding a glint of both satisfaction and surprise. "These codes," he began slowly, "are the key to Julian's hidden accounts. They hold the locations of his stashed wealth and sensitive information, which he didn't want falling into the wrong hands."

Valerie's mind raced with the implications of his words. "So, these codes are worth a fortune?"

He nodded.

"So you killed him for his money?" she asked, unable to hide her disgust. "Didn't you have enough of your own?"

Valerie stood frozen as she waited for his answer. Antonio's gaze bore into hers, his eyes dark and unreadable.

"Is that what you think of me, Valerie?" Antonio's voice was

The Necklace

low and dangerous, a stark contrast to the smile that had adorned his lips moments ago. He got out of the bed and walked toward her.

She swallowed hard, her heart pounding uncomfortably loud in her ears. She held Landon close to her chest, finding solace in her warmth. "I... I don't know what to think anymore," she admitted, feeling the weight of her own doubt pressing down on her.

Antonio's eyes softened slightly, a flicker of something vulnerable passing through them before he masked it with his usual stoicism. "It's not about the money, Valerie," he said firmly. "It's about power. Julian held secrets that would've brought down everything I'd built. I sent my men there to retrieve the codes so I could protect myself. Things went sideways and he got killed."

Valerie chewed on her lower lip uncomfortably. She couldn't blame Antonio for his actions. He and Julian are both criminals, and these things happen in their world.

She was mostly angry at Julian now for hiding all the money he had access to. He pretended that he didn't have enough to support her and made her work at sleazy clubs. Sometimes he made her do things that she wanted to erase from her mind.

"I understand," she finally managed to whisper, the weight of his gaze almost suffocating her. "I... I am not angry at you for killing him."

Antonio's expression softened for a fleeting moment, revealing a vulnerability that seemed out of place on his usually composed face. In that brief instant, Valerie caught a glimpse of the man behind the mask he wore so effortlessly.

"Good," he said quietly. "I wouldn't want you to resent me."

"So... now that you have the codes, does it mean you don't need me anymore?" she asked.

Antonio's lips curled into a small smile. "What do you think?"

After Antonio's question, Valerie could feel a knot forming in her stomach. The air between them crackled with tension, like a storm waiting to break loose. She struggled to read his expression, the subtle shift in his features leaving her unnerved.

"I think..." she hesitated, unsure of what to say next. The weight of his gaze bore down on her, urging her to speak. "I think you'll always find an excuse to keep me around," she finally replied.

Antonio chuckled. "I am glad you figured that out, mia cara. You can't get rid of me. And don't forget whose name is written on your son's birth certificate." He winked.

Valerie rolled her eyes.

Antonio's voice was hesitant as he spoke to her. "Can I ask you something?"

The Necklace

"What's that?"

"Why aren't you angry at me for killing Julian?" he asked.

His question caught her off guard. Valerie hesitated before answering. "I don't know," she lied.

"Why do you bottle everything inside, mi amore? You can tell me the truth, you know," he said.

"I don't know what you are talking about, Antonio," Valerie said defiantly.

"I just think it's strange that you don't seem terribly upset about his death. Even though he was the father of your child," he asked, tilting his eyebrow.

"It's none of your business, Antonio," Valerie barked.

Antonio's eyes darkened at her retort, a flicker of hurt crossing his face before he masked it with his usual indifference. He took a step closer to Valerie, causing her to instinctively back away until she was cornered.

"Everything about you is my business, Valerie," he whispered, the intensity of his gaze piercing through her defenses. "You can pretend all you want, but we both know the truth."

Valerie swallowed hard, refusing to break eye contact with Antonio. "I may not mourn Julian's death, but that doesn't mean I owe you anything."

Antonio reached out to tuck a loose strand of hair behind her ear. "Did he hurt you?"

Valerie jerked her head away from his touch, her eyes blazing with a mix of defiance. "That's none of your concern," she snapped, her heart pounding in her chest.

Antonio's jaw clenched, his patience wearing thin. "It is my concern, Valerie. Because whether you admit it or not, you belong to me now."

She laughed bitterly, the sound devoid of any humor. "Belong to you? You think because you let me live at your house, you own me? Let's get one thing straight, Antonio," Valerie said, her voice dripping with venom. "I am not a possession to be owned or controlled by anyone. Not by you, not by Julian, not by anyone."

She squared her shoulders, meeting his intense gaze head-on.

Antonio's expression hardened at her defiance, a muscle ticking in his jaw as he fought to maintain his composure. "You may have a sharp tongue, Valerie, but don't mistake my patience for weakness," he warned, his tone low and dangerous.

Valerie let out a bitter laugh, unafraid of the storm brewing in his eyes. "And don't mistake my compliance for acceptance, Antonio. We have kissed once or twice, but that doesn't mean we are in a relationship or something."

The Necklace

Antonio's lips curved up. "Oh, we did much more than just kissing once or twice cara mia."

Valerie's cheeks heated, and her stomach clenched as she remembered what she had done to him in the bathtub last night. "That was…I don't know what that was. It was a mistake. It will never happen again."

Antonio's eyes darkened at her words, a dangerous glint flickering in their depths. "We will see about that."

Thirty

Special Day

The moment Ellie's eyes fluttered open, a surge of excitement pulsed through her. She rolled over, glancing at the empty space beside her where River usually lay.

Today was different, special—it was her birthday. She pushed off the sheets and sat up, her heart thrumming with anticipation.

"Morning," she called out as she stepped into the kitchen. River stood there, his back to her, his hands busy fixing his coffee. No sign of recognition flashed across his face—no 'happy birthday,' no smile. Just the clink of his spoon against the mug.

"Sleep well?" she asked, leaning against the counter, eyeing

Special Day

the calendar on the fridge where she had circled the date in red.

"Like a rock," he replied, not turning around. The steam from his mug rose in the air, disappearing without a trace—just like her hopes that he would remember.

"Big day today," she said, trying not to let the disappointment seep into her voice.

"Is it?" River finally looked at her, his eyebrows raised, a question in his gaze but missing the point entirely.

"Thought we might do something... celebratory," she hinted, her fingers drumming a quick, impatient rhythm on the countertop.

"Celebratory," he said distractedly, sipping his coffee, "What's the occasion?"

Ellie's heart sank. He totally forgot!

"Anything wrong?" River asked, finally looking at her.

"Nothing," she replied, too quick, too sharp. Her foot tapped an impatient beat on the hardwood floor.

"Okay then." He scribbled something on a document, oblivious.

"Busy with work?" she probed, her voice edging toward

confrontation.

"Yeah," he muttered, not missing a beat.

"Right." Her fingers curled into fists at her sides.

She stormed to the window, staring out at nothing. The glass fogged with her breath, each exhale a silent scream. Betrayal simmered beneath her skin, thoughts of loyalty and revenge battling for dominance. How could he forget?

"Nice view today," she said aloud, hoping to snag his attention.

"Uh-huh." River's voice floated from the table, detached.

"Clear skies, bright sun… kind of like a day for celebrating, don't you think?" Her tone spiked with sarcasm, her body tense, ready to spring.

"Sure, Ellie." He didn't look up. "Celebrate away."

Ellie whirled around, fists clenched. "You'd like that, wouldn't you? Me, celebrating all by myself while you bury yourself in work!"

"Hey, what's gotten into you?" River stood, papers forgotten, his expression a mix of confusion and concern.

"Nothing, River," she spat out his name like it was poison. "Absolutely nothing has gotten into me today. Not one thing."

Special Day

"You really have no idea, do you?" she whispered, her voice trembling with a mix of anger and hurt.

River took a step toward her, his brow furrowed in genuine confusion. "Ellie, I—"

"Happy Birthday, Mommy!" two voices sang near the door, making River look at her with wide eyes.

"Your birthday—" River's voice faltered. "Today?"

Tiffany slapped her palm against her forehead. "Oh, Dad. You forgot, didn't you?"

"Shit, Ellie, I—" He started, but Ellie wasn't in the mood for excuses.

"No, you know what? Don't bother." She spun on her heel, ready to storm out of the room, feeling the sting of tears threatening to betray her anger.

"Ellie, wait, please." His chair scraped against the floor as he stood abruptly, reaching for her.

"Let go," she snapped, jerking her arm away from his grasp. "Just forget it, River. Like you forgot me."

"You better have a great way to make up for it, Dad," Tiffany commented. Lucas was standing next to her, looking clueless.

"Ellie! Please, just… listen to me."

The Mafia Boss's Pregnant Bride

She spun around to face River, arms crossed, her glare icy. He stood there, hair disheveled, his usual composure shattered. The sight almost made her falter—almost.

"Sorry doesn't cut it, River."

His eyes were wide, the horror in them unmistakable. "I know, I know," he rushed out, stepping closer. "I can't believe I forgot. There's no excuse."

"Damn right, there isn't." Her voice was low, a dangerous edge creeping into every word.

He ran a hand through his hair, a gesture of distress she'd come to recognize. "Let me make it up to you. Please, Ellie."

"Make it up to me?" she scoffed, disbelief sharp in her tone. "How? You can't turn back time."

"Give me a chance to fix this. I'll throw you the best birthday party, I promise." His desperation was palpable, his words tripping over themselves as he sought to mend the rift between them.

"A party?" She raised an eyebrow, skeptical. "You think a party will make everything okay?"

"That's a great idea, Mom!" Tiffany chirped.

"I love parties!" Lucas joined in.

Special Day

"Yes. A party." River reached for her hand, and this time, she didn't pull away.

"Alright," she said, the word heavy on her tongue. "But it better be good, River. Really good."

"Trust me, it will be." His grip tightened, a silent vow passing between them. "I won't let you down again."

"See that you don't." She pulled her hand back.

Maybe she was being too hard on him, but he deserved it!

"Ellie," River's voice was softer now, filled with regret. "I really am sorry. Let me make this right. I'll clear my schedule, we'll do whatever you want today."

She glanced back at him, seeing the sincerity in his eyes. "I want to invite Lila."

River nodded. "Of course. She is your best friend."

"Valerie and Landon. Antonio can be here too," she said. She knew River didn't like Antonio, but that didn't matter. She had a feeling Valerie was softening toward Antonio.

River nodded again. "Yes. Valerie and Landon have to be here."

"And…" She hesitated.

River looked uncomfortable. "And Antonio."

Ellie rolled her eyes. "Don't look so horrified. He is not a bad guy."

"He is every bit of a bad guy, Ellie," River argued.

Ellie insisted, her eyes pleading with him to understand. "Just give him a chance."

River sighed, knowing he couldn't win this battle. "Fine, invite Antonio too."

A weight lifted off Ellie's shoulders as she smiled gratefully at River. Maybe this party could be the fresh start they all needed.

Thirty-One

Shiny Things

Antonio slid the sleek device across the kitchen counter toward Valerie, a glint of mischief in his eyes.

She stared at the brand-new phone, its screen reflecting the dim light, her heart skipping a beat.

"Is this for me?" Her voice barely rose above a whisper, confusion knotting her brows. Why would Antonio give her such an expensive gift out of the blue?

"Of course, it's for you." He leaned back against the counter, arms crossed, a smile tugging at the corner of his mouth.

Valerie picked up the phone, its cool surface foreign in her palm. "Antonio, why are you giving me this?" The words rushed out in a torrent, fueled by a mix of surprise and a nagging sense of unease.

He laughed, the sound rich and warm, filling the space between them. "Just because."

"Stop trying to buy my affection," she snapped. "And, if I'm not your pet, so maybe stop throwing shiny things at me," she snapped, folding her arms tightly across her chest.

A chuckle rumbled from his throat as he pushed off the counter and sauntered closer. "Ah, but even humans like shiny things," he said, reaching out to tilt her chin up, forcing her to meet his playful eyes.

"I am not kind of human," she retorted, dodging his touch and stepping back. Their little dance of words quickened her pulse.

"Perhaps," he conceded with a raised eyebrow, "but I want you to have it. As a peace offering."

"Peace offering?" she scoffed.

"Yes. I didn't mean to argue with you this morning." He took another step, closing the small gap she had created, his voice dropping to a teasing whisper.

"I don't need a new phone," she shot back, but despite herself, her lips betrayed her, curving into a reluctant smile.

"See?" Antonio grinned, triumphant. "You are smiling. Just stop being so stubborn and accept the damn gift."

"Fine," she huffed, the tension easing as she reached for the phone once more, unable to fully resist the charm of his challenge. "But if I find out this thing is bugged…"

"Then you'll have earned the right to throw it at me," he finished for her, the corners of his eyes crinkling with laughter.

"Consider it your first warning," she warned, though the threat sounded hollow even to her own ears.

"Fair enough," he agreed, and for a moment, they stood there, just looking at each other, the undercurrent of something deeper pulsing beneath their light-hearted sparring.

"Truce?" he offered, extending his hand.

"Truce," she agreed, taking it, feeling the warmth of his fingers wrapping around hers.

"I put in my number already, of course," he said.

"Of course," she repeated. "I don't have any friends. So my address book will look sad." She looked down at the phone and frowned. "No one to call. No one to text."

Antonio's expression softened as he watched her, the earlier playfulness giving way to something more serious. "Valerie," he said quietly, "you have me. And your family, River and Ellie."

She sighed, tracing her finger over the sleek screen. "Thank you." For some reason, she felt like crying.

"By the way," he said, a note of something new threading through his voice. "River's thrown out an invite. His place. Ellie's birthday party."

She paused, a ripple of surprise breaking through the calm surface of the moment. "Ellie's birthday?"

"Tonight." He leaned against the doorframe, arms folded, watching her closely.

"Really?" Excitement surged, unexpected and fierce. A party meant laughter, meant forgetting the tightrope walk of her life for just a few hours. "That's... that's great!" she exclaimed.

"Thought you might say that." There was a glint in his eye, a shared secret in the curl of his lip. "You up for it?"

"Definitely." She pushed off from where she sat, feeling a spark ignite. The idea of celebrating, of being part of something so normal, it was like a lifeline tossed into the stormy sea of recent events. "Can't miss Ellie turning another year sassier."

He straightened, a silent laugh in his throat. "Then it's settled."

Shiny Things

"Settled," she parroted back, but before the word fully left her mouth, he was pushing off from the doorframe and striding towards her with purpose.

"However," he started, and she could feel the shift in the air, the playfulness giving way to something else. "It comes at a price."

She blinked up at him. He towered over her, close enough that she could see the faint lines etched at the corners of his eyes. The kitchen felt smaller with him so near, his presence an undeniable force.

"Price?" Her eyebrows knitted together, suspicion threading through the single word.

A half-smile played on his lips, but his eyes held hers with an intensity that made her heart skip unevenly. "Yep. If you want me to drive you there. I want you to kiss me again." He leaned down, his breath fanning her face.

"Extortionist," she accused, but even to her ears, the word lacked heat.

"Opportunist," he corrected, and his lips twitched as if holding back a full-blown smile.

"Fine," she relented with a huff that wasn't entirely feigned. "One kiss."

His grin broke free then, triumphant and devilish. And before she could contemplate the cost of such currency, his lips found hers.

The kiss was soft and gentle at first, teasing and testing the waters. But soon it became something more.

His hands cupped her face, his thumbs stroking her cheeks as his lips moved against hers with a practiced ease.

She could feel herself getting lost in the moment, the warmth of his body seeping into hers, making her forget about everything else but this feeling. But just as she started to give in completely, he pulled back with a smirk.

"Payment accepted," he murmured, pulling back just far enough to study her face.

"Happy now?" she managed, trying to ignore the way her own lips tingled, betraying her attempt at indifference.

"Ecstatic," he replied, the word heavy with unspoken promises. And for a split second, she allowed herself to wonder what it would be like to stay with this man forever.

"I...I will go get dressed," she said and hurried away from him.

She rushed inside her room and rummaged through her clothes.

She didn't have much, so she had to dig to find something

Shiny Things

nice to wear to Ellie's party. Suddenly, a flash of emerald green caught her eye, causing her to halt abruptly.

It was the dress Antonio sent to her, along with things for Landon.

The emerald green dress lay in a perfect, folded heap at the bottom of the bag, untouched since the day Antonio had left it for her. She hesitated, her fingers hovering over the soft fabric.

And then, she stripped off her everyday clothes and slipped into the dress. The emerald silk cascaded down, hugging her curves in a way that made her feel both vulnerable and powerful. She stared at herself in the mirror, surprised by the woman looking back at her—a woman who could still feel desire despite all she had lost.

She took her time doing her hair and makeup then stepped out of her room to find Antonio waiting by the door, his eyes widening as they met hers.

For a moment, they simply stared at each other, both aware of the unspoken tension crackling between them.

"Wow," Antonio finally breathed out, his gaze flickering over her.

"I...uh...thought it would be appropriate for Ellie's party," she stammered, suddenly self-conscious under his intense scrutiny. "Is it too much?"

The Mafia Boss's Pregnant Bride

His eyes burned into hers. "You are breathtaking, Valerie."

The sincerity in his voice caught her off guard, melting some of the walls she had built around herself.

"Thank you," she murmured.

She quickly averted her gaze, feeling his eyes boring into her face. Antonio's expression shifted, a flicker of something primal sparking in his eyes as he took a step closer, his proximity making her pulse quicken.

"You know," he began, his voice low and husky, "you are a dangerous woman, mio amore. I feel like losing all control when I am near you."

His words sent a shiver down her spine, and she tried to maintain her composure.

"Antonio, we should head to River's house for Ellie's birthday," she managed to say, attempting to steer the conversation away from the dangerous path it was turning toward. But Antonio wasn't easily deterred.

Leaning in closer, his breath ghosting over her ear, he murmured in a tone that made her knees weak, "I can't stop thinking about ripping this dress right off your body." His hand slid around her waist, pulling her flush against him.

She could feel the rapid beat of her heart against her ribcage, the heady scent of Antonio's cologne enveloping her like a cloak.

Despite the warning bells ringing in her mind, she couldn't deny the undeniable pull between them, the magnetic force drawing them closer with each passing second.

"Antonio," Valerie managed to whisper. She tried to push against his solid frame, attempting to regain some semblance of control over the situation.

His gaze bore into hers, dark and intense, stripping away any pretense or facade she had carefully constructed around herself. "I am counting the days until I can have you in my bed," he rasped, his lips hovering dangerously close to hers.

Valerie swallowed hard. Before she could form a coherent response, a sharp knock on the door broke the spell that bound them together. Antonio's grip loosened slightly, allowing her a fraction of space to gather her thoughts.

With a final lingering glance, he released her reluctantly, stepping back as if creating a physical distance could temper the emotional storm brewing within them.

"That must be Sam. I asked him to get the car ready. Is Landon ready to go?" he asked.

Valerie nodded silently and took his hand.

Thirty-Two

Beautiful and Elegant

Antonio stood by the luxurious Rolls Royce, gesturing towards the sleek black car waiting at the curb. The exterior gleamed under the city lights. "You may stay back here," he instructed Sam.

"Capo?" Sam looked at Antonio questioningly.

"I will be driving them myself tonight," Antonio announced, opening the door.

"Va bene. I will follow closely behind," Sam said.

Antonio nodded. "That's fine."

He helped Valerie secure Landon in the back seat before opening the passenger door for her. "After you, my love," he said, offering his hand. Valerie took it with a smile and climbed into the car, settling into the plush leather seats.

Antonio closed the door behind her and walked around to the driver's side, wanting to enjoy their drive without his men watching.

Halfway to their destination, Valerie suddenly gasped. Antonio looked at her with concern. "What is it?"

"I didn't get Ellie a gift!" she exclaimed.

"It's alright, love," Antonio reassured her, glancing at her worried expression. "We will pick something up on the way." He reached out to gently squeeze her hand, his eyes focused on the road ahead.

As they pulled up to an elegant boutique, Valerie's eyes lit up with excitement at the sight of the window displays filled with sparkling jewelry and luxurious accessories. Antonio parked the car and turned to her, unable to resist a smile at her enthusiasm.

Ah, so little Miss Firecracker wasn't immune to shiny things after all!

He got out of the car and opened the door for her. Valerie practically skipped out, her face glowing with delight. But then she looked back and furrowed her brows. "Landon…"

"I will carry him," Antonio said, taking Landon out of the car seat.

"Are you sure? I can carry him," Valerie said hesitantly.

"I can handle him," Antonio replied firmly. "Please, go ahead and find Ellie a present."

Valerie stared at him intently but then nodded in agreement.

As they walked into the boutique, the shop assistant greeted them with a polite nod and a warm smile. Valerie wandered off to a display of delicate necklaces, each one twinkling under the soft lights.

A silver locket caught her eyes. It was something Ellie would surely like.

"Would you like to get this one?" Antonio asked.

Valerie looked unsure. "It looks expensive."

"Don't worry about the cost," Antonio interjected.

"But..," Valerie started to argue, but Antonio stopped her.

"No more argument tonight, Bella," he said.

Valerie still looked at Antonio with an unsure expression. "I will pay you back...eventually."

Antonio shook his head, a smile playing on his lips. "Consider

Beautiful and Elegant

it a gift from both of us. And besides," he paused and caressed her cheek, "you will never have to worry about paying me back, Bella. Ever."

"Thank you, Antonio," she whispered.

"Don't mention it. Why don't you go back to the car while I pay for this?" Antonio instructed, his voice firm but gentle. Valerie nodded, her long red hair falling in loose waves over her shoulders as she took Landon outside.

Antonio waited for a few moments, then made his way towards a display where Valerie had been lingering earlier. His eyes fell on a magnificent emerald necklace glistening under the soft light, casting a mesmerizing glow.

He could picture Valerie wearing it, the emeralds complementing her eyes. With a sense of determination, he called over the jeweler. "I would like to purchase that emerald necklace with this locket," he said.

The jeweler carefully lifted the necklace from its display case. With both gifts in hand, Antonio made his way back to the car where Valerie and the children were waiting.

"Ready to go?" he asked once he settled into the driver's seat.

Valerie nodded, and Antonio started driving.

As they stopped in front of River's mansion, Valerie tried to get out of the car, eager to see her brother, but Antonio grabbed her arm. "Wait," he husked.

She looked at him questioningly. "What's wrong?"

"There is something I need to do first," he said. "Close your eyes," he whispered.

Valerie looked at him suspiciously. "Why?"

"Just do it. I promise you won't regret it," he said, smiling mischievously.

With a small laugh, Valerie indulged him and closed her eyes. Antonio carefully fastened the beautiful emerald necklace around her neck, feeling her pulse quicken beneath his fingertips.

"You can open your eyes now," he said.

Valerie's eyes fluttered open, and as she caught sight of the dazzling emerald necklace in the rearview mirror, her breath caught in her throat. Her hand instinctively flew to her chest, feeling the weight of the precious stones against her collarbone.

"Oh my goodness," Valerie gasped, her eyes widening in disbelief. "Antonio, this is... It's too much."

Antonio could see the emotions swirling in her eyes – gratitude, astonishment, and a hint of unease. She turned to him, her expression dark.

Beautiful and Elegant

"I can't accept something this expensive," Valerie murmured softly, her fingers tracing the contours of the necklace.

Antonio raised an eyebrow. "You are trying to reject my gift, Bella? I thought we were starting to become friends?"

"Y…yes…but. This necklace. It's so beautiful and elegant. I don't deserve something like this. It doesn't suit me and…" she started to ramble, but Antonio decided to shut her up by covering her mouth with his.

The softness of her lips against his silenced her protests as he poured all the passion and adoration he held for her into the kiss. When they finally broke apart, Valerie's eyes were wide with surprise, her cheeks flushed with a delicate pink hue.

"You deserve the world, cara mia," Antonio whispered, his voice filled with sincerity. "And if this necklace is what it takes to show you even a fraction of how much you mean to me, then it's worth every gem and every penny."

Valerie's eyes glistened with unshed tears, shimmering like the emeralds adorning her neck. Her touch on his cheek was gentle and warm. "Antonio, I…I don't know what to say," she whispered.

"Then don't say anything," Antonio replied softly, bringing her delicate hand to his lips and placing a tender kiss on her knuckles. "Just know that you are cherished beyond measure."

Her voice trembled as she spoke again. "I…if you are trying to buy my affection with jewelry and pretty words, then it's…it's kind of working."

Antonio chuckled at her honesty and vulnerability.

Thirty-Three

Birthday Celebration

When River opened the door, Valerie entered confidently. Antonio trailed behind, carrying the stroller holding little Landon.

"Good evening, Foster," Antonio said, flashing his irritating grin at him.

River couldn't help but stare at his sister in utter amazement. She was a stunning sight in her emerald green dress, which perfectly complemented her red hair and striking green eyes.

A delicate emerald necklace adorned her neck, matching her dress and undoubtedly costing a pretty penny. But what truly took his breath away was the radiant smile on her face as she looked at him. He had never seen her so…happy. It left him speechless.

The Mafia Boss's Pregnant Bride

In that moment, River knew he might have to swallow his pride and thank Antonio for whatever he had done to make Valerie look like this.

"Glad you two could make it," River said.

Valerie's footsteps quickened as she approached them, her breaths coming in short bursts of excitement. "River, Ellie!" she exclaimed, her voice laced with barely contained joy.

"Thanks for the invite," Antonio said dryly.

River nodded and grinned at Antonio to let him know he wasn't planning to start a fight. Antonio's shoulders relaxed a bit.

Valerie hugged Ellie first. "Happy Birthday, Ellie," she said.

"Thank you. I am so glad you are here," Ellie replied, returning the embrace.

As Valerie released her from the hug, she turned to River with a smile. Without hesitation, he wrapped his arms around her in a comforting hug. "You okay, Elle?" he asked, even though the answer was written all over her radiant face and sparkling eyes, mirroring the joy and excitement radiating from within her.

Valerie smiled at River as she stepped back from the hug. "I'm okay, River. I'm really happy to be here," she beamed, her eyes shining with joy. "And to see you again so soon."

Birthday Celebration

River couldn't help but smile at her infectious enthusiasm, feeling a sense of relief wash over him. Whatever Antonio had done to bring this glow to his sister's face was worth it. Maybe he wasn't as bad as River had thought.

Antonio cleared his throat, drawing their attention. "We have a gift for the birthday girl, don't we, Valerie?" he asked, looking down at her.

"Oh, yes!" Valerie chirped.

Ellie beamed. "Really? You didn't have to bring me anything."

Valerie handed her the small box. "I couldn't come here empty-handed."

"I am sure it's lovely. Thank you," Ellie said as she held the box like it was the most precious thing in the world.

River led Valerie and Antonio inside. He couldn't help stealing glances at his sister, who seemed to be walking on air. Her laughter filled the air, warming his heart.

They entered the living room, and Ellie eagerly opened the gift from Valerie and Antonio. Ellie gasped in delight, her eyes wide as she held the necklace up to the light, watching it sparkle.

"It's beautiful," she whispered, her voice full of awe.

Valerie beamed at her reaction, pleased that her gift had been well received. "I saw it and thought of you instantly," she explained, a warm smile on her face.

Ellie turned to Antonio, gratitude shining in her eyes. "Thank you so much, both of you. I will cherish it always."

Antonio nodded, a hint of a smile playing on his lips. "You're welcome, Ellie. Happy Birthday."

"It's time to cut the cake," Tiffany announced from the doorway.

"Come on, Mommy!" Lucas yelled.

Ellie giggled at his eagerness. "Yes, yes, I am coming."

The group gathered around the beautifully decorated birthday cake, Ellie's eyes sparkling with anticipation. She took a deep breath and made a wish before blowing out the candles, everyone cheering around her.

Antonio nudged Valerie. "And when is your birthday?"

Valerie raised an eyebrow. "Why do you ask? Are you planning on throwing me a grand party?"

Antonio chuckled. "Maybe I will. But only if you are a good girl."

Valerie snorted. "No, thank you. I don't need all of that. The last thing I need is to be reminded of how old I am."

Birthday Celebration

Antonio grabbed her waist and pulled her closer. "I bet you will age like a fine wine, Bella."

"Stop flirting over there and come get some cake," River growled from across the room.

Valerie giggled and pushed him away and strode toward her brother.

~-~

All eyes were fixed on River and Ellie, caught up in the joy of their birthday celebration. But Antonio's attention was drawn to Valerie.

His Valerie.

Valerie's smile illuminated the room like sunshine, bringing warmth to Antonio's heart.

At that moment, Antonio silently vowed to himself—that he would make this woman his wife.

But Antonio knew he couldn't rush it. He wanted Valerie to come to him willingly, to fully surrender herself. He sensed her longing in every glance they shared, in the unspoken words that lingered between them. When the time was right, he would propose, and he knew she would accept without hesitation.

In that moment, they would evolve from two individuals

brought together by fate into a true family.

Antonio reached over and gently touched Valerie's hand, half-expecting her to pull away. Instead, she intertwined her fingers with his.

"Isn't this wonderful?" she whispered.

"It truly is," Antonio replied quietly, giving her hand a reassuring squeeze.

"I love them so much," Valerie continued. "River took care of me since we were teenagers. Our parents died already and I had no one."

Antonio felt a deep respect for River Blackwood then. "Is that so?"

Valerie nodded. "Yes. He had to grow up too fast because of me."

"He did a great job raising you because you are perfect," Antonio said in a low and husky voice.

Valerie rolled her eyes. "You are full of it, Antonio."

"I'm telling the truth," Antonio admitted with a smile.

Valerie shook her head in playful disagreement but leaned closer to him. A comforting warmth enveloped Antonio as she leaned on his arm, their hands still intertwined.

Thirty-Four

Nightmares

"I think you're growing on me, Antonio," Valerie whispered softly.

"I hope so," he replied sincerely, his voice filled with warmth. "Because you've already become a part of me, Valerie."

Their eyes locked, and in that moment, Antonio sensed a deep and genuine connection that transcended words. Despite the lively atmosphere of the engagement party around them, it felt as though they were in their own private world.

"Alright! Who's ready for some dancing!" Ellie's cheerful voice interrupted, interrupting the moment.

Valerie withdrew her hand quickly, her expression momen-

The Mafia Boss's Pregnant Bride

tarily startled. Antonio noticed the shift in her demeanor, a subtle retreat that left him longing for her touch once more.

But just as swiftly as it had vanished, the connection reasserted itself, and Valerie put on a smile for Ellie's sake.

River approached Antonio right then. "Can we talk, Antonio? In private," he asked, his face inscrutable.

"Of course," Antonio agreed, nodding towards a quieter corner of the room. Valerie's gaze followed them as they walked away, a mix of curiosity and concern flickering in her eyes.

Once they found a quiet corner away from the bustling engagement party, River cleared his throat, his expression serious. "I know you care about Valerie," he began, his voice low.

Antonio raised an eyebrow, a hint of amusement in his eyes. "Then you're not as clueless as I thought, Foster."

River glared back at him. "Don't push me, Costello."

Antonio grinned, a touch of apology in his tone. "My apologies. Please, continue."

"I can see that you care for her and the baby," River continued, his gaze searching. "My question is, why? What do you get out of this?"

Nightmares

"I care because Valerie deserves to be cared for," Antonio replied calmly, his voice steady and resolute. "She's a strong woman and a good mother. Anyone with sense can see that. But no matter her strength, she and Landon need someone who will stand by them, protect them, love them. I want to be that person for them."

River studied Antonio's eyes, as if assessing his sincerity. "You've had your own share of darkness, Antonio. How can I trust you won't bring Valerie into more danger?"

Antonio held his gaze firmly. "I would never do anything to harm Valerie or the baby. My past might be questionable, but my intentions towards them are genuine. You have my word on that."

River nodded slowly, weighing Antonio's words carefully. "Alright, Antonio. I'll trust you... for now."

"If only your sister could see what you see," Antonio chuckled lightly.

River smirked knowingly. "She doesn't trust you yet, huh? Can't blame her. Valerie's been through a lot."

"Would you care to share?" Antonio inquired, his tone respectful.

A shadow passed over River's face. "Now's not the time or place for that discussion. And I'm sure Valerie wouldn't appreciate me airing her secrets. When she's ready, she'll tell you herself. Just know, she's been broken once before, so make damn sure it doesn't happen again."

"I understand," Antonio replied solemnly. "I promise I'll do everything in my power to ensure Valerie never experiences that kind of pain again."

River studied Antonio for a moment longer, then nodded. "Good. That's all I needed to hear."

As they rejoined the group, Antonio couldn't help but notice Valerie watching them from across the room. She gave him a small, hesitant smile, and he returned it, feeling a surge of determination to earn her trust completely.

The rest of the evening passed in a blur of laughter, toasts, and shared memories. As the night drew to a close, Antonio approached Valerie quietly and placed a hand on her back. "Ready to go home, Bella?"

She looked at him and smiled softly. "Yes," she replied in a quiet voice.

They gathered the kids, who were already drowsy from the excitement of the evening, and made their way to the car. The drive home was peaceful, the city lights blurring into a comforting glow outside the windows. Valerie leaned her head against the window, lost in thought, while the kids slept soundly in their car seats.

When they arrived home, Antonio carefully lifted Landon

Nightmares

from the back seat, cradling him in his arms.

Once he put him in his crib, Antonio and Valerie found themselves alone in the quiet of the living room.

"Tonight was wonderful," Valerie said, breaking the silence. She looked at him, her eyes reflecting the softness of her words.

"It was," Antonio agreed, stepping closer. "And you looked ravishing. Seeing you so happy... it made me realize just how much I want to see that smile on your face every day."

Valerie blushed, looking down at her hands. "You've already done so much for me and Landon, Antonio. I don't know how to thank you."

Antonio reached out, gently lifting her chin so their eyes met. "You don't need to thank me, Valerie. I am doing this for myself too."

For a moment, they stood there, the intensity of their connection palpable. Then, Antonio leaned in and pressed a gentle kiss to her forehead. Valerie closed her eyes, a sigh escaping her lips as she leaned into the touch.

"Goodnight, Bella," Antonio whispered softly. "Sweet dreams."

~-~

Late at night, Antonio stirred awake at the sound of muffled sobs cutting through the silence. His heart clenched as he recognized the familiar sound of Valerie's cries. She must be having another nightmare.

Quietly slipping out of bed, he made his way to her room. The door stood slightly ajar, offering a glimpse of Valerie's silhouette trembling under the blankets. Her soft cries were getting louder, stirring an urgent need in him to comfort her.

Gently pushing the door open, Antonio approached her bedside with cautious steps, mindful not to startle her. "Valerie," he whispered softly, touching her shoulder. "It's okay, Bella. I'm here."

"Go away," she breathed, her voice fragile, like a wounded child. "Please…"

Antonio persisted, his tone gentle yet unwavering. "Valerie, who are you talking to?"

Her eyes fluttered open, momentarily unfocused and clouded with fear. "Please, just leave me alone," she pleaded, her voice quivering as if still trapped in the throes of her nightmare. "Can't you just leave? Just for tonight?"

"Valerie," Antonio spoke again, his voice a touch firmer this time. "Who are you talking to?"

She paused, her breath catching, before recognition slowly dawned in her eyes. "Antonio?" she murmured, uncertainty

Nightmares

mingling with relief.

"Yes, it's me," he confirmed, leaning closer to her.

Valerie sat up, drawing her knees to her chest, her gaze darting around the dimly lit room as if searching for unseen threats. "It felt so real," she whispered hoarsely, her voice barely audible. "I was back there, with him... I couldn't get away."

Antonio reached out, gently taking her hand in his, offering a reassuring anchor. "You're here now, Valerie. You're safe with me."

She glanced down at their joined hands, her fingers trembling slightly. "I'm sorry," she murmured, her voice laden with guilt and vulnerability.

"Don't apologize, mio amore," Antonio replied, his voice firm yet tender. "You have nothing to be sorry for."

"You can leave now. I'm fine," Valerie whispered, barely meeting his gaze.

"I'm not going anywhere," Antonio asserted firmly, refusing to heed her request.

Their eyes locked, Valerie torn between her instinct to push him away and the overwhelming need for the comfort and reassurance he offered.

The Mafia Boss's Pregnant Bride

"Valerie? Can I stay?" Antonio asked.

"Yes," she whispered with tears in her eyes.

Thirty-Five

I Need You

"I'm not going anywhere," Antonio said firmly, and Valerie released a sigh of relief. Thank god this man was as stubborn as he was kind.

Kind. It was such a strange word to describe Antonio. A few weeks ago, she would have never thought to use that word for him.

"You will stay?" she asked weakly.

He shifted beside her, his fingers brushing a stray lock of hair from her face with a tenderness that belied the harshness she had come to associate with him. "Yes, my love. I thought you said Julian never hurt you," he said softly, though she could hear the anger in his voice.

"He didn't," she lied.

"Then care to tell me who you were pushing away in your nightmare? Who had you terrified like a little girl?" Antonio asked, pulling her onto his lap.

"I...no one," she said. She didn't want to talk about Julian or anyone with Antonio right now.

"Valerie," he started.

Valerie's voice rose in desperation. "I don't want to talk about it with you, okay?" she nearly screamed. Hot tears started to flow down her cheeks before she could stop them, and her body started to shake again. This time, it wasn't because she was scared. It was because she was angry.

She didn't want Antonio to see her like this! She didn't want him to think of her as some weak little girl.

Antonio wrapped his arms around her and held her tight against his chest. "Hush now, cara mia. You don't have to tell me if you're not ready," he said, his voice a whisper laced with understanding.

But his patience only stoked the embers of her anger, sparking a fire within her that she struggled to contain. "I don't need your pity," she snapped, her words sharp like broken glass.

Antonio didn't let go.

I Need You

"I can take care of myself," she insisted, pushing away from him. But even as she distanced herself physically, his presence still loomed large over her fractured resolve.

"Why won't you let me in, Valerie?" Antonio's voice was gentle but insistent.

"Why should I?" she whispered, barely able to meet his gaze.

Antonio's expression softened, his eyes searching hers as if seeking the answers to questions he hadn't yet formed. His fingers grazed her cheek, a touch so tender it felt like a balm on her raw emotions. "Because I care about you, Valerie. More than I ever thought possible."

A shiver ran down her spine at his words, the vulnerability in his voice cutting through the barriers she had so carefully erected. "I never asked you to care," she retorted, her tone laced with defiance.

His gaze held hers, unwavering. "You didn't have to ask. It just happened."

She looked away, unable to bear the intensity of his stare. How could he care when he knew so little of the darkness that resided within her? "You shouldn't," she whispered, a plea more to herself than to him.

"But I do," Antonio insisted, his hand reaching out to tilt her chin up, forcing her to meet his gaze once more. "And I won't apologize for it."

The Mafia Boss's Pregnant Bride

The sincerity in his eyes was like a lifeline in the storm of her emotions. Part of her wanted to push him away, to shield herself from the possibility of hurt. But another part... another part longed to surrender to the warmth he offered, to let go of the burdens she had carried alone for so long.

"I'm broken, Antonio," the confession slipped past her defenses before she could stop it, each word heavy with the weight of years of pain.

He didn't flinch. Instead, he pulled her closer, wrapping her in an embrace again. "We're all broken in our own ways, Valerie. But sometimes, two broken pieces can fit together and make something whole."

Tears welled up in Valerie's eyes again, but she didn't want to sit there and cry all night. She put her arms around Antonio's neck and kissed him.

Their lips met in a clash of need and desperation, the taste of salt from her tears mingling with the warmth of his mouth. Antonio responded eagerly, his hands cradling her face with a tenderness that belied the intensity of their kiss.

"I won't let anyone hurt you, Valerie," Antonio murmured against her lips. "Not now, not ever."

Valerie reached down between his legs to feel his length in her hand. He let out a soft groan, his eyes widening in surprise. "What are you doing?" he hissed.

I Need You

She pushed him back against the bed, straddling his waist as she kissed him hungrily. Thankfully, he wasn't wearing a shirt, so she was free to roam her hands around his naked chest and stomach.

She felt his several jagged scars under her fingers, and it sent a strange thrill through her. This was a man who had been through pain like her. Maybe not emotionally but physically. The thought gave her comfort.

Antonio's hands moved to her hips, his touch sending a shiver down her spine. "Valerie, wait," he breathed between kisses, trying to slow her pace.

But she couldn't hold back. Every touch, every caress was a blazing trail against her skin that fueled the fire within her. She needed this connection, this intimacy, to drown out the echoes of her nightmares.

"I need you, Antonio," she whimpered. "I need to…I need to feel."

"We shouldn't," he said, his voice tight.

"Don't you want me? Am I not desirable?" she pouted.

He almost smiled, but he didn't. "Oh, my love, I do," he admitted. "More than anything, I want you. But I remember you telling me that it's been barely six weeks since you gave birth. I don't want to hurt you, and I know that your body needs time to heal."

She knew he was right, but the longing in her mind was too powerful. She could barely breathe, let alone think rationally.

"It's okay if I feel pain. I don't care. I need you to fuck me, Antonio," she whispered, hoping he could feel the truth in her voice.

He searched her eyes, his own pools of darkness deepening. "Valerie, my love…"

"Stop it! Stop calling me that. I am not your love. You don't love me," she snapped. She knew she was acting like an insane woman, but she couldn't control herself tonight.

His words carried a fierce growl laced with passion and intensity. "Do not underestimate my feelings for you, mia cara," he declared. Her heart skipped a beat at the raw emotion in his voice. "I have loved you from the moment I held your hand in the delivery room, and I love you now!"

Valerie gaped at him. Did he have any idea what he had just done? She was speaking out of anger and emotions, but he had just declared that he loved her!

Thirty-Six

You Can't Say That!

"Y... you can't just say that!" Valerie exclaimed, her voice quivering as her heart beat erratically.

Antonio brushed a strand of hair away from her face, stroking her cheek gently. "I can't say what?"

"You can't just say you love me," she said hoarsely.

He leaned over, his lips brushing her earlobe. "Why can't I say I love you?"

"Because!" Valerie gasped as he kissed her neck. "Because you don't actually love me."

"Is that so? And how did you come to that conclusion, Mia Cara?" he asked, smiling at her devilishly.

"I know you don't love me because… because…" Valerie stammered, searching for an answer but finding none.

He raised an eyebrow, his dark eyes twinkling with amusement. "Because what?"

"I don't know," she replied weakly.

Antonio chuckled, his breath sending shivers down her spine. "You don't know? Well, let me tell you, my sweet Valerie. I know exactly why I love you. I love your fiery spirit, your sharp tongue, and your beautiful heart. I love the way you make me feel, like I'm home, like I'm exactly where I'm meant to be."

Antonio pulled Valerie closer, his lips inches from hers. "And I love the way you taste, like sweetness and sin all mixed together. I love you, Valerie, and I will prove it to you, no matter what it takes."

Valerie felt like she was drowning in his words, lost in the depths of his eyes. She couldn't think, couldn't breathe. All she could do was feel, and what she felt was desire, pure and simple.

"Antonio," she whispered, her voice barely audible.

His hands roamed her body, caressing her as he whispered sweet nothings in her ear. He kissed her gently, his lips soft and lingering. Valerie closed her eyes, savoring the moment, reveling in the feeling of being loved and desired.

You Can't Say That!

As the kiss continued, she felt his hands exploring her body, his touch sending electricity through her. She wrapped her arms around him, pulling him closer, wanting to feel every inch of him against her.

Her breath caught in her throat as his hand slid between her legs, tugging her panties aside. His touch was electric, sending shivers through her body. "It's a shame I can't be inside you tonight," he whispered, his voice low and husky.

A fire burned in his eyes as he continued, "But don't worry, my darling, I won't leave you unsatisfied." His words sent a wave of desire coursing through Valerie, leaving her trembling with anticipation for what would come next.

His lips were warm and inviting as they trailed down her neck, sending shivers down her spine. "I promise you, I won't let you down tonight," he murmured, his breath hot against her skin.

Valerie felt a mix of fear and excitement at the thought of what was to come. But as his fingers gently caressed her, she knew she was in safe hands. His touch was tender and loving, yet possessive.

It was clear that he wanted her in a way that left her breathless. And as he continued to explore her, Valerie couldn't help but feel a sense of pleasure and desire that she had never experienced before.

"Antonio, please," Valerie begged, her body trembling with

anticipation.

He smiled wickedly, his eyes locked on hers. "I'm just getting started, my love. But when I'm done with you, you won't remember your own name."

Valerie shuddered at the thought, unable to deny the heat building between them. Antonio yanked her shirt off, then pulled off her panties, leaving her naked and vulnerable.

She gasped. "No, don't look at me! I thought I told you my body was…"

"Perfect," he growled, staring at her hungrily. "Your body is absolutely perfect."

Valerie closed her eyes and let out a moan as Antonio began to worship her with his mouth, his tongue darting out to trace the delicate lines of her body. His hands were everywhere, caressing her, exploring her, making her feel alive in ways she never thought possible.

Antonio slid his fingers over Valerie's clit, now slicked with her juices but not entering her. As he continued to tease and torment her, she could feel the intensity building within her, the desire growing stronger with each passing second.

Her body was begging for more, craving the release that she knew was just moments away. But Antonio was toying with her, denying her the pleasure that she so desperately sought.

You Can't Say That!

Finally, she could take no more. "Antonio, please!" Valerie begged, her voice shaking with need.

He smiled wickedly, his eyes locked onto hers. He pushed himself off of her and unzipped his pants.

Her heart raced as she watched him pull out his erection, taking it in with wide eyes. It was massive, and she knew she was nowhere near ready for it now. But she wanted it so badly that her body ached.

Antonio's eyes never left hers as he slowly slid his cock over her pussy, teasing her even more.

Valerie could feel the head of his penis brushing against her wet folds, sending shivers down her spine. It was a torment she had never experienced before. She wanted him so badly, but Antonio was in control now.

Every fiber of Valerie's being screamed for him to thrust into her, to give her the release she so desperately craved. But he continued to tease her, moving his cock back and forth, just barely touching her entrance. Valerie moaned loudly, pleading with him to take her.

But he was determined not to hurt her.

"Please, Antonio!" Valerie cried out, her voice breaking with desperation. "You're driving me insane!"

Antonio smirked, his eyes never leaving her face. "You're wet for me, my sweet Valerie. I don't want to hurt you. Wrap your legs around me."

Valerie did as he asked, wrapping her legs around his hips and pulling him closer. She could feel his erection pressing against her pussy, exquisite torture.

Antonio looked her in the eye as he began to slide over her again. Valerie moaned and writhed beneath him, her hips bucking against his.

"Yes…like this. Please don't stop," she breathed, feeling her orgasm building slowly.

Antonio whispered, his voice low and seductive. "I'm not going to stop, I promise you that."

Valerie's breaths came in ragged gasps as her body began to tremble with anticipation. She could feel her orgasm building, threatening to consume her.

Antonio leaned down, his lips hovering just above hers, whispering into her ear. "I'm going to make you come, sweetheart. Just let go and let me take you there."

His words were like a match to a flame, igniting something deep within her. Valerie felt herself lose control, her body arching up to meet his as he continued to tease her, his cock sliding over her clit. The pleasure was intense, overwhelming. She could feel the orgasm building, a tidal wave of sensation that threatened to consume her.

You Can't Say That!

Antonio's hands gripped her hips, holding her steady as she writhed beneath him. Valerie's nails dug into his back, her breath coming in ragged gasps. "Ohh, Antonio... please," she begged, her voice hoarse with need.

He responded by increasing his pace, his hips moving in a steady rhythm that matched the pounding of her heart.

"You're so close, my sweet," he breathed, his voice filled with lustful promise.

And then, just as she felt she couldn't take anymore, Antonio's lips met hers, his tongue sliding into her mouth with a passionate intensity that sent her over the edge.

The explosion of pleasure was like nothing Valerie had ever experienced before. It was all-consuming, a tide of ecstasy that washed over her, leaving her helpless and breathless.

And the man didn't even enter her the whole time!

His tongue continued to dance with hers, as his body trembled and his hips moved with greater intensity. She could feel the telltale signs of his own impending climax.

He groaned into her mouth and then suddenly his body went still. They stayed wrapped around in each other's arms for a while.

"Did you like that, sweetheart?" Antonio asked, his voice thick with satisfaction.

Valerie managed a weak smile and nodded, her voice still too hoarse to speak.

"I promise you'll always feel like this with me, Valerie," he said, his gaze locked onto hers.

My voice was weak and trembling as I spoke. "I...I can't believe you weren't even inside me this whole time."

He laughed, the sound rich and deep. "Oh, Valerie. Don't worry. After six long weeks, I fully intend to be inside you, claiming you as mine in every way." His eyes held a glint of playful mischief but also something more primal and possessive. The promise in his words sent shivers through her entire body, her heartbeat quickening with anticipation.

Thirty-Seven

Lullaby Type

~~~~~~~~~~~~~~~~~~~~~

Valerie snuggled closer to Antonio, his steady heartbeat calming her in the quiet night.

His arms were her safe haven, strong yet gentle. His warmth eased away all of her fear and tension, and she couldn't resist falling asleep in his embrace, feeling completely secure.

She slept through the night and only woke up when the sunlight hit her eyes through the curtains.

Her eyes snapped open to find his side of the bed empty, the impression of his body still haunting the mattress. "Antonio?" she whispered. No answer came.

She pushed herself up. He was gone. She felt oddly

disappointed because a part of her wanted to wake up next to him.

A blush crept up her cheeks as she remembered last night. He had made love to her without even penetrating her. She didn't know it was even possible, but with Antonio, anything seemed possible.

"Dammit," she muttered, the word a sharp exhale of frustration. She swung her legs over the side of the bed, the cold floor a jarring contrast against her skin. And then, cutting through the silence, a melody seeped into the room. Soft, more felt than heard, it was a song threaded with a tenderness that seemed out of place in this room.

"Where is that coming from?" Her voice was barely a whisper, her heartbeat loud in her ears. The singing continued, so she decided to check it out.

It was coming from Landon's room. She moved toward the door, slowly and carefully. The melody grew stronger, the voice behind it rich and resonant with a depth that warmed her body.

Without a sound, she padded across the room. Her hand reached for the door, fingertips brushing the wood before grasping the handle. She nudged the door open.

There he was, his back to her, standing in the middle of the room with Landon nestled against his chest, his tiny fist curled around his finger. The melody he hummed was low, a series of soothing notes that filled the space between them.

"Shh," Antonio whispered to Landon, a soft command that stilled the room. His voice, usually so commanding, now laced with tenderness, wrapped around each note, cradling it as gently as he held her son. Landon's eyelids fluttered, fighting sleep, then succumbing to the lullaby, to the comfort of his arms.

They looked too much like a father and son, Valerie thought to herself and felt a pang in her chest.

"Sleep, little one," Antonio murmured, his words barely audible. Valerie watched, rooted to the spot, as he swayed gently.

"He might be hungry," her voice sounded too loud, breaking the spell, slicing into the quiet.

Antonio turned, surprise etching his features. "Valerie," he started, "you're awake."

"Yes," she whispered, ignoring the pressure in her chest. "Were you singing just now?"

She took an involuntary step closer, drawn by the tenderness of the scene unfolding before her.

"Never took you for the lullaby type," she managed.

He shifted, the motion gentle to keep from waking Landon.

"There's a lot you don't know about me, Valerie."

"What else don't I know about you?" she asked.

Antonio grinned wickedly. "You will find out, slowly."

Valerie pouted. "Why slowly? Why can't I find out now?"

"What's the fun in that? If I tell you all of my secrets, I might have to…"

"Kill me?" she finished for him.

Antonio laughed out loud, making Landon stir in his arms. "No, Valerie," his voice was low, a dangerous edge to it that sent a shiver down her spine. "If I tell you all my secrets at once, you might just run away."

Valerie lifted her chin defiantly, refusing to let his words intimidate her. "I might still run away."

His stare bore into hers, searching for something she couldn't quite name. "Why would you want to do that? Didn't I satisfy you last night?"

She blushed and looked down. "Last night was wonderful," she whispered.

Antonio chuckled again, the sound rich and velvety in the quiet room. "Then I will trust you to stay with me, yeah?"

Lullaby Type

She didn't answer. She took a deep breath and nodded, looking up to meet his eyes. "Where did you learn to sing?"

Antonio smiled brightly at that. "My Nonna taught me. She used to sing to me when I had nightmares or couldn't sleep. Sometimes, she would have me sing with her."

His voice softened as he spoke of his grandmother.

"You have a beautiful voice," Valerie finally said, the words coming out more sincere than she had intended.

Antonio met her gaze then, the vulnerability still lingering in his eyes. "Thank you," he murmured, almost shyly. "I don't often share that part of me with others."

Valerie felt a sudden rush of understanding for this man who had been so guarded and distant. His music was a bridge between the walls he had built around himself and the outside world, a glimpse into the depths of his soul that he rarely allowed anyone to see.

"I'm glad I got to hear it," she admitted.

Antonio's lips curved into a small smile. "And what about you? Any special talent, mia cara?"

Valerie shook her head.

"No? Nothing at all?" he asked.

The Mafia Boss's Pregnant Bride

She hesitated. "Well…I do like to paint a little."

Antonio's dark eyes twinkled with interest. "Paint, you say? What do you paint?"

Feeling a bit self-conscious under his intense gaze, Valerie shrugged and avoided eye contact. "Just… things. I don't really get to do it much."

A slow smile spread across his lips as he studied her. "Hmm," he hummed, his voice low and velvety. "I'd love to see your paintings sometime."

She shot him a warning look, suddenly feeling vulnerable and exposed. "What? No way. I don't like showing anyone my work. It's not good enough," she said, the memories of past ridicule flooding her mind.

A harsh voice from her past cut through her thoughts, breaking the moment. "Stop wasting time on stupid shit and get the dinner ready." Julian's words barked out at her, causing her to shiver involuntarily.

Antonio narrowed his eyes. "What's wrong?"

"N…nothing. I will take Landon. It's time for his breakfast," she said, holding her arms out.

Antonio handed Landon to her, his gaze lingering on her face, searching for answers to questions he didn't voice. As she cradled the sleeping baby, a wave of protectiveness washed

Lullaby Type

over her, a fierce determination to shield him from any harm.

Valerie made her way back to the rocking chair in the room and settled down.

She cradled Landon in her arms, relishing the warmth and softness of his body. Landon stirred slightly, letting out a tiny whimper. With a gentle touch, Valerie held him closer, feeling his breath against her chest.

Shifting her position, she guided Landon to her breast, where he latched on effortlessly. Soon, the room was filled with the soothing sound of his suckling.

Glancing over at Antonio, Valerie saw the adoring look in his eyes as he watched them. "Are you just going to stand there and stare? You're making me self-conscious," she joked.

"It's a beautiful sight, a mother feeding her child. There's nothing more pure and natural," he said sincerely.

"Well, maybe you should find yourself a wife and experience this joy some more," she teased playfully. But deep down, she couldn't fathom the thought of Antonio with anyone else. In fact, she might have to keep him all to herself and never let go.

Antonio's expression turned serious. "Are you trying to propose, Bella?"

Valerie giggled, feeling the heat rise to her cheeks. "Propose?

Let's not get ahead of ourselves, Antonio."

He arched an eyebrow, a playful smirk dancing on his lips. "Why not? I could be the most devoted husband, you know."

Valerie couldn't help but roll her eyes. "Devoted husband, huh? That remains to be seen," she teased.

Antonio stepped closer, his gaze intense. "I will show you. You can count on that."

Thirty-Eight

He is Sick

L andon's cries suddenly pierced the peaceful moment, causing Valerie to wince. He had detached himself from her breast, his tiny hands still grasping at the air in search of comfort. As she held him close, she felt the heat radiating off his feverish body.

"He feels warm," Valerie murmured, worry lacing her voice as she pressed a hand to Landon's forehead. "Something's not right. I think he might be sick."

As if on cue, Landon let out another whimper, his face scrunching up in discomfort. Valerie's heart clenched at the sight.

"I'll call the doctor," Anthony declared, already picking up his phone.

The doctor arrived promptly and started to examine Landon. His movements were methodical, yet there was a hint of concern in his eyes that Valerie couldn't ignore.

"What's going on? Is he okay?" Valerie breathed.

"I'm afraid little Landon is quite ill," the doctor began, his voice gentle yet firm. "It appears to be a serious infection. We will have to take him to the hospital."

Valerie felt a wave of panic wash over her as she clutched Landon closer to her chest, his ragged breathing tugging at her heartstrings.

Antonio immediately took charge, swiftly calling for the car.

A few minutes later, they sat together in the hospital waiting room while they examined Landon.

Tears streamed down her cheeks. She couldn't lose Landon. He was the most precious thing in the world for her.

"Valerie," Antonio's deep voice murmured near her ear.

She turned to look at him, his eyes filled with tenderness.

"He'll be okay," he assured her, his hand resting gently on her back. "The doctors here are some of the best."

Valerie nodded, trying to absorb his calmness. "What if… what if he is not?"

He is Sick

"He will be," he said firmly.

"I can't lose him. I just can't. He is all I have," Valerie sobbed.

Antonio pulled her closer, wrapping his arms around her in a protective embrace. "You won't lose him, Valerie. We won't let that happen. He's strong, just like his mother."

She buried her face in his shoulder, her tears soaking into his shirt.

The minutes dragged on, each one feeling like an eternity. Finally, a nurse approached them with a soft smile. "You can see him now."

Valerie and Antonio followed the nurse to a small room where Landon lay in a crib, his tiny chest rising and falling steadily. The sight of him looking so small and vulnerable tugged at Valerie's heart.

"He's stable and responding to the treatment," the nurse explained. "We'll keep monitoring him closely, but he's going to be okay."

Valerie let out a breath she didn't realize she'd been holding. "Thank you," she said, her voice thick with emotion.

She approached the crib, reaching out to gently touch Landon's hand. He stirred slightly, his eyes fluttering open for a moment before closing again.

"Hey there, little guy," she whispered, a tear slipping down her cheek. "Mommy's here. You're going to be just fine."

Antonio stood by her side, his hand resting on her shoulder. "See? He's a fighter."

Valerie nodded, feeling a glimmer of hope. "Yes, he is."

"You can take him home now, but monitor him closely. I have prescribed some medicines as well," the doctor said before handing over the prescription list.

"Thank you, Doctor," Antonio said grimly. He looked at Valerie. "Ready?"

Valerie nodded. "Yes."

Antonio gently picked up Landon, cradling him in his strong arms. Valerie gathered their things, her movements slow and deliberate as she tried to steady her racing heart. With the prescription list in hand, they made their way out of the hospital and back to the car.

The drive home was quiet, the tension in the air palpable. Valerie couldn't take her eyes off Landon, her mind racing with worries and prayers for his swift recovery. Antonio placed an arm around her shoulders. "He's going to be okay, Valerie."

"I hope so," she whispered, her voice trembling. "I just want him to be healthy and happy."

He is Sick

"He will be," Antonio reassured her.

When they arrived home, Antonio carefully carried Landon inside and put him in his crib. Valerie hovered near as if she couldn't stand to be away from Landon.

"Madonna mia! What happened, my dear Valerie?" Nonna rushed into the room.

"It's Landon. He is…he is sick," Valerie said, unshed tears glistening in her eyes.

"Oh, sweetheart, come here," Nonna said and pulled her into an embrace.

"He is going to be fine. The doctor prescribed him some medicines," Antonio explained.

"Bene. Valerie, my love. Why don't you lie down and get some rest? You look exhausted," Nonna suggested.

Valerie shook her head. "No, I want to stay awake and watch over Landon. What if he wakes up and needs me?"

Nonna nodded understandingly, her eyes filled with sympathy. "I understand. But you need your strength too. Let us help you. I'll stay with Landon while you rest. Just for a little while."

Valerie hesitated, glancing back at Landon, who was sleeping peacefully in his crib. She knew Nonna was right, but the thought of leaving her son, even for a moment, was unbearable.

Antonio stepped in, his voice gentle but firm. "Come with me, Valerie. You can lie down in my bed."

Antonio led Valerie to his bedroom. Valerie hesitated at the threshold, blushing slightly as she remembered what she had done with Antonio last night.

"Thank you, Antonio," she murmured. She sank onto the edge of his bed, the mattress invitingly plush beneath her.

Antonio lingered in the doorway, his gaze searching hers with an intensity that made her heart skip a beat.

"Do you, um…do you want to lie down next to me?" she asked.

Antonio's eyes softened. "I am afraid I can't right now. I have to go take care of some business."

Disappointment washed over her. "Oh."

"But I will be back tonight and you can call me anytime you want," Antonio quickly added.

Valerie nodded.

And then, she was all alone in his room.

Thirty-Nine

Photographs

Valerie lay on Antonio's bed, the soft sheets enveloping her in a cocoon of warmth. She closed her eyes, letting the quiet of the room seep into her bones. The events of the past few days had left her drained, both physically and emotionally.

As she lay there, feeling the rise and fall of her own breaths, a restlessness began to stir within her. She knew she should be resting, as Nonna had advised, but the stillness only seemed to amplify the unease that gnawed at her insides.

With a cautious glance towards the door, Valerie sat up slowly, glancing around Antonio's room.

Curiosity getting the better of her, Valerie rose from the bed and began to explore the room.

He probably would hate her snooping around like this, she thought to herself. But she knew nothing about him, and she wanted to know more.

Valerie's eyes scanned the room, taking in the details. She walked over to the dresser and lightly touched the first drawer.

She really shouldn't, she thought, taking he hand off it for a few minutes.

But the temptation was too strong. She felt a strong need to understand the man who had shown her so much care and support.

Valerie hesitated a moment longer, then gently pulled the drawer open. Inside, she found neatly folded clothes and nothing else. She closed the drawer and walked across the room toward the closet.

Valerie hesitated again, her hand hovering over the closet door handle. She felt a pang of guilt for invading Antonio's privacy, but her curiosity won out. She opened the closet door slowly, revealing a row of neatly hung suits and shirts. Everything was meticulously organized, reflecting Antonio's disciplined nature.

On the top shelf, she noticed a small, unmarked box. It seemed out of place amidst the orderly arrangement. Valerie reached up and carefully pulled it down. She sat on the floor and opened the box, her heart racing with anticipation.

Photographs

Inside, she found a few old photographs.

She picked up one of the photographs, recognizing a younger Antonio standing proudly in front of what looked like a vineyard.

She smiled absentmindedly as she looked at it. He looked about eight or nine in this picture. She recognized his jet-black hair, long and wild in the picture, and his boyish smile. And his face...

Well, the right side of his face was unscarred. It was a reminder of how much he had changed since this photo was taken when he was a boy.

"How did you get that scar on your face, Antonio?" she murmured to herself.

Last time she asked him about his scars, he had given her a vague answer. But she wanted to know more. She wanted to know everything about him with all the gory details.

Valerie's mind raced with questions as she carefully examined each photograph in the box.

One showed Antonio standing next to his Nonna. Another captured him as a teenager, looking determined and focused as he worked on a car engine. But it was the last photograph that caught her attention the most.

It was a faded picture of Antonio with a man and a woman.

The man looked strikingly similar to Antonio with his black hair and dark brown eyes that almost looked black. And the woman...she was beautiful with her strawberry blond hair and bright blue eyes.

His mother? Antonio didn't look like her at a first glance but when Valerie looked closely, she saw they had similar nose and smiles.

As Valerie studied the photograph, she noticed something she hadn't seen before. A subtle tension in Antonio's posture, a haunted look in his eyes that hinted at untold stories and hidden scars beyond the visible ones on his face.

She felt a surge of empathy wash over her as she realized that Antonio carried more weight on his shoulders than she had ever imagined.

Closing the box reverently, Valerie placed it back on the shelf and rose to her feet, her mind buzzing with curiosity. Maybe she will ask him more about his mother. He wouldn't deny her that, would he? She knew he wanted to be closer to her so why wouldn't he tell her about his childhood?

Valerie walked back to her bedroom and opened the door slightly to look inside.

Landon was still sleeping in his crib and Nonna sat on a chair next to him. She didn't look up as she was focused on her knitting. Valerie quietly stepped away and went back to Antonio's room.

Photographs

Valerie lay back down, closing her eyes and trying to imagine what it would be like if she stayed with Antonio. If she did it would mean trusting him completely. Last time she gave it all to a man, it didn't turn out well.

She drifted off into a light sleep, her mind still swirling her thoughts of the future.

She stirred awake when she felt a brush of lips on her forehead. She opened her eyes to find Antonio standing over her, a devilish smirk painted on his lips.

She jerked open her eyes entirely. "How long had I been asleep?"

"For a few hours. Don't worry, Landon was awake for only a few minutes. Lucia had made sure he was fed from the breast milk you stored in the freezer. He went right back to sleep after that," Antonio said.

Valerie sat up and yawned. Her entire body felt relaxed now. It had been a while since she had a nice rest like this. "I will be sure to thank her for taking care of Landon."

Antonio nodded. "I didn't want to wake you up but it's dinner time. Why don't you freshen up and join me?" he asked.

"Okay. I will be right there," Valerie said.

Forty

Sleep with Me

Valerie sat at the dinner table, her eyes stealing glances at Antonio. The aroma from the steaming plates of pasta filled the room as they prepared to eat together.

"Valerie," Antonio said, his gaze meeting hers. "I would like us to have dinner together every night. Family time is important."

"Okay," she agreed, her voice catching in her throat. She still wasn't used the word family associated with Antonio. Could she really do this?

Antonio looked down at the food, then back up at her. "Promise me, Valerie. Promise this will be our routine."

"Promise," she whispered, her heart pounding in her chest.

The steam from the plate of vegetables rose, filling the air with a comforting warmth.

Valerie's thoughts were a whirlwind of emotions. The little happiness she felt with Antonio here and there was tainted with the fear of losing this newfound stability they had created. The stakes felt higher than ever, and she struggled to find a balance between her attachment to Antonio and the ever-present risk of heartache.

"Valerie, are you okay?" Antonio's question snapped her out of her thoughts.

"Y-yes, sorry," she stammered, trying to mask the uncertainty that plagued her.

"Worried about Landon?" he inquired gently.

"Yes," she said.

"He seems stable the last time I checked on him. Don't worry, if he doesn't get better with the medicines, I will make sure to take him to another specialist," he said.

"Thank you," she said.

"I meant it when I said he was my son now," he said firmly. He reached over and grabbed her hand.

Valerie bit her lower lip and fought back her anxiety. She wanted to believe him and give in.

After dinner, Valerie went to check on Landon one last time before going to bed. He was sound asleep as the medication made him drowsy. Valerie sighed and started to get ready for bed.

She suddenly heard footsteps so she turned around. Antonio was standing by the door, his expression serious.

"Is the baby asleep?" he asked, his eyes meeting hers with concern.

"Yes, the medicines make him drowsy, so he had been sleeping a lot," she replied.

"Good, he needs his rest," Antonio said.

Valerie waited for him to walk away, but instead of leaving, Antonio walked toward her.

"Valerie," Antonio began, reaching out to take her hand. "Are you going to tell me what's wrong now?"

"Nothing is wr-.." Before she could finish, Antonio covered her mouth with his.

His kiss was unexpected, fierce and unyielding. It sent her heart racing and her mind reeling as she struggled to keep up with the overwhelming rush of emotions—relief at finally being touched, warmth from his desperate lips, and a lingering fear of what would come next. As Antonio pulled back slightly, his intense gaze bore into hers.

"Don't lie to me, mia cara," he growled.

"I am not lying. I-I'm just scared," she managed to whisper, her voice trembling under his intense gaze that seemed to see right through her.

Antonio's expression softened ever so slightly, his thumb gently tracing the line of her jaw. "Scared of what, Valerie?"

"Of getting used to this... to us," she admitted, the words feeling heavy as they left her lips. "I don't want to get too comfortable and then have it all taken away."

His eyes searched hers for a moment before a determined look crossed his face. "You won't lose me, Valerie. I promise you that."

She wanted to believe him, to let herself be swept away by his assurance, but the fear lingered at the back of her mind like a shadow.

"I'll always protect you and the boy," Antonio said firmly, his voice unwavering. "You will not leave my side. I won't allow it."

Valerie stared at him. The back of her eyelids burned, but she refused to cry.

"And you will be sleeping in my bed from now on," he said. "With me," he added.

She blinked. "What?"

"You heard me, my love. I want you to move into my bedroom," he said.

Valerie swallowed hard, trying to process Antonio's sudden declaration. Her mind raced with conflicting emotions—fear, doubt, but also a flicker of hope that maybe this could be a new beginning for them.

"I...why would you..." she stammered.

"Hush," he scolded her. "I won't hear any arguments."

She wrinkled her forehead and frowned. "You can't just order me around, Antonio. And you can't make me move into your bedroom. I won't..." she yelped as he suddenly bent down and picked her up in his arms.

She squirmed in his grasp, her protests falling on deaf ears as Antonio effortlessly carried her to his bedroom.

Antonio gently lowered Valerie onto the edge of his bed before stepping back, his intense gaze never leaving hers. She sat there, feeling small and vulnerable under his scrutiny.

"You will sleep here tonight," Antonio stated firmly, his voice brooking no argument. "And don't try to run away because every time you step foot out of this room, I will pick you up and bring you back right here."

Valerie opened her mouth to protest again, but the look in his eyes silenced her. "But why do you want me to sleep here?" she asked.

"So I can hold you at night, of course," he said nonchalantly.

"Who do you think I am? Your side pillow?" she pouted.

Antonio chuckled, a deep, rumbling sound that sent a shiver down her spine every time. "Something like that. And besides, with those nightmares you've been having, I ended up sleeping in your bed most times anyway," he shrugged.

"So what? You will become my hero and save me from my nightmares?" she retorted.

"Maybe I will," Antonio replied, his tone teasing but with an underlying seriousness that sent a chill down Valerie's spine. "Maybe I'll chase away all your demons and make sure you sleep peacefully."

Valerie stared at him, uncertain whether to be annoyed by his presumptuousness or touched by his concern. Antonio's gaze softened as he took a step closer, his hand reaching out to gently tuck a lock of hair behind her ear.

"You don't have to be strong all the time, Valerie," he murmured, his thumb brushing against her cheek.

His words struck a chord deep within her, a longing for someone to share the burden of her fears and insecurities. But could she trust him with her vulnerabilities? Could she let herself depend on Antonio when the walls she had built around her heart were so fragile?

Before Valerie could voice her doubts, Antonio leaned in and pressed a soft kiss to her forehead, his touch gentle yet reassuring. She closed her eyes, allowing herself to bask in the warmth of his embrace, the scent of his cologne wrapped around her like a comforting blanket.

With a sigh, she whispered softly, "Okay, Antonio. I'll sleep here with you."

A smile curved his lips as he pulled her closer, enfolding her in his arms as if promising to shield her from all harm. "Don't make me regret this," she mumbled against his chest.

"Wouldn't dream of it," he said.

She looked up, her eyes wide. "But what about Landon? He will be alone in the room!"

"His room isn't far and there's a baby monitor," he replied. "We will know if he cries."

"But still…" she started.

"Would you like me to bring the crib in here?" Antonio asked, sighing.

Sleep with Me

Valerie nodded vigorously. She was not ready to leave her baby alone just yet.

"Alright, as you wish," Antonio said, giving up.

Forty-One

Spending Time

The morning sun invaded the room, assaulting Valerie's closed eyelids. She stirred, groggy and disoriented, only to find that she couldn't move her body. Panic bubbled inside her as she tried to wiggle free, but it was no use.

But as soon as she opened her eyes, her tension was released.

She was trapped in Antonio's tight embrace. "Antonio," she whispered. She tried to wriggle out again, but he was too strong.

"Hmm," he murmured, his grip unwavering. Was he doing this on purpose?

"It's morning," she said, her voice barely audible. His arms

Spending Time

remained steadfast, keeping her pinned to him.

She suddenly realized something: there were no nightmares haunting her sleep this time. It was a strange relief, but she needed to focus on the fact that she was captive in his strong arms.

"Are you going to let me go?" she asked, attempting to sound assertive, but her voice came out shaky.

"Too early," he mumbled.

Jeez...

Valerie inhaled deeply, taking in Antonio's familiar scent. He smelled like sandalwood and...man. She felt his breath tickle the nape of her neck, sending shivers down her spine. His chest rose and fell with each steady breath, pressing her back against his firm body.

As she shifted slightly, Valerie became acutely aware of his stiff cock pressing against her. A wave of heat rushed through her, flushing her cheeks as a soft giggle escaped her lips. Antonio stirred at the sound, his grip tightening around her possessively.

"Ticklish, are we?" he murmured huskily, his warm breath fanning over her ear.

She could feel a blush creeping down her neck as she squirmed against him, trying to suppress another giggle

The Mafia Boss's Pregnant Bride

threatening to bubble up.

"Antonio, come on. We need to get up," she tried again.

"It's not time yet," he growled, his voice low and rumbling. "Just a few more minutes, Bella."

Valerie tried to reason with him, but there was something about his tone that made her reluctant to argue. Instead, she closed her eyes and allowed herself to enjoy the warmth of his body against hers, his scent surrounding her.

Suddenly, his phone started ringing, the sound jarring her senses back. Antonio muttered a curse and shifted beneath her, his hand tightening around her waist as he reached for his phone.

"What?" he barked as an answer.

The conversation on the phone seemed to be brief, but Antonio's demeanor changed as he hung up. "I have to go," he said, tension creeping into his voice.

"Is everything alright?" Valerie asked, her voice gentle.

He ran a hand through his unruly hair. "Just business stuff. I might be gone all day, but I'll leave some of my men here to keep watch."

Valerie's heart sank. He may leave some men for protection, but it's not the same as having him by her side all day long.

Spending Time

The thought made her bones ache with longing.

God, she felt like a lovestruck teenage girl just now!

He hesitated before speaking again. "Would you mind doing me a favor?"

"What's that?" Valerie asked.

"Would you mind spending some time with Nonna? I hadn't been able to spend much time with the old lady and she has not been feeling well," Antonio asked, looking at her expectantly.

"Of course," she replied softly.

Antonio nodded, his expression softening. "Good."

He leaned in and pressed a kiss to her forehead.

Antonio pulled back and gave her a reassuring smile. "I'll be back. We'll have dinner together tonight, just like promised."

All she could do was nod.

As Antonio left the room, Valerie watched him walk away. With a sigh, she forced herself out of bed and started her day. She fed Landon and then walked around carrying him to her chest.

After a while, Valerie took them to see Nonna in her room.

Nonna was thrilled to see them, her eyes twinkling with joy.

"Oh, it's you, Valerie. And you brought the baby!" Nonna exclaimed.

Valerie looked at her and smiled. "Thank you for taking care of Landon the other day. I needed that sleep."

"Oh, sweetie. It was my pleasure," Nonna said, waving her hands in dismissal.

Nonna took Landon from Valerie's arms and cradled him gently, cooing and whispering in Italian as she stroked his soft black hair.

"And you, mio amore. Come sit by me," Nonna said to Valerie.

She settled down next to her.

"Ah, the child didn't inherit your beautiful red hair, but he sure is beautiful," Nonna said.

Valerie laughed softly. As she sat there, watching Nonna interact with Landon, a sense of peace washed over her. It was in these moments that she truly felt like part of the family - Antonio's family.

"I like his raven black hair," Valerie said.

Nonna chuckled softly, her eyes twinkling with a warmth that made Valerie feel instantly welcome. "Ah, he will be

Spending Time

a beautiful boy and grow into a handsome man," Nonna said, gently rocking Landon. The baby cooed, his tiny hand reaching up to grasp Nonna's finger.

Valerie smiled. She thought the same thing. Though some may argue she was biased since she was his mother.

"Nonna, how have you been feeling?" Valerie asked gently, watching the way Nonna's eyes crinkled with amusement at Landon's cooing.

Nonna's expression turned more serious, though her smile never completely faded. "Oh, you know, my dear. The usual aches and pains of old age. But having you here brings me such joy. It's the best medicine."

Valerie reached out to squeeze her hand. "I'm glad we can be here with you. Antonio mentioned you haven't been feeling well, and I wanted to make sure you were alright."

Nonna patted her hand affectionately. "Antonio worries too much. But I appreciate his concern. This family has needed a bit of sunshine, and you and the children have brought that."

Valerie felt that familiar warmth in her stomach at the mention of Antonio. "Will you tell me more about Antonio? His childhood?"

Nonna's expression darkened slightly. "I suppose I could tell you now that you've become part of the family." She paused to take a deep breath.

Forty-Two

Tell Me His Story

"Antonio's upbringing was fraught with challenges," she began, her voice becoming more somber.

"He was born into a life he did not choose, a life dictated by circumstance and the expectations of his father. His childhood was one of constant tension and fear. He carried the weight of his father's legacy on his shoulders, knowing the expectations that came with it. But he never let it show. Antonio always held his head high, a resilient young boy with a sense of duty and honor that never faltered."

As she spoke, Valerie could almost see the young Antonio, a boy with a bright future before him, but his path was already set. The harsh reality of his environment weighed down on him, shaping him into the man he is today.

"His mother, my dear Isabella, she tried to protect him from the darkness that surrounded them. But even her love couldn't shield him from the harsh realities of the life he was born into." Nonna's eyes welled up with tears as she spoke of her daughter-in-law.

"What was she like?" Valerie asked quietly.

"Sweet Isabella, she was a kind and loving soul," Nonna said, her voice trembling with emotion. "She was always full of life, with a smile that could light up a room. She loved Antonio deeply, and she tried her best to give him the life he deserved."

"Antonio was always a good boy," Nonna continued, wiping away a tear. "But sometimes, life is cruel, and it tests even the strongest of spirits. He had to grow up fast and learn to deal with a world that wasn't always fair."

Landon gurgled, drawing their attention back to her. Nonna kissed her cheek, and the baby cooed, content in her arms.

"How did someone like his mother end up with a man like Antonio's father?" Valerie asked, her curiosity growing.

Nonna sighed, her face a mix of sadness and pride. "Antonio's father, Alexander, was a powerful man in the city. He was a man of influence and wealth, but his heart was as black as the night."

Valerie held her breath, listening to the story. "Did...did he force Isabella?"

Nonna's eyes drooped for a moment before regaining focus. "No, not quite like that. You see, their love was genuine, but circumstance played a cruel hand. Alexander was ruthless in his pursuit of power, and Isabella, with her gentle heart, was an obstacle he could not bear."

Valerie felt a chill run down her spine, thinking about the kind, gentle Isabella caught in such a predicament. "What happened to her?"

Nonna's face twisted with pain as she remembered her dear daughter-in-law. "Isabella, she couldn't take the pressure anymore. She had tried to leave Alexander, but the city was his playground, and he would not let her go easily."

"Why did she want to leave her husband?" Valerie asked, fearing the answer.

"It was because of the way he treated Antonio. He didn't just want a son; he wanted a son who could rule his empire. And to ensure that, he put Antonio through torture," Nonna said, shaking her head.

Valerie couldn't breathe. Her heart raced, and a knot formed in her throat as she tried to swallow the lump that had appeared there. "What kind of torture?" It was hard to speak, but she needed to know.

Nonna sighed, the pain in her eyes palpable. "It was physical, emotional, and psychological. Alexander would do anything to ensure his son would never fall short of his expectations.

Tell Me His Story

He would beat Antonio and make him endure endless humiliation, all in the name of preparing him for his future role."

Valerie couldn't believe what she was hearing. This was the man who had raised Antonio, who had shaped him into the man he was today? "So, this... this violence is the reason behind his anger and the scars on his body?"

Nonna nodded, her eyes filled with sorrow. "Yes, my dear. And to make matters worse, Isabella couldn't bear to see her son suffer. She tried to protect him, but that only made things worse for both of them. It was a vicious cycle."

Valerie's heart ached for the young Antonio, for his dear mother, and for what they must have gone through. "How did Isabella die?"

Nonna closed her eyes and breathed slowly. "Alexander had sent Antonio on a mission when he was merely sixteen. Isabella cried and pleaded, but he never listened. The mission went wrong, and many of Alexander's men ended up killed. When Isabella heard, she was in hysterics. She completely lost it when Antonio didn't return home."

Nonna continued, her voice choked with emotion, "Alexander was furious. He searched for Antonio, but he was nowhere to be found. He was missing for a week. When he finally returned, it was too late. Isabella had taken her own life, thinking her son was dead. It was a tragic end to a desperate situation."

Valerie's stomach twisted in knots as she listened to the story. "What happened to Alexander after that?"

Nonna finally looked up, her eyes clear and determined. "Alexander went on to rise to the top of his empire, but he never found happiness."

Valerie was silent for a moment, her throat constricted with the enormity of the story she had just heard. "What about Antonio? How did he survive all that?"

Nonna's eyes softened, and her lips curled into a warm smile. "Antonio, he was a survivor. He rose to the top like his father and took over his business, but he never lost his humanity like Alexander did."

Valerie nodded. "He is… kind to Landon. But what if…" She stopped, unable to find the right words to express her lingering fears.

Nonna's smile was reassuring as she addressed Valerie's unspoken fears. "I know what you're thinking, dear. Will Antonio treat your son like how his father treated him? I can assure you he won't."

"But how can you be sure?" Valerie asked, her voice tinged with doubt.

"Antonio is not his father," Nonna replied firmly. "He's a man who's been through hell and back but has held on to his humanity. He understands pain, and he won't inflict it upon others. Antonio will love your son and you."

Valerie felt a blush creep across her cheeks at Nonna's words.

"In fact," Nonna continued, "I believe he already loves you."

Valerie bit her lip, about to argue, but then stopped herself. Instead, she asked, "But what about you, Nonna? How did you survive all that?"

Nonna smiled and patted Valerie's hand gently. "I survived because I chose to. I raised Antonio alongside Isabella. She was like a daughter to me, and I loved her dearly, and I could not give up on her. I had to be strong for her, and I believed in her. It wasn't easy, but it was what I needed to do."

Valerie couldn't help but smile at Nonna's determination. She began to understand Antonio better and the reasons behind his deep desire for a loving family.

"Sometimes, life can be cruel, my dear," Nonna said, her face lined with wisdom and experience. "But it's the choices we make that determine how we handle it. Give my boy a chance to prove to you that he can be a better man."

Valerie was left without words, contemplating the depth of Nonna's wisdom and the possibilities of their future.

Forty-Three

Marry Him

Antonio stood there, seething.

The shop was a war zone—glass shards glinted like treacherous ice on the floor, necklaces and rings lay scattered amidst velvet displays torn apart. He cursed out loud, his hands curling into fists at his sides, nails digging into his palms hard enough to leave crescent marks.

Anger surged through his veins like hot steel, pulsing with each rapid beat of his heart.

"Who the fuck tried to mess with my business?" he spat, tasting the bitterness of betrayal.

"Someone with a death wish," Sam muttered.

Antonio moved deeper into the chaos, eyes scanning the disaster before him. Everything was in disarray, from the toppled showcases to the shattered display cases. It was clear that whoever had done this wanted to send a message. But to whom?

He couldn't shake the feeling that this was personal. His mind raced, trying to connect the dots, but anger clouded his thoughts. Maybe it was one of Slava's men, someone who decided to stay loyal even after his death.

"Sam, who do you think did this?" Antonio asked gruffly.

Sam's eyes narrowed as he surveyed the wreckage, his jaw clenched tightly. "Julian's men are a possibility," he said, his voice measured but tinged with anger. "Even though he was a small time criminal compared to us, he could still have someone who wanted revenge. Could be one of his loyalists trying to send a message."

Antonio nodded, his thoughts whirling. "We need to find out who exactly did this and why," he said, his voice steely with determination. "We can't let this stand."

Sam nodded in agreement, his expression hardening.

Antonio rolled up his sleeves, ready to dive into the mess that lay before him. The shattered glass crunched under his boots as he surveyed the damage, the metallic scent of blood lingering in the air. He could feel the rage bubbling inside him, a fire fueled by betrayal and the threat to his family.

With Sam by his side, Antonio spent hours speaking to the insurance company and law enforcement, whom he usually avoided like the plague.

Toward the end of the day, his phone started to ring. He looked down and saw it was Viktor, one of the guards he had left at the house.

"What is it, Viktor?" he barked.

"You have to come home, Capo. The house was under attack," Viktor said urgently.

Antonio's heart stopped. The chaos at the shop suddenly seemed insignificant compared to the terror of the thought that his family might be in danger.

He didn't waste a second. "Let's go," he ordered Sam, his voice clipped with urgency.

Antonio and Sam raced through the streets, every sound amplified, every shadow a potential threat. The tires screeched as they pulled up to the house, Antonio's pulse thundering in his ears. He burst through the gate, and what he saw made his blood run cold. Ambulances were everywhere. He rushed inside the house.

Valerie stood there, her eyes wide with fear but unharmed. She had Landon clutched against her chest, tears staining her cheeks.

Marry Him

"Antonio," Valerie whispered, her voice trembling.

Antonio's heart clenched at the sight of Valerie and the baby, safe but terrified. Relief flooded through him, momentarily easing the tight knot of fear that had gripped him since Viktor's call.

"What happened? Are you all okay?" he demanded, his voice rough with emotion.

Valerie rushed into his arms, burying her face in his chest. "We are okay. Someone attacked us, but I was able to hide with the baby."

Antonio's heart swelled with gratitude and protectiveness for Valerie as he held her tight. "You did well," he murmured, pressing a kiss to her forehead.

"Why are the ambulances here?" Antonio asked.

Valerie's eyes filled with tears as she looked up at him. "It's Nonna, Antonio. She had a heart attack. They rushed her to the hospital. The rest of the ambulances are here to take some of your injured men away."

Antonio's blood turned cold at the news. Nonna, the one who had always been his pillar of strength, lay in a hospital bed, fighting for her life.

"I have to go see her," he said.

"We want to come with you," Valerie said quickly.

Antonio looked at Valerie. He didn't trust anyone to leave her alone here, so he nodded. "Yes, you are coming with me."

Valerie nodded, relief and worry mingling in her eyes. "Let's go then," she said, gathering the kids quickly.

They moved swiftly, the urgency of the situation driving them forward. Antonio ensured Viktor and the remaining guards were on high alert, their expressions grim and resolute. This wasn't over.

The drive to the hospital was tense. Landon whimpered softly in his car seat, sensing the anxiety in the air.

As they arrived at the hospital, Antonio parked as close to the entrance as possible. "Stay close to me," he instructed Valerie as they hurried inside.

Inside, the antiseptic smell and the hum of activity greeted them. Antonio approached the nurse's station, his heart pounding. "I'm here for my grandmother, Isabella Costello. She was brought in after a heart attack."

The nurse nodded, checking her records quickly. "She's in the ICU. Room 304," she said, pointing down the hall.

"Thank you," Antonio muttered, leading Valerie toward the room.

Marry Him

When they reached the ICU, the sight of Nonna hooked up to various machines nearly brought Antonio to his knees. She looked so fragile, a stark contrast to the indomitable woman who had always been his rock.

"Nonna," he whispered, taking her hand gently. Her eyes fluttered open, and a weak smile touched her lips when she saw them.

"Antonio," she murmured, her voice barely audible. "You came."

"Of course, Nonna," Antonio said, his voice choked with emotion. "We're all here."

Valerie stepped forward, holding Landon close. "Hello, Nonna," she said softly, her eyes filled with compassion.

Nonna's eyes moved to Valerie and the children, and a faint smile touched her lips. "So glad you are safe," she whispered.

"We're here for you, Nonna," Valerie said gently.

"I don't have long, I'm afraid," Nonna said weakly.

"Don't say that, Nonna," Antonio pleaded, gripping her hand tighter. "You're strong. You'll get through this."

Nonna's eyes, still bright with a lifetime of wisdom and love, met his. "Antonio, my dear, there's no escaping fate. I've lived a full life and seen you grow. That is all I could ever ask for."

Antonio fought to keep his composure. "Don't die on me, old woman."

She smiled weakly. "My sweet boy. How I wish I could see you settle down before I died."

Antonio shot a quick glance at Valerie, who was looking at them with tears in her eyes. He squeezed his grandmother's hand, willing her to stay with them a little longer. "You will, Nonna. We'll get through this, and you'll see it all."

Nonna's gaze softened as she looked at Valerie, then back at Antonio. "Valerie is a good woman, Antonio. Trust her, lean on her. She will be your rock, just as I've been."

Nonna's breathing grew more labored, and her grip on Antonio's hand weakened. "Valerie, my dear, you will have to forgive me for asking this much of you, but could you promise me something?"

Valerie stepped closer, her voice gentle but steady. "Anything, Nonna."

"Promise me you'll take care of Antonio in my absence. He looks like a terrifying beast, but he has a good heart. And promise me you'll find your own happiness, too."

Valerie nodded, tears streaming down her face. "I promise, Nonna."

Marry Him

"Then you will marry him?" Nonna asked.

Valerie looked taken aback, her eyes widening as she glanced at Antonio. He felt a jolt of surprise too, but he quickly masked it, focusing on Nonna's face.

"Marry him, Valerie," Nonna repeated, her voice frail but determined. "Give him the love and support he needs. Be the family he deserves."

"Err...Nonna..." Antonio tried to interrupt, but Nonna glared at him.

"Stai zitto, bambino!" she barked.

Antonio narrowed his eyes. For someone who was dying, she sure looked like she could bite his head off.

"Um...I..." Valerie hesitated.

"Of course, you couldn't do this, Valerie. It was cruel of me to ask of you," Nonna said in a sorrowful voice. "I am sorry, dear. I know I'm being unreasonable. It's just that...this has always been my wish. To see my boy have a family," she said.

Antonio furrowed his brows. Was this old lady scheming right now?

Forty-Four

Accept Me

Valerie was completely taken aback by Nonna's sudden request.

Marry Antonio? The words echoed in her mind, sending a jolt of shock through her body.

Her mind whirred with conflicting emotions, torn between the weight of her dying wish and her own feelings. On one hand, she wanted to honor Nonna's final request. She had grown fond of the old lady in this short period of time.

But on the other hand, the thought of marrying Antonio so suddenly felt overwhelming and daunting.

As she struggled to find her voice, Antonio reached out and gently squeezed her hand. His touch was warm and

Accept Me

reassuring, bringing a sense of calmness over her. Leaning in close, he whispered, "You don't have to marry me if you don't want to. I will not force you."

Valerie turned back to Nonna. "But you don't know anything about me. What if I'm not good enough for your grandson?" she whispered, making sure only Nonna could hear.

Nonna's eyes softened even more, and she managed a faint smile. "Valerie, my dear, I see more than you realize. I see the way Antonio looks at you, the way he speaks to you. He respects you, and that's something not easily earned. And I see the kindness in your eyes, the strength in your heart. Trust me, you are more than good enough for my Antonio."

Her words wrapped around Valerie's heart, filling it with a mixture of hope and fear. She glanced at Antonio again, who was watching them intently. The weight of Nonna's trust and Antonio's unspoken feelings pressed down on her.

"Nonna," Valerie said softly, "you are putting me in a really tough position, you know? One could almost argue that you are blackmailing me."

Nonna laughed softly. "We Italian women can be cunning sometimes, but we mean well."

Valerie couldn't help but smile through her tears. "Okay," she whispered.

Nonna raised an eyebrow. "You agree?"

"I will marry him," Valerie heard herself say. Oh God, she had gone crazy.

Nonna's face lit up with a fragile joy. "You have made an old woman very happy," she said, her voice barely above a whisper. "Antonio, take care of her. She is your greatest treasure."

Antonio looked at Valerie, his dark eyes twinkling. "I will, Nonna," he promised.

Nonna closed her eyes, a peaceful expression settling on her face. "Thank you, Valerie. Thank you both," she murmured, her breathing slowing.

Valerie squeezed her hand gently, feeling the weight of her trust and love. "Rest now, Nonna. We'll be okay."

As soon as they walked down the hallway, Antonio grabbed Valerie's shoulders and turned her to face him. "Do you realize what you just did, Valerie?"

She took a deep breath, trying to steady her racing heart. "Yes, Antonio, I do," she replied, her voice trembling slightly. "I made a promise to your Nonna."

"But Valerie," he said, his grip tightening slightly, "this is a huge decision. You don't have to marry me just because she asked you to."

"I know," she said, looking into his eyes. "But I couldn't just

Accept Me

ignore a dying woman's wish! Unless..." she paused and looked at him. "Did you change your mind? You asked me to marry you at the hospital, but..."

"No! I did not change my mind." Antonio's expression hardened. "She won't die. I am going to provide her with the best care possible."

"But what if that's not enough?" Valerie argued.

Antonio's lips twisted into a small smile. "Yes, you are right. We can't take any chances. I guess you will be my wife, Valerie."

Her heart skipped a beat at the word "wife." "Y-yes... I suppose I will be."

"Ah, don't look so distressed," he chuckled.

Valerie frowned. "What? I don't look distressed!" she breathed.

He looked at her, his eyes intense and unwavering. "It won't be so bad married to me. I intend to take care of you until I die. And even if I die, I will have enough resources to make sure you never have to worry about a thing ever again."

Tears welled up in Valerie's eyes as she absorbed the magnitude of what he was saying. "Antonio, this is... it's too much. You don't have to take on so much responsibility."

Antonio cupped her face in his hands, his touch gentle but firm. "I won't hear your protests. Let's go home now. We have things to prepare."

Valerie walked with him in a daze.

As they reached his car, he opened the door for her, his demeanor steady and resolute. Sitting beside him, she couldn't help but steal glances at him, trying to read the emotions playing across his face. His jaw was set, and his eyes focused on the road ahead as they drove through the streets back to their home.

Once they arrived, Valerie gently settled Landon into her crib, making sure he was comfortable and safe. She went back to Antonio so they could talk.

Antonio took her to his bedroom. "Wait here," he instructed, disappearing into his closet.

Valerie stood by the bed, her heart racing with curiosity and nervousness. What was he up to?

Moments later, Antonio emerged from the closet, holding a small box in his hands. His expression was serious yet tender as he approached her.

He opened the box, revealing a ring nestled inside. It was delicate and elegant, with a ruby in the center and diamonds surrounding it. Valerie's breath caught in her throat as she realized the significance of what Antonio was about to do.

Accept Me

He took her hand, his touch gentle yet firm, and slid the ring onto her finger.

"Antonio..." she murmured, overwhelmed by the moment.

He looked into her eyes. "My mother's ring. It's yours now."

Tears welled up in Valerie's eyes as she looked down at the ring, remembering what his grandmother had said about his mother. "I...I can't take your mother's ring! It's..."

"Yours," Antonio repeated. "My mother wanted me to give it to my future wife, and that's you, Valerie. Please accept it. Accept being my wife."

Valerie took a deep breath, her heart filled with warmth. She nodded slowly, her voice trembling with both uncertainty and determination. "I accept, Antonio. I will be your wife."

He pulled her into a tender embrace. "Non capirai mai quanto ti amo," he whispered against her hair.

"What did you say?" she asked, her voice shaky.

"Nothing, mi amore," he replied.

Forty-Five

Approval

Ellie's joyful cry echoed through the room as she threw her arms around Valerie, squeezing tightly. Her blue eyes sparkled with excitement and happiness. "Oh, Valerie, I am beyond thrilled for you!" she exclaimed.

A small smile tugged at Valerie's lips. "You are?"

"Of course! You're getting married!" Ellie said cheerfully. "I am here to help you with everything. I hope you know that."

Valerie's laughter rang out, replacing the knot of nerves that had been twisting in her stomach. "I know. And I think Antonio and I would prefer a more intimate ceremony," she replied fondly.

The warmth of Ellie's embrace and her genuine enthusiasm

Approval

made Valerie feel less anxious about the whole thing.

"Wait until River hears about it," Ellie said.

And...just like that, Valerie's anxiety was back.

Ellie frowned. "Why are you looking at me like that? Don't tell me you are worried about River knowing."

"River knowing what?"

A deep voice made both women jump. "R-River, hi," Valerie said nervously.

"What's going on? Why is Valerie here?" River asked, eyeing her suspiciously.

"Can't a sister visit her brother?" Valerie pouted.

River smirked. "Of course she can," he said, stepping forward to hug her.

River's embrace was warm and reassuring, but Valerie couldn't help feeling a pang of anxiety. His protective nature always made him wary of any changes, especially when they involved her.

Ellie, ever the enthusiastic one, jumped in to diffuse the tension. "River, you won't believe the news!" she said, her eyes twinkling with excitement. "Valerie and Antonio are getting married!"

River's hug froze for a second before he pulled back, his eyes narrowing as he looked between Ellie and Valerie. "Married? Since when?"

Valerie's heart hammered against her chest, threatening to burst through as she swallowed hard. "It… it just happened, River," her voice trembled as she spoke. "His grandmother… she asked us to."

River's brows furrowed in confusion and concern as he processed the information. His gaze softened slightly as he looked at Valerie. "His grandmother's dying wish was for you to marry Antonio?"

Valerie's response came out like a desperate plea for reassurance. "Yes?"

River's lips curled into a slight smirk as he scoffed. "I don't blame her. If she didn't do that, Antonio could never find a wife. Because who would willingly marry that insufferable asshole?" His words were laced with contempt, and his tone held no sympathy for Antonio.

Ellie chimed in, playfully punching River's arm while laughing. "River!" She scolded but couldn't contain her own amusement at his blunt honesty.

Valerie couldn't help but giggle. "He is not so bad, you know. He loves Landon, oddly enough." She didn't mention how Antonio confessed to loving her too. She couldn't imagine River taking that seriously.

Approval

River raised an eyebrow, his smirk softening into a more thoughtful expression. "He does, huh?" he said, his tone shifting slightly. "Well, that's something, I suppose. He was awfully happy about accidentally signing Landon's birth certificate."

Ellie linked her arm with Valerie's, her eyes twinkling with mischief. "See, River? There's more to Antonio than meets the eye. Besides, he's good for Valerie and Landon. That's all that matters."

River sighed, rubbing the back of his neck. "And does he love you?"

Valerie looked down. "I don't know," she whispered. She wasn't lying. Despite him telling her, she couldn't figure out whether he was telling the truth or not. Or maybe it was a temporary feeling he was feeling for her.

River's eyes softened further, and he took a step closer to Valerie, placing a reassuring hand on her shoulder. "Valerie, you deserve someone who loves you wholeheartedly. If Antonio isn't that person, then this marriage… it shouldn't be forced."

Valerie nodded slowly, taking a deep breath. "I know it's not a conventional love story, but his grandmother's wish and his care for my son… it means something. And I… I don't hate the idea of being his wife."

River smiled. "Alright, Valerie. Just promise me you'll always put yourself and Landon first. If things ever feel wrong, you come to me, okay?"

"I promise," Valerie said, her voice steadier now. "Thank you, River. Your support means the world to me."

River pulled Valerie into a tight hug, and for a moment, all her uncertainty faded away. When he finally released her, Ellie took her hand again, her excitement bubbling over.

"So," Ellie said, grinning, "how about we start planning this wedding? It doesn't have to be huge, but it should be special."

River chuckled, the tension easing from his shoulders. "Yeah, and you know what that means, Ellie? You'll get to be the maid of honor."

Ellie's eyes sparkled with joy. "Really, Valerie? Can I?"

Valerie smiled, feeling a sense of warmth and hope. "Of course, Ellie. I'd love for you to be my maid of honor."

Ellie squealed with excitement, pulling Valerie into another hug. "This is going to be amazing, Valerie! We're going to make sure your wedding is perfect."

Valerie nodded. Ellie's enthusiasm was contagious, and Valerie was starting to allow herself to feel happy for once.

A small part of her was scared, though. Antonio had told her he would protect them from the men who had attacked the

Approval

house, but what if more came back?

"River, don't freak out, but I need to tell you something," Valerie said.

Ellie's beaming expression faltered as River's eyes narrowed in concern. "What is it, Valerie? What happened?" His voice was sharp, instantly on high alert.

Taking a deep breath, Valerie tried to steady her voice. "There was an attack on Antonio's house. His men managed to fight them off, and we weren't hurt, but I thought you should know."

River's jaw clenched. "He should've told me. I'll make some calls and ensure you have extra security around the house. You need to be safe, Valerie."

"Antonio won't like that," Valerie reminded him. She knew he wouldn't like River's interference in his territory. Maybe she shouldn't have said anything.

River's expression hardened, his eyes glinting with determination. "I don't care what Antonio likes or doesn't like. Your safety come first, Valerie. I promised to protect you, and that's what I intend to do."

Ellie stood by Valerie's side, her hand squeezing hers in silent support. "He's right, Valerie. Don't worry about Antonio. River will handle this."

Valerie felt a surge of gratitude for their unwavering loyalty and care. Despite the complications of her situation, having River and Ellie by her side made her feel stronger than she ever thought possible.

River turned to Valerie, his voice firm yet reassuring. "I'll talk to Antonio. You just worry about yourself and focus on being his wife."

Valerie raised an eyebrow. "You are being a little too cool about this marriage. Should I be worried?"

River chuckled, a wry smile playing on his lips. "Don't get me wrong, Valerie. I may seem calm, but I'm watching Antonio closely. If he ever steps out of line or puts you or Landon in danger, he'll have me to answer to." His tone was sharp, emphasizing his words.

Ellie nodded in agreement, her gaze unwavering. "River's not one to make idle threats, Valerie. We've got your back, no matter what."

Valerie had no doubt about that.

She called Antonio to pick her up when she was ready to go back.

As Antonio's car pulled up, Valerie couldn't shake the tension gripping her chest. The recent attacks had put her on edge, and she knew Antonio was equally unsettled by the threats to their family.

Approval

"How did Foster take the news?" Antonio's voice was low, concern etched in his features as he glanced at her. His eyes searched hers for any sign of distress.

Valerie smiled. "A lot better than expected."

He reached out and tucked a loose strand of hair behind her ear. "Good," he said.

A surge of emotion rippled through Valerie, and she had the sudden urge to kiss him.

She leaned into Antonio's touch, feeling his warmth seep into her skin. As his hand lingered on her cheek, she met his gaze, the intensity in his eyes mirroring the storm of emotions swirling within her.

Without a word, she closed the distance between them and pressed her lips to his. Antonio's arms encircled her, pulling her closer as if he never wanted to let go.

For a heartbeat, the world fell away, leaving only the two of them suspended in time. His lips moved against hers with a tenderness that made her head spin.

As they finally pulled away, Antonio looked at her with his dark eyes, and in that moment, everything felt right.

Forty-Six

Tell Me Everything

A sharp, sinking feeling pierced Antonio's chest when he watched the slow trail of tears falling down Valerie's face. No, he didn't like it when Valerie cried. He didn't like that at all.

He told the driver, John, to pull over so he could focus on her. "Give us some privacy," he ordered. John nodded before stepping away.

Antonio quickly pulled Valerie onto his lap. "What's wrong, my love?" he asked urgently, wiping the tears from her face.

"I… I just…" she choked out.

"Shh… breathe, mia cara. Whatever it is, you can tell me," he crooned, kissing her forehead.

Tell Me Everything

Valerie took a deep, shuddering breath, trying to steady herself. "I... I just feel overwhelmed," she finally admitted.

Disappointment washed over Antonio. "You don't want to marry me," he said gravely. "I told you I won't force you to do this, my love."

Valerie looked up at Antonio, her eyes wide with surprise. "No, Antonio, it's not that," she said. "I want to marry you."

A grin escaped Antonio before he could stop it. "You do?"

She nodded.

"Then what's wrong? What can I do to make it better?" he asked, turning serious.

"You already did so much for me!" she said.

He chuckled. "You sound as if it's a bad thing."

"I don't deserve it," she said, her voice barely audible.

"No, that's not—"

"No, Antonio, listen to me. I have to tell you something. Something you don't know," she said in a hoarse voice.

Valerie took another deep breath, her voice trembling. "There are things I haven't told you about my past. I'm afraid that if you knew everything, you wouldn't want to marry me."

Antonio caressed her cheek. "Tell me," he said in a calm and steady tone.

"Julian was an alcoholic, and he used to stumble home every night in a drunken rage. He would take out his anger on me," she confessed, her eyes filled with pain and fear.

Antonio kept his eyes on her, trying to read the emotions flickering across her face. Her eyes were downcast, and tears streamed steadily from their corners.

"Did he beat you?" Antonio asked, his voice barely above a whisper.

Valerie nodded, her hair falling around her face like a curtain of sadness.

More tears cascaded down her cheeks as she spoke, her voice trembling. "He beat me and sometimes had me do things I didn't want to do," she admitted, the pain evident in her words.

"What kind of things?" he asked slowly.

"Sometimes he forced me to have sex with me when I didn't want to." She let out a humorless laugh. "But that's not where he stopped. He loved making money, but he was bad at business. He had a lot of debts because of it. So he made me strip at his club sometimes even though I said I didn't want to do that."

Antonio felt a rage building up inside him. His hands clenched into fists, and he could feel the tension coursing through his veins, but he remained calm to avoid scaring her.

"My love," he said hoarsely, his voice laced with emotion and longing.

"He didn't stop there, Antonio." she continued, her words trembling. "He would make deals with the men he owed money to, and he would let them fuck me to…to…delay paying them back."

Her voice wavered with raw vulnerability, but her gaze remained steady.

At that moment, Antonio was flooded with a black, destructive fury that threatened to consume him. Every muscle in his body tensed, and his hands clenched into fists. "I am glad that fucker is dead, then," he said through gritted teeth.

"I couldn't leave. I was a coward. I thought he would kill me if I did. That's what he told me," Valerie said timidly, her voice barely audible above the pounding of his own heartbeat.

"Where was your brother? Why didn't he kill that bastard?" Antonio asked.

"River and I weren't always close." Valerie sighed. "Our relationship fell apart when we were teenagers and when I turned eighteen, I went to live with Julian. But when I got pregnant with Julian, and then he died, I sought River out.

He took me in without hesitation and promised to protect me."

"You should've gone to him when Julian was abusing you," Antonio said.

Valerie shot him a glare. "Don't you think I know that? I just...I couldn't. I thought I loved him."

"Do you?" Antonio asked.

"No! I don't love him. I never loved him. I was only infatuated with him. I made a mistake," she said, breathing heavily.

"So Landon. Are you sure he is Julian's baby?" Antonio asked.

Valerie didn't get angry at the question. The thought had come to her before. "Maybe he is, maybe he isn't. I was a whore that Julian passed around whenever he pleased so the father could be anyone," she said bitterly.

"You are not a goddamn whore, Valerie. Too bad my men killed him because I wish I could tear him apart, limb by limb," Antonio growled.

Tears welled up in Valerie's eyes as she slowly reached for something on her finger. "I'm sorry I didn't tell you sooner," she whispered, sliding off a ring and holding it out to him.

"What do you think you are doing?" he growled.

"I... I thought you would like to have your mother's ring back," Valerie said hesitantly, her hand still extended toward him.

"Why the fuck would I want that?" Antonio said with a tight jaw.

"You can't possibly want to marry me now. Aren't you disgusted by me?" she asked.

"Valerie. You are being ridiculous," he said, almost scolding her now.

"I was used, and I am not even sure who fathered Landon. Why would you want to marry someone like me?" she declared.

Antonio stared at her. His heart pounded in his chest, and he felt his breath catch in his throat. He looked down at the ring still clasped in her fingers, feeling a strange mixture of emotions—anger, sorrow, and protectiveness.

"You think I care about that?" Antonio growled.

"Don't you?" Valerie snapped. "Can you really accept me and truly love me after knowing about all the men I've been with?"

"You haven't been with those men, Valerie. Your so-called boyfriend pushed you to them. And as far as Landon is concerned. He is my son now," Antonio said, sliding the ring back onto Valerie's finger. "And don't try to slink your way out of this marriage because I won't let you go, mia cara."

"But Antonio," she began to protest, but he pressed his lips against hers.

"Don't speak," he whispered against her lips, his arms wrapping around her tightly. "I don't want to hear any more protests."

"But wouldn't you rather be with someone who isn't... ruined?" she asked.

"Good god, Valerie," Antonio nearly growled. "You are absolutely insane, but you are not ruined. You are beautiful, and you are perfect."

She sniffled and wiped her face. "You are full of shit, Antonio."

"Maybe," he admitted, leaning in and pressing his forehead against hers.

Tears glistened in her eyes as she looked up at him, her lips trembling.

"Will you tell me what happened when you went missing at sixteen?" she asked.

Antonio halted. "How do you know about that?"

"Nonna told me. She mentioned how you were gone for a week, and because of that, your mother..."

Tell Me Everything

"Killed herself," Antonio said flatly.

"Yes," Valerie breathed. "Will you tell me what happened?"

For years, Antonio had shoved that memory deep down, pretending it never existed. But after hearing Valerie's own dark and vulnerable experiences, he knew he couldn't keep his secret any longer. She had opened up to him, and now it was his turn to reveal the darkest part of his past. It was only fair.

"I will tell you everything. But first, I should call John back to drive us home. I'm sure he's freezing out there," Antonio said, a small laugh escaping him.

Valerie smiled for the first time. "Okay," she said, leaning on him and closing her eyes.

Forty-Seven

What Do You Want to Do?

~~~~~~~~~~~~~~

Mary, Antonio's housekeeper, sat in a rocking chair beside Landon's crib, gently swaying back and forth. She turned to Valerie with a warm smile as she entered the room.

"Was he a good boy?" Valerie asked.

"A perfect baby, this one is," Mary replied. "Didn't cry much and went right to sleep after feeding."

Valerie smiled proudly. "I am glad to hear it."

"He is good just like his mother," Antonio's voice boomed near Valerie's ear. Valerie felt Antonio's warmth seeping through her as Antonio wrapped his fingers around her waist and pulled her against his body.

What Do You Want to Do?

Mary got up. "I will return to my room now, Signor Costello and Signora Foster. Is there anything else you need from me?"

Valerie shook her head. "Thank you for watching Landon, Mary."

"It's my pleasure," Mary said before exiting the room.

Antonio kissed Valerie's neck, and a shock of pleasure shook her to her core. "The baby is sleeping already," he whispered.

"Yes, he is," Valerie said, shivering as he placed another kiss on her neck.

"But we are awake," he said, tightening his grip on her.

"Wide awake," she whispered.

"What should we do about it?" he asked, turning her around slowly to face him.

Valerie's heart raced as Antonio turned her to face him. His eyes, dark and intense, locked onto hers. The warmth of his body pressed against her, and the intensity of his gaze made her breath catch in her throat.

"We could... watch TV," she suggested, though her voice betrayed her true feelings, trembling with anticipation.

He smirked, a playful glint in his eyes. "There's nothing on

TV I want to watch."

"We could… um… play chess?" Valerie said, trying not to laugh.

Antonio chuckled softly, his breath warm against her skin. "Chess, huh? I didn't know you were a strategist," he teased, his fingers tracing gentle patterns on her waist.

Valerie giggled, trying to keep the mood light. "I could surprise you with my moves."

"Oh, I'm sure you could," he replied, his voice dropping to a husky whisper. "But I have a better idea."

Before Valerie could respond, Antonio scooped her up into his arms, carrying her toward the bedroom with effortless grace. "Antonio!" she exclaimed, laughing as he carried her. "What are you doing?"

"Taking us somewhere more comfortable," he said with a mischievous grin.

Antonio gently laid Valerie down on the soft sheets. His eyes, usually so hard and intense, now held a warmth that made her heart flutter.

"This is not a very good position for a chess tournament," she teased, tracing a finger along his jawline.

Antonio's smile softened, his gaze lingering on her face with a

What Do You Want to Do?

tenderness that spoke volumes. "You drive me crazy, woman," he murmured, leaning in to capture her lips in a tender kiss.

Valerie forgot about everything else then. Antonio's hands roamed her body hungrily as if he wanted to feel every inch.

He kissed her with a passion that ignited a fire within her. The worries of the day melted away. "Antonio," she whispered against his lips. "You were supposed to tell me about your past once we got home. Are you trying to distract me?"

Antonio paused, his breath hitching slightly as he pulled back just enough to look into Valerie's eyes. "My stories come with a price."

Valerie pouted. "No fair."

Antonio chuckled softly, his eyes twinkling with amusement. "Life isn't always fair, mia cara," he said, tracing a finger along her jawline.

Valerie pouted again, her lower lip jutting out in a playful gesture. "No fair at all," she repeated, trying to maintain a serious expression but failing as a smile tugged at the corners of her mouth.

Antonio's eyes darkened with desire as he leaned closer, his voice a low, hungry growl. "I want to taste you," he said, his breath warm against her ear.

A shiver ran down Valerie's spine, and her heart raced with

anticipation. "Antonio..." she whispered, her voice trembling with a mix of excitement and nervousness.

"I can't make love to you for another two weeks and four days, but that doesn't mean I can't have my fill other ways," he said, grinning devilishly.

Valerie's breath caught in her throat as Antonio's words sent a thrill through her. The intensity in his eyes left no room for doubt about what he wanted.

"You have been counting?" Valerie whispered, her voice a blend of anticipation and shyness.

Antonio's grin widened, his eyes twinkling with mischief. "Every single day," he replied, his voice low and husky. "I've been counting down to the moment I can have you completely."

Valerie's heart skipped a beat at Antonio's words, a mix of excitement and nervousness swirling within her. "Antonio..."

He leaned in, his lips brushing against her ear. "But for now," he whispered, "I'll just have to savor every other part of you."

With that, he began a slow, deliberate exploration, his hands and lips leaving a trail of fire across her skin. His touch was both gentle and possessive, making her feel cherished and desired.

Antonio pulled off Valerie's dress, exposing her completely.

What Do You Want to Do?

"Antonio," she moaned softly, her hands clutching at his shoulders as she surrendered to the sensations he was creating.

He kissed his way down her body, his lips worshiping every inch of her skin. The anticipation built with every moment, every kiss and caress heightening her senses.

When he finally reached his destination, he paused, looking up at her with a mixture of tenderness and hunger. "You're so lovely, Valerie," he said softly, his breath warm against her skin.

Before she could respond, he dipped down and pressed his mouth on her sex.

"Ohh!" Valerie moaned as she felt his tongue against her wet pussy. Valerie closed her eyes, feeling a rush of heat and desire course through her body. Antonio's mouth began to move, his lips parting her folds, exploring every inch with agonizing slowness.

Valerie let out another low moan, arching her back as he continued his exploration. Every touch was exquisite, every kiss sending waves of pleasure coursing through her. She could feel his tongue tracing patterns on her folds, her little sensitive nub, sending jolts of pleasure in her belly and all the way down to her toes.

Antonio's hands moved to her thighs, gripping them firmly, spreading her legs wider, giving him better access. His tongue dipped inside her, lapping up her juices as if savoring a decadent dessert. Valerie cried out, her body writhing under his expert touch.

Antonio continued his assault, his mouth moving up and down, his tongue sliding in and out in a rhythm that was driving her wild. Valerie could feel her climax building, the tension knotting up inside her, threatening to explode.

Valerie reached down, gripping his hair, pulling him closer to her, needing him to feel the full force of her pleasure. "Antonio," she panted, her voice hoarse with desire. "Antonio, please."

He responded by increasing his efforts, his tongue moving faster, his lips pressing harder against her. She could feel his teeth grazing her skin, sending sparks of sensation through her. Valerie's climax was upon her, building up to a crescendo that threatened to split her in two.

"Antonio!" Valerie cried out, her voice echoing through the room. "I'm going to come!"

And then it happened, her body convulsing, her orgasm washing over her in waves of ecstasy. Antonio kept going, his mouth never leaving her, his tongue never stopping, milking every last drop of pleasure from her.

When it was over, Valerie lay there, panting, her body still trembling from the intensity of the experience. Antonio looked up at her, a satisfied smile on his face.

What Do You Want to Do?

"Well," he started in a husky voice. "Now we can talk."

Forty-Eight

Rip Them Apart

"When I had just turned sixteen, my father sent me to one of his clubs to collect the money the manager owed him," Antonio began. "I hated going to those clubs. The scent of alcohol and perfume made my eyes water and it was suffocating."

Valerie listened to him with wide eyes and not interrupting. She realized how hard it was for him to tell her the story just by looking into his eyes.

"My eyes scanned the room, searching for the man I was looking for," he said. "I found him then, the manager, laughing at the bar with a glass in hand, carefree. He hadn't seen me yet. I approached him, ready to remind him of his debts."

Rip Them Apart

Antonio paused and wrinkled his forehead as if to recall the event scene by scene.

"The man asked me how old I was and who I was so I told him who my father was," Antonio continued. "I called one of my father's henchmen as a backup. This wasn't the first time I wasn't taken seriously because of my age, and it won't be the last. But that didn't mean my father would stop throwing me into these situations." Antonio sighed.

"But you were so young," Valerie whispered.

Antonio laughed bitterly. "As I said, my father didn't care about my age. Jenkins understood what I needed and moved forward to grab the manager's collar."

"Suddenly, armed men stormed in and attacked us. Get down!" someone screamed. I heard Glass shattering. And then, another shot, closer to me."

"Oh!" Valerie gasped.

"I saw people scrambling to get out of there, a mess of screams and fear. Tables were overturned, and drinks were forgotten as everyone sought the same thing—escape. A woman tripped, her cries smothered by the stampede of those desperate to survive. It was quite the scene." Antonio chuckled as if he was talking about a funny movie.

"Where you scared?" Valerie asked.

"No. I thought it was exciting! A man barked at me and shoved past me. I could tell he was afraid. Jenkins told me to calm down and he was trying to protect me. But…"

"But what?" Valerie asked eagerly.

"People were shooting at me, so I ducked. But the club was a trap now. I was not going to get out of there alive, it seemed," Antonio said.

"As the sound of shattering glass rang in my ears, I quickly ducked behind the bar, feeling the sharp shards crunch beneath my feet. The acrid smell of burning alcohol mixed with the pungent scent of fear as bullets tore through bottles, sending liquid and fragments flying in all directions. With adrenaline pumping through my veins, I didn't have time to process the chaos around me before vaulting over the counter and making a mad dash for the back door."

"That's horrible," Valerie whispered again as if she was scared of talking out loud.

"I barked at some cowering busboy and started to run toward the front door but some hands reached for me, grasping, clawing. My breath came in ragged gasps as I pushed on, nearly at the door, the sweet promise of escape just beyond—" he paused.

Valerie urged him with her eyes to go on.

"A heavy weight slammed into me from behind, crushing me

to the ground. The air whooshed from my lungs. I struggled and fought against the iron grip that pinned me down."

"Gotcha, a rough voice growled above me. It wasn't just one; it was many. They were on me, overpowering me with sheer force."

"I fought to get out of their grasp, but it was useless. My fists flew, connecting with flesh, but they were relentless. More hands dragged me back, away from freedom, back into the bowels of the club."

"They kidnapped you," Valerie breathed.

Antonio nodded. "I didn't know these men. They hauled me up, dragging me with force. Someone hit me on the head to make me unconscious." He paused and Valerie could tell it was hard for him to tell the story.

"You can stop and tell me the story another time if you want," Valerie said gently.

"No, I want to tell you this. When I slowly regained consciousness, I realized I was in some dark room. The earthy smell of damp soil and musty air filled my nostrils. And then, I heard a voice. He asked me if I was ready to talk."

Valerie's heart skipped a beat as she listened to the story. She couldn't imagine how terrified Antonio must've been at that age.

"The man told me I was important so I asked him what he wanted," he said.

"What did he want from you?" Valerie asked.

"I want you to suffer. That's what he told me," Antonio replied.

Valerie shivered.

"The first blow was very painful. Air whooshed out, and I gasped, struggling to draw breath as another blow followed. I'd never felt such pain before," Antonio said.

"The man's face twisted into a cruel grin as he spoke. I could tell he was enjoying this. The man taunted me and my father. But I just clenched my jaw, refusing to give them the satisfaction. I wouldn't break—not for them, not for anyone," Antonio laughed.

His laugh didn't sound warm like it usually was, Valerie thought to herself.

"Their blows kept coming, each one more powerful than the last until the world became a dizzying blur of pain. Through gritted teeth, I managed to speak. Enough, I said. I told them my father would come after them."

"What did the man do then?" Valerie asked.

"The man's mocking smile widened and he told me he was

counting on my father to come to my rescue," Antonio replied.

"When I lay there, battered and bruised, I knew I had to escape. My father would never forgive me if I allowed these men to defeat me. I had to find a way out of this darkness."

Valerie couldn't fathom the thought. How could Antonio think about his father's disapproval when he was being beaten to death?

"The torture continued for days. All I could think about was revenge and how to escape it," Antonio said.

Valerie's emerald green eyes widened in shock as she stared at him. Her lips parted and a soft gasp escaped them. "How did you escape?" she whispered, barely audible.

"I didn't," Antonio admitted. "They let me go after a week. I was disoriented and had no idea how to find my way back home, but somehow I managed it."

"And then what happened?" Valerie asked, her eyes filled with concern.

Antonio couldn't hide the bitterness in his voice as he answered, "When I got home, I found an even bigger surprise waiting for me."

A look of realization crossed Valerie's face. "Your mother..." she started, unable to finish her sentence.

"Committed suicide," Antonio finished for her, the words heavy on his tongue. "Didn't even get to say goodbye to her."

Valerie reached out and took his hand, her touch offering a sense of comfort amidst the storm of memories crashing through him. "I'm so sorry, Antonio," she said softly.

Antonio clenched his jaw, the anger simmering just beneath the surface as he continued, "It was nothing I couldn't handle."

"You were only sixteen," she reminded him.

Antonio pulled her to his chest and stroked her hair. "You've endured much worse than I did and survived. What I've been through is nothing compared to your bravery."

Valerie lifted her head from his chest, her eyes meeting his. "You don't have to compare, Antonio. We've both faced our own battles," she said, her voice determined. "But we made it through."

Antonio nodded. "No one will hurt you anymore, mia cara."

She absentmindedly toyed with his chest hair. "And if they do?"

"I will rip them apart with my bare hands," he said coolly.

Forty-Nine

Secret Talent

"Antonio," Valerie said. "Can I ask you something?"

Antonio raised his eyebrows, intrigued by her question. "Of course, what do you want to know?"

"Why me? Why do you like me? Is it simply because you think I'm pretty? Or is it because you want to be a father and adopting Landon was…easy?" she asked.

He looked into Valerie's beautiful green eyes, his heart swelling with emotions he didn't know he could feel. "I liked…no, I loved you because of who you are, not what you look like. And I wanted to be with you because I saw a depth to your soul that I couldn't resist. You're strong, resilient, and full of love. That's why I chose you. Not because it was easy, but because it was right."

The Mafia Boss's Pregnant Bride

Valerie's expression softened, and she smiled at him. "You don't actually love me. You're just saying that, right?"

"No." His tone was firm. What would it take to convince this woman how much he loved her? He had been smitten with her since day one, and she was questioning whether he was just saying that.

"I do love you, Valerie," he said, his voice filled with sincerity. "Every moment, every breath, every beat of my heart is for you."

Valerie blushed and rested her head on his chest.

"Did you ever find out who kidnapped you that day?" Valerie asked.

His chest constricted. That was the part he wanted to avoid telling her, but for some reason, he found it difficult to lie to Valerie. "Yes," he said hoarsely.

"Who was it?" she breathed.

"My father," he confessed, his voice heavy with the weight of betrayal. "He orchestrated the whole thing, wanting to toughen me up, make me more like him. He thought it was a lesson, but all it did was drive a wedge between us that can never be mended."

Valerie's eyes widened in shock and disbelief. "Your own father?" she repeated, her voice barely a whisper.

Secret Talent

Antonio nodded grimly, the memories flooding back with a vengeance. "He wanted me to become a part of his underworld empire, follow in his footsteps. And I did that. I gained power, strength, skills, everything he wanted me to gain, and lost everything at the same time."

Tears glistened in Valerie's eyes as she reached out to touch his face gently. "I'm so sorry, Antonio. That's...that's unforgivable."

A bitter smile tugged at his lips. "That's the thing, Valerie. I don't forgive him. And I never will for killing my mother."

Valerie's eyes met his, and they shared a moment of understanding. He could see the pain in her gaze, the scars left by her the one she loved, and he knew that what they had in common was deeper than just their difficult pasts.

"I guess we both got shitty people to deal with, eh?" he said in a teasing tone, trying to lighten up the mood.

"Probably the only thing we have in common," she retorted with a small smile.

Antonio chuckled, but then his expression turned serious again. "I have something for you."

Valerie got up and leaned against the headboard. "I don't need anything else."

He simply smiled and got up. He walked over to his closet

and came out holding his present for her.

He handed the box to Valerie, who looked at him with curiosity dancing in her eyes. She untied the ribbon and carefully opened the box.

Inside was a hand-knitted cashmere sweater, its soft red fabric complementing Valerie's eyes perfectly. She gasped softly, her fingers brushing over the knit with wonder.

"It's beautiful," she whispered, her voice filled with awe.

Antonio couldn't help but feel a surge of pride at her reaction. It wasn't just a gift. "I've been meaning to give that to you. It's going to be winter soon, so I thought it would be useful."

Valerie held the sweater up to her chest, and a smile bloomed on her face, lighting up the room.

"Thank you, Antonio," she said softly. "Did Nonna make this?"

Antonio blinked. "Nonna?"

"Yes, I saw her knitting before. Did she make this?" she asked.

"Ah…yes. Anyway, let's get some sleep now," he said.

Nodding in agreement, she folded the sweater lovingly and set it aside before turning back to him.

Secret Talent

Antonio put his arms around Valerie, pulling her close to him. They lay in bed together in silence, and eventually, they both drifted into sleep.

The next day, Antonio woke up before Valerie and went to see Nonna in her room. He squinted his eyes as he saw her sitting up in bed, reading a book, looking fresher than ever.

Strange...he thought she was dying...

Nonna looked up from her book, a sly twinkle in her eyes. "Oh, Antonio, you know how it is. Old age plays tricks on the mind and body. One day I'm on death's door, the next I'm running marathons." She chuckled softly, but there was a mischievous glint in her gaze.

Antonio raised an eyebrow, sensing that Nonna was up to something. "Running marathons, you say? I must have missed that on the news."

She patted the empty spot on the bed beside her, gesturing for him to sit. With a shrug, he obliged, curious about what game she was playing this time.

"You faked it, didn't you?" he said coyly.

"Faked what?" she asked.

"Don't look so shocked. You know what I'm talking about. You acted like you were dying so Valerie would agree to marry me." He smirked.

The Mafia Boss's Pregnant Bride

She feigned innocence. "Oh, dear. I'd never do that."

"Sure, you won't. But hey, you won't catch me complaining," he said.

She stroked his hair. "You really love her, don't you, nipote?"

"Si. I do. And I won't let her go, no matter what," he said determinedly.

"Bene. I like her. She is a good woman," she said.

"Anyway, I didn't just come here to accuse you of lying. I wanted to ask you for a favor," he said in a low and conspiratorial tone.

"What is it?" she asked, narrowing her eyes in suspicion.

"If Valerie thanks you for knitting her a sweater, could you just…err…play along?" he asked, scratching his neck uncomfortably.

Nonna's eyes widened with curiosity, and then she burst into laughter. "Hiding your secret talent, Antonio?"

"Nonna, please…"

Nonna's laughter subsided into a warm, knowing smile. "Oh, Antonio. Alright, I'll play along. But remember, you owe me one."

Secret Talent

"Deal," he said, leaning in to kiss her cheek. "Grazie, Nonna. You always know how to help me out."

Nonna patted his hand affectionately. "Anything for my favorite grandson."

He chuckled. "I'm your only grandson."

"All the more reason to take care of you," she replied with a wink.

They shared a moment of quiet understanding before Antonio stood up to leave. "I need to take care of some business. Remember what we discussed."

"Yes, yes. I will keep your secret," she said. "As long as you don't tell Valerie I am not actually dying."

He sighed and left the room.

Fifty

What to Wear

The first light of morning trickled through the curtains, and Valerie's eyes fluttered open. For a moment, she lay there, disoriented.

"Damn," she whispered, her body tensing from the residual sadness she felt from hearing Antonio's story.

She could still see the pain in his eyes. They were not much different, she and Antonio. Both had suffered at the hands of someone who was supposed to love and protect them.

Antonio must have already left, so she pushed herself out of bed and began her new routine.

First, she went to Landon's room, where the baby lay, cooing softly in his crib. As Valerie picked him up and cradled him

What to Wear

in her arms, she felt a surge of love for this tiny being. She sat down in the rocking chair, allowing Landon to latch onto her breast as he drank hungrily.

Valerie's thoughts kept drifting to Antonio, his caring nature shining through even in the darkest moments of her life.

"Landon, your adopted father is an incredible man," she whispered softly, kissing his forehead as she finished feeding.

With Landon settled back in his crib, Valerie walked to the kitchen to eat some breakfast.

She couldn't wait for him to come home, so she could hold him close and let him know just how much he meant to her—and their family.

As the day went on, every action she took and every thought she had was filled with anticipation of their upcoming wedding and the future they would share together. Her heart raced at the idea of standing beside Antonio, united as husband and wife, ready to face whatever challenges life had in store for them.

A sudden realization hit her. She had fallen in love with Antonio.

Valerie reached for her phone, her fingers trembling slightly as she dialed Ellie's number. The excitement of planning their wedding was mixed with a touch of nervousness. As the call connected, she took a deep breath.

The Mafia Boss's Pregnant Bride

"Hey, Ellie, it's Valerie," she said when Ellie picked up.

"Valerie! How are you? What's going on?" Ellie's voice was filled with curiosity and concern.

"I... I need your help. I want to go dress shopping for my wedding," she confessed, her voice shaking with anticipation.

"Of course I'll help you find a dress! Do you want to go later today?" Ellie asked.

"Yes," Valerie said, feeling slightly overwhelmed but still thrilled at the prospect of finding the perfect dress for her big day.

"Absolutely, let's do it. I can't wait to see you walking down the aisle in a stunning wedding gown," Ellie replied, her enthusiasm practically radiating through the phone.

"Thank you, Ellie. I'm so glad you're going to be there with me." Valerie's voice wavered with emotion as she thought about how much Ellie's support meant to her throughout this entire journey.

"Of course, Valerie. I wouldn't miss it for the world. Now, let's get you that dress!" Ellie declared, her excitement contagious.

They made plans to meet up at a bridal boutique in the afternoon, and Valerie hung up the phone with a sense of relief that she wasn't alone in this.

What to Wear

The morning passed in a blur of preparations and taking care of Landon.

As the afternoon approached, Valerie got ready, slipping on the red sweater Antonio had gifted her the night before. It fit her perfectly. She had never really liked shopping, but this time, things were different. She was going to be a bride.

His Bride.

When Ellie and Valerie arrived at the shop, Ellie's enthusiasm was infectious. They greeted each other with a hug, and Ellie immediately launched into discussing dress styles, colors, and themes. Walking into the bridal boutique together felt surreal yet exciting.

Ellie led Valerie through the rows of gowns, each more beautiful than the last. The soft rustle of fabric and the faint scent of lavender filled the air. Valerie couldn't help but feel a rush of nerves mixed with excitement bubbling up inside her.

"Valerie, this one," Ellie exclaimed, holding up a gown with delicate lace that sparkled in the light. Valerie ran her fingers over the intricate details, marveling at how it caught the light and seemed to shimmer like magic.

As Valerie stepped into the gown and looked at herself in the mirror, she was stunned. The dress hugged her figure in all the right places, the ivory color making her red hair and green eyes pop. She felt like a princess from a fairy tale.

Ellie's eyes widened with delight, her smile reflecting Valerie's own joy. "Oh, Valerie, this is the one. You look absolutely stunning."

Valerie twirled in front of the mirror, watching how the skirt billowed out around her like a cloud. It was as if this gown was made just for her, as if it was meant to be worn on her special day.

Tears pricked at Valerie's eyes as she realized that this dress was more than just fabric and lace—it was a symbol of love, hope, and a new beginning.

"River and I will be buying this for you, of course," Ellie said.

Valerie looked at her with surprise. "Wait… what?"

"Don't protest, Valerie. You are his only sister, and he wants to take care of everything, so let him," Ellie said firmly.

Ellie's generosity overwhelmed Valerie, and tears welled up in her eyes. "Ellie, I don't know what to say…"

"You don't have to say anything," Ellie said, her voice warm and reassuring. "River insisted. He wants this day to be perfect for you, just like you deserve."

Valerie nodded, feeling incredibly grateful for Ellie and her brother's kindness. "Thank you, Ellie. Please tell River how much this means to me."

What to Wear

"I will," Ellie replied with a smile. "Now, let's get you all set up for your fitting. We have to make sure everything is perfect for the big day."

As they left the boutique, Ellie linked her arm with Valerie's. "I'm so happy for you, Valerie. Antonio is a lucky man."

"Thank you, Ellie," Valerie said, fighting back tears.

~-~

Later that night, Valerie sat on the bed, waiting for Antonio. She wondered if he thought about their wedding day as she did. The image of herself in that beautiful gown lingered in her mind, reminding her of the love and hope that filled her heart.

She glanced at the clock, realizing Antonio was late.

A knock on the door interrupted her thoughts, and her heart skipped a beat. She looked at the door and found Antonio standing there, a tired but warm smile on his face.

Without a word, Valerie stepped into his embrace, feeling his arms wrap around her in a familiar and comforting hold.

"Hey," he murmured into her hair, his voice soft and filled with tenderness.

"Hey," she whispered back, holding onto him tightly as if afraid he might disappear.

"Miss me, amore?" Antonio asked, pulling back slightly to look into her eyes.

"Yes," Valerie replied without hesitation. "I found the most amazing wedding dress today, Antonio. I can't wait..." She stopped as she realized she was starting to sound like a giddy schoolgirl. She felt so silly.

Antonio narrowed his eyes. "Finish your sentence. You can't wait to what?"

"I...I can't wait to wear it," she breathed.

"And I can't wait to see you in it," he said, brushing a gentle hand over her cheek. His touch sent a wave of warmth through her, easing any lingering nerves.

"Oh!" Valerie exclaimed. "What will you wear? Should we get you a suit?"

Antonio chuckled softly. "I will wear whatever you want me to, mia cara. I will show up naked if you asked me to."

"Maybe not naked," Valerie teased, pressing a playful kiss to his cheek. "You might scare off the priest."

He grinned, his eyes twinkling with amusement. "Can't have that."

"I love you, Antonio," she whispered, feeling the words slip out of her easily.

What to Wear

His dark eyes widened in surprise, and for a moment, he didn't say anything.

"This is the part where you say, 'I love you too, Valerie,'" she teased.

Antonio's expression softened, and he cupped her face in his hands. "I love you too, Valerie," he said, his voice filled with sincerity and a depth of emotion that took her breath away.

Those words echoed in her heart, warming every corner with their truth. Valerie felt like everything was exactly as it should be.

Fifty-One

Wedding Night

Three weeks later...

Valerie stood before the full-length mirror, her hands trembling as she adjusted the delicate lace of her wedding gown. Nervousness and excitement coursed through her veins like wildfire.

This was the day she had been dreaming of, and now that it was here, she couldn't help but feel a pang of panic.

"Nervous?" Ellie asked.

Valerie nodded.

"Don't be. You look amazing. Antonio might pass out when he sees you," Ellie said seriously.

Wedding Night

Valerie giggled.

The door creaked open, and River stepped into the room. His presence instantly calmed her nerves. He offered a reassuring smile, his eyes filled with understanding. "Wow, Valerie. You look stunning."

"Thank you," she whispered, trying to steady her shaking hands.

"Are you ready?" River asked, extending his arm for her to take.

Valerie took a deep breath, gripping River's arm tightly as if it were a lifeline. "As ready as I'll ever be."

"Good," he said, his voice firm yet gentle. "Antonio better know how lucky he is," he muttered, giving her arm a gentle squeeze. "Now, let's get you married."

With one last glance in the mirror, Valerie allowed River to lead her out of the room and toward her future with Antonio.

As they walked, she focused on the sound of their footsteps echoing through the quiet halls, reminding herself that today was a new beginning—a chance to leave behind past betrayals and embrace the life that lay ahead.

"Ready?" River whispered as they reached the entrance to the garden where the ceremony would take place.

"Ready," Valerie confirmed, her grip on his arm tightening as determination settled in her chest.

The garden was beautiful, the scent of blooming roses filling the air as Valerie stepped into it. White chairs were neatly arranged, facing an elegant arch adorned with fresh flowers, where Antonio stood, looking devastatingly handsome in his tailored suit.

As he heard their approach, Antonio turned, his eyes locking onto Valerie's with a mix of awe and adoration. River gently guided Valerie toward him, and with each step closer, her heart swelled with a profound sense of happiness and anticipation.

Antonio's expression softened into a tender smile as they finally stood face to face. His hand reached out, trembling slightly, to cup her cheek. "You're... absolutely breathtaking," he murmured, his voice thick with emotion.

"Thank you," Valerie managed to whisper, feeling a rush of warmth at his touch.

The ceremony began. There weren't many people present—just Ellie, River, their kids, Nonna, and Mary. Mary was holding Landon in her arms, a big smile playing on her lips. A few of Antonio's men stood in the background, keeping watch.

Valerie couldn't stop the tears from falling when the officiant pronounced them husband and wife, and Antonio gently slid

Wedding Night

a ring onto her finger.

"Don't cry, mi amore," Antonio leaned down and whispered in her ear.

"I can't help it," Valerie whispered back, trying to contain her overflowing emotions.

Antonio's gaze softened even more, his eyes full of love and tenderness. "I'll spend a lifetime making you happy, I promise," he vowed, his voice unwavering.

Valerie's tears flowed even harder at his words. She couldn't believe this was real—that she was standing here, married to Antonio, the man who had captured her heart against all odds.

Antonio pulled her towards him and kissed her, making her tears stop in an instant. She heard Ellie cheering in the background and smiled against Antonio's lips.

A small tug at her skirt made her look down. It was Lucas, staring up with wide eyes, his expression a mix of wonder and innocence. As Antonio and Valerie broke apart from their kiss, she crouched down to meet his gaze.

"Hey, buddy," Valerie said softly, brushing a lock of hair out of his eyes. "Did you like the wedding?"

Lucas nodded vigorously, his face breaking into a gap-toothed grin. "It was like in the movies!" he exclaimed, bouncing on his heels with excitement.

Valerie couldn't help but giggle at his enthusiasm.

"Well, it's even better in real life," Antonio said, giving him a playful wink.

Antonio looked at her and smiled. Valerie blushed and looked down. She couldn't believe this was happening.

He held out his hand. "May I have this dance, Signora Costello?"

"Of course," Valerie replied, placing her hand in his. As he led her to the center of the garden, the music began—a soft, romantic melody that enveloped them like a warm embrace.

They moved together, swaying gently in each other's arms. Antonio's eyes never left Valerie's, and she felt like the luckiest woman in the world.

"I can't believe this is real," Valerie whispered, resting her head against his chest.

"It's real, Valerie," Antonio murmured, his voice a soothing balm to her heart. "And it's just the beginning."

Valerie rested her head on his broad chest, closing her eyes.

Antonio leaned in, his breath warm against Valerie's ear. "I have something more important to discuss with you."

Wedding Night

Valerie's heart raced with anticipation as she gazed up at him, curiosity bright in her eyes. "And what might that be?" she asked.

A sly grin formed on Antonio's lips as he whispered, "I want you to prepare yourself for all the things I will do to you tonight." His voice dripped with seduction, and Valerie felt her knees go weak.

"What... what will you do to me?" she replied, her voice a hoarse whisper.

Her cheeks flushed with heat at his words. Antonio's grin widened, his eyes darkening with desire as he leaned in even closer.

"You'll have to wait and find out, Valerie," he murmured huskily, sending shivers down her spine. His fingers traced a feather-light path from her cheek to her neck, igniting a trail of fire in their wake.

Valerie gulped, feeling a delicious mix of nervousness and anticipation pooling in her stomach. The world around them seemed to fade away, leaving only Antonio and her in their own bubble of desire.

His lips brushed against hers in a tantalizing promise, his breath warm on her skin. "Tonight is way past our deadline; I hope you haven't forgotten."

"The deadline?" she asked, confused.

Antonio's eyes gleamed with hunger as he held her close. "If I did my math correctly, it has been six weeks already. And that means, I get to have you tonight." He smirked.

Valerie pouted. "You act like I'm some kind of food."

Antonio chuckled. "It's just that…I've waited so long for this moment, Valerie," he confessed, his voice low and filled with longing.

A rush of desire mingled with nervousness surged through Valerie at the thought of finally being with him in that way.

"I'm going to make you mine tonight," Antonio murmured huskily, his voice sending shivers down her spine. "In ways you've never experienced before."

"Oh," Valerie breathed, her heart racing at the intensity of his gaze. Antonio's expression was one of unwavering desire, his eyes drilling into hers with a hunger that sent waves of heat through her. His hand reached out to caress her cheek, the touch sending electric currents down her spine.

He looked like he wanted to devour her right there and then, and Valerie could hardly contain the excitement and anticipation building inside her.

Fifty-Two

He Will Pay

A loud crash shattered the perfect moment, drawing everyone's attention to the garden's entrance. Antonio's men tensed, their hands moving instinctively toward their concealed weapons. Antonio's grip on Valerie tightened protectively.

"What was that?" Valerie whispered, her heart pounding with fear.

Antonio's jaw clenched. "Stay close to me," he ordered, his voice low and urgent.

Were they being attacked?

River jumped up from his seat, his eyes blazing. "It seems we have uninvited guests," he said, his voice laced with tension.

Before anyone could react, a group of masked men burst into the garden, their faces hidden behind black balaclavas. They were armed, their presence menacing as they advanced toward the gathering.

"Everyone, get down!" Antonio barked, his voice commanding and authoritative.

Valerie's heart raced with terror. She clung to his arm, her fingers digging into his suit jacket.

"I won't let anything happen to you," Antonio quickly reassured her.

Gunfire erupted, the sharp cracks splitting the air as the intruders began shooting. Antonio's men swiftly responded, engaging the attackers with precision and determination. The serene garden transformed into a chaotic battleground.

Valerie's breath came in short, panicked gasps as she feared for her life.

And her family.

"Landon! Where is Mary with Landon?" she gasped. Mary was nowhere to be seen. Maybe she ran to safety, but what if that wasn't the case? What if those men got them?

Antonio's eyes darted around, scanning the chaotic scene.

River, who had been crouching nearby, caught Antonio's eye.

"I'll find them. You stay with her," he said, his tone leaving no room for argument.

Antonio nodded, his grip on Valerie tightening. "Be careful," he urged River.

River gave a determined nod before slipping into the fray, his movements swift and purposeful. Antonio focused on keeping Valerie safe, pulling her behind a row of chairs to shield her from the gunfire.

Valerie's heart pounded. She clung to Antonio, her mind racing with worry for Mary and Landon. She couldn't lose her son, not now, not ever.

"Stay hidden. I am going to find the ringleader," Antonio growled.

Valerie's grip on his arm tightened. "No, don't! I have a bad feeling about this," she pleaded, her voice trembling.

Antonio leaned in, pressing a quick kiss to her forehead. "I have to kill whoever did this," he whispered before slipping away, his movements stealthy and purposeful.

Valerie crouched behind the chairs, her heart pounding in her chest as she watched Antonio disappear into the chaos. The sound of gunfire and shouting filled the air, making it hard to think. She held her breath, praying for everyone's safety.

Oh god, where were Ellie, Tiffany, and Lucas? If something happened to them...

River reappeared moments later, his face set in a grim expression. "I found Mary with Landon. They're safe inside the house," he said, crouching beside Valerie. "Antonio's men have secured the area. We need to get you to safety too. I can sneak you out of here and take you to my one of my safehouse."

Valerie nodded, her relief mingling with fear. "Thank you, River. But I can't leave without knowing Antonio is okay."

"He'll be fine," River assured her, his voice steady. "But we need to move now. I'll come back for him once you're safe."

Valerie hesitated but then nodded, trusting River's judgment. She followed him. "Where are Ellie and the kids?"

River's eyes scanned the area as he led Valerie through the chaos. "I saw Max taking Lucas and Tiffany to the car. I am sure they are safe now."

"But what about..."

River's eyes widened in alarm as the man emerged from the shadows, pointing a gun directly at Valerie. Time seemed to slow as the reality of the threat sank in.

"Don't move," the masked man growled, his voice cold and menacing. "Or she dies."

He Will Pay

Valerie's breath caught in her throat, fear gripping her heart. River's gaze flickered between Valerie and the gunman, his mind racing for a solution.

"Listen," River began, his voice calm and measured. "You don't know who you're trying to fuck with."

The man sneered, tightening his grip on the gun. "Oh no? Trust me, hombre. I know exactly who you are. And who Antonio Costello is."

~-~

River's heart pounded as he assessed the situation. The masked man was too close to Valerie, and any sudden move could end in tragedy. He needed to buy time.

"Then you know what will happen to you if you hurt her," River said.

The man chuckled darkly. "I'm not afraid of Antonio or you. This is bigger than your little empire."

River's eyes flickered to Valerie, whose face was pale with fear. He had to think fast. "What do you want?" he asked, trying to keep the man talking.

"Revenge," the man spat, his eyes glinting with anger. "Antonio destroyed my life. Now, I'm going to destroy his. I am going to kill the love of his life."

The Mafia Boss's Pregnant Bride

The man aimed the gun at Valerie and squeezed the trigger. River froze. Time seemed to slow down as the shot rang out. Valerie's eyes widened in horror.

But before the bullet could reach her, Ellie appeared out of nowhere, throwing herself in front of Valerie.

The bullet struck Ellie in the chest, and she crumpled to the ground, blood blooming across her dress.

The sight of Ellie crumpling to the ground, blood staining her dress, was too much for Valerie to bear. She screamed as she fell to her knees. "Ellie!"

No, River thought. This could not be happening.

He stood frozen in shock and disbelief, his world crumbling before his eyes.

Antonio appeared right then and lunged forward in a fury, disarming the man with a swift, brutal motion. It wasn't until he had the man pinned to the ground that River snapped back into reality. He rushed to Ellie's side, his hands trembling as he tried to stop the bleeding. "Ellie, stay with me," he pleaded, tears streaming down his face. "Someone call an ambulance!"

Valerie could only watch helplessly as her best friend and sister-in-law fought for her life. Tears streamed down her face as she held onto Ellie's hand, praying for a miracle. "Hang on, Ellie," she whispered, her heart shattering into a million pieces.

He Will Pay

River's voice broke as he spoke again, unable to fathom losing the woman he loved more than anything else in this world. "What have you done, Ellie?" he choked out. He couldn't let her die. She was his everything - his wife, the mother of his children. Losing her would be losing a part of himself forever.

River's trembling hands were stained with Ellie's blood, his heart aching as he desperately tried to stop the flow. "Stay with me, Ellie. You have to fight. Think about Lucas and Tiffany."

Ellie's eyes flickered weakly, struggling to focus on River's face. A small whimper escaped her lips and she managed to utter, "Take care of them." Her hand reached out feebly, clinging onto River's with what little strength she had left.

"Ellie, my love. Please, don't leave us," River pleaded, tears streaming down his face.

"It's too late...please, promise me you'll protect our children," Ellie's voice was barely audible, her breaths becoming shallower with each passing moment.

"No, no, it's not too late, honey. You will be fine. Then we can both keep Tiffany and Lucas safe," River insisted.

Ellie's lips quivered into a weak smile. She tried to squeeze River's hand, a final gesture of love and reassurance, but her strength was fading fast.

"P...promise me," Ellie repeated.

"I promise, okay! Tiffany and Lucas will be just fine. But Ellie, you can't just..."

But Ellie's strength was gone. Her hand fell limp in River's grasp, her body growing still. River's heart shattered as he felt her warmth slipping away, leaving him alone in his anguish.

"River," Valerie said softly, his voice filled with a deep sadness, "I'm so sorry."

River could only manage a broken nod, his eyes locked on Ellie's peaceful but lifeless form. "She loved you like you were her own little sister, you know," he said hoarsely. "She always had such a big heart, always caring for everyone around her. And now..." River stopped.

Gone. She was gone forever.

Valerie remained kneeling next to him. "Sh...she saved my life," she whispered.

"What will I tell Tiffany? And Lucas? What do I tell them?" River asked no one in particular.

The gunshots had stopped, and the garden was now eerily quiet. Antonio's men must've taken care of the assailants.

River looked at Antonio, who still had Ellie's killer pinned to the ground.

He Will Pay

"What do you want me to do with this asshole?" Antonio hissed.

"Give him to me," River said, his voice cold and hard. "I want to show him what happens when you cross River Foster."

Antonio's gaze hardened as he looked at River. The pain and anger in River's eyes were unmistakable, and he could see the depth of his loss. "Very well. He is all yours."

Fifty-Three

Take Care of Them

Antonio dragged the man to his feet, pushing him towards River, who stood up slowly, his body shaking either from rage or loss, it was hard to tell. As the man stumbled in front of him, River stared into his eyes, searching for any sign of remorse. There was none.

"Look at her!" River roared, pointing at Ellie's body. "Look at what you've done!"

The man's eyes darted toward Ellie, then quickly away, but not before a flash of satisfaction flickered across his face.

That was all River needed. He lunged forward, grabbing the man by the collar and connecting his fist with the man's jaw.

The man groaned. Blood trickled down his nose, but the

Take Care of Them

smirk on his face didn't change.

River pulled back his fist and struck the man again. And then again.

"River! Stop!" Antonio intervened, pulling him back. "Not here."

He paused, breathing heavily, his fist still raised. Slowly, the fire in his eyes dimmed as he looked over at Ellie again.

"You're right," River said hoarsely, turning away from his captive and toward Valerie and Antonio. "Get one of my men to take him to the dungeon. I need to…I need to take care of my wife." His voice broke.

Valerie could only stand there and watch. This was the happiest day of her life, and now, there was nothing but sadness.

She moved closer to River, offering him a sympathetic touch on the shoulder.

"We should get back inside," she suggested softly. "We have to tell Tiffany and Lucas what happened."

River nodded mutely and picked up Ellie in his arms. River felt numb as he walked toward the house. Tiffany and Lucas were waiting in there, their innocent faces unaware of the tragedy that had just occurred. River's heart ached at the sight of them, knowing he would have to break their hearts.

"Daddy, what's going on?" Tiffany asked, her eyes wide with worry. "What's wrong with Mom?"

River's throat tightened at Tiffany's innocent question. He gently laid Ellie's body on the couch, brushing a strand of hair from her face. His mind raced for the right words, but there were none that could soften the blow.

"Come here, kids," he said softly, his voice cracking. He knelt down to their level, pulling them close. "Mommy... Mommy was hurt very badly."

Lucas's eyes filled with confusion. "Is she going to be okay?"

River shook his head, tears streaming down his cheeks. "No, Lucas. Mommy... she's not coming back. She was very brave and tried to protect us, but... she's gone."

Tiffany's face crumpled as she burst into tears, clutching River's arm. "No! Mommy can't be gone! She can't!"

River hugged his children tightly. "I know, sweethearts. I know. But we have to be strong for Mommy. She loved us so much, and she would want us to take care of each other."

Valerie knelt beside them, her own heart breaking for the family. She wrapped her arms around the grieving trio, offering what comfort she could. "We're going to get through this together," she whispered. "Ellie wouldn't want us to give up."

Take Care of Them

Antonio stood silently nearby, his expression a mix of grief and anger. He cleared his throat, trying to maintain his composure. "River, I've taken care of the immediate threat. My men are securing the perimeter. We'll keep everyone safe."

River nodded, still holding his children close. "Thank you, Antonio. I appreciate it."

Mary took Tiffany and Lucas to another room for a while. River sat by Ellie's side, holding her lifeless hand and whispering words of love and promises to her. He knew he had to be strong for Tiffany and Lucas, but the pain of losing Ellie was almost too much to bear.

"We can't keep her here all night, Foster. Let me take her away and…" Antonio started, but River growled at him. "Don't you fucking touch her, Costello!"

Valerie placed her hand on his shoulder. "River, please. Let Antonio take care of her."

"She is my wife. I can't…I can't just let him take her, Val," River said raspily.

Valerie knelt beside him, her eyes filled with empathy. "I know, River. But Ellie deserves to be taken care of properly. And you are not in the right mind to do that."

River looked down at Ellie's peaceful face, his heart shattering all over again. He knew Valerie was right, but the thought of letting go was unbearable.

"Okay," he finally whispered, his voice barely audible. "But... be gentle with her."

Antonio nodded solemnly. "I promise, River. I'll take care of her with the utmost respect."

With a heavy heart, River kissed Ellie's forehead one last time before standing up. Antonio and a few of his men carefully lifted Ellie's body, carrying her out of the house. River watched them go, feeling as though a part of his soul was being ripped away.

Valerie stayed by his side, offering silent support. "We'll get through this, River," she said softly. "We'll get through this together."

River nodded, though the words felt hollow. He knew he had to be strong for his children, but in that moment, all he could feel was the immense void left by Ellie's absence.

"I won't kill that bastard," River said absentmindedly. "The death is too easy for him. By the time I am done with him, he will wish he was dead."

"I know," Valerie whispered.

"But first, I need to find out why he did it." River stood up straight. "He said he wanted to kill you because he wanted to punish Antonio."

Take Care of Them

Fear flickered in Valerie's eyes. "Y-you don't blame Antonio, do you? River, he couldn't have known," she said in a hoarse whisper.

River sighed, the weight of the situation pressing heavily on his shoulders. "No, I don't blame Antonio. This is the life we both chose. But I need to understand why this happened. I need to make sure it never happens again."

Valerie nodded, relief washing over her face.

"I need you to do me a favor, Val," River said grimly.

"Anything," Valerie said quickly.

"Could you let Tiffany and Lucas stay with you for a few days until I sort things out?" he asked.

Valerie's eyes softened with understanding. "Of course, River. I'll take care of them. You know I love these kids to death."

River's shoulders sagged with relief. "Thank you, Val. I don't know what I'd do without you."

Valerie gave him a reassuring smile. "We'll get through this together, River. Just focus on what you need to do. I'll handle the kids."

River nodded. "I will say goodbye to the kids before I go."

River took a deep breath, steeling himself. He walked back

into the room where Tiffany and Lucas were sitting, their eyes red from crying. He knelt down in front of them, taking their small hands in his.

"Daddy has to go for a little while," he said gently. "But Aunt Valerie will take care of you. I need you to be brave for me, okay?"

Tiffany nodded, her lower lip trembling. "Will you come back soon, Dad?"

River swallowed hard, forcing a smile. "As soon as I can, sweetheart. I promise. Take care of your brother, please."

Lucas clung to his father's neck. "Don't go, Daddy."

River's heart broke all over again. "I need to, buddy. I have to make sure we're all safe. Trust Aunt Valerie and listen to her, okay?"

Reluctantly, the children nodded. River kissed their foreheads one last time before standing up and turning to Valerie. "Thank you, Val," he said, his voice thick with emotion.

Valerie squeezed his hand. "Go do what you need to do, River. They'll be here when you get back."

"I'm coming for you, asshole," River murmured before leaving the house.

Fifty-Four

I Love You

Valerie was overcome by grief. Ellie was not just a sister-in-law to her. She was also her best friend. They had been friends since high school, she was River's first love and now…

She was gone.

Will River be okay? Valerie sobbed at her brother's loss. And the kids. Oh my god, they lost their mother!

She had tucked Tiffany and Lucas into their beds. They were all cried out for the night, and exhaustion slowly took over them. And now, she was standing outside of their closed door, contemplating.

"Mi amore." Antonio's voice brought her back.

She looked at him with her eyes full of tears. "What will happen to River and the kids? How will they cope?"

Antonio stroked her cheek. "It will get easier with time. And we will be there for them."

Valerie nodded. "I am sorry."

Antonio lifted his brow. "For what?"

"I can't help but feel responsible for Ellie's death. She died because...because she tried to save me," she choked out.

Antonio suddenly bent down and lifted Valerie into his arms, cradling her in a bridal-style embrace. Her heart pounded in her chest, threatening to burst out of her ribcage. His eyes locked onto hers, dark and intense, filled with sadness.

"It wasn't your fault," he said, his voice low and husky. "She was brave for taking the bullet on your behalf and I will forever be in her debt for saving the love of my life."

"I think I love you, Antonio," she whispered.

Antonio carried her up the staircase, each step bringing them closer to his room – and to their undeniable longing for one another. She could feel the heat radiating off his body and longed for him to touch her, to bring her even closer to him.

"Here we are," he said as they reached the landing. He carried her across the room, her heart racing with every step.

I Love You

He laid her down on the bed, his touch sending shivers down her spine. Her breath hitched as their gazes met once more, both of them yearning for the same thing.

"You need sleep," he said. "I will leave you alone to rest if you wish," he said.

This was all wrong. This wasn't how their wedding night was supposed to turn out.

"No, please don't leave me, Antonio," she said in a hoarse whisper.

"Tell me what you want, Valerie," Antonio demanded, his voice raw with passion.

"You," she replied without hesitation. "I want you, Antonio."

She felt the heat of Antonio's body as he leaned in, capturing her lips in a passionate kiss. Their mouths moved in sync, tongues dancing together in an intimate rhythm that left her breathless and wanting more.

"Valerie," he murmured against her lips, the sound of her name sending shivers down her spine.

"Please, Antonio," she whispered, unsure of what she was asking for but knowing that she needed it. He seemed to understand, his fingers finding the intricate buttons on her wedding dress, deftly undoing them one by one. The fabric slipped off her shoulders, pooling around her waist as the cool air kissed her exposed skin.

"Are you sure?" Antonio asked once more, his eyes searching Valerie's for any hint of hesitation. Despite the whirlwind of emotions swirling inside her, she knew that this was the path she wanted – no, needed – to take.

"Yes," she breathed.

Antonio slowly started to unlace her dress and Valerie couldn't help but feel vulnerable under Antonio's intense gaze. But there was something about the way he looked at her – like she was the most precious thing in the world – that set her fears at ease.

"Valerie, you're so beautiful," he said softly, his eyes never leaving hers as he continued to undress her.

"Antonio," she whispered, unable to hold back as his strong hands delicately explored her body. Her breath hitched in anticipation of every caress.

"Valerie," he murmured against her skin, his lips leaving a trail of hot kisses along her neck. The sensation was electrifying, and she couldn't help but arch her back, craving more of him. Their eyes locked for a moment, the passion between them nearly tangible.

"Tell me what you want," he prompted, his voice low and husky.

I Love You

"More," she gasped, feeling bolder with each second that passed. "I need more of you, Antonio."

She needed to feel like nothing bad had happened this day. She wanted to feel good.

"Your wish is my command," he replied, his fingers gliding over her curves, teasing and tantalizing her in ways she never thought possible. It felt as if they were losing themselves in the moment, all thoughts of betrayal, loyalty, and revenge fading away.

Valerie felt her fingers tangle in Antonio's hair, holding his head close as he moved lower, his lips igniting a trail of fire along her collarbone and down to her breasts. The pleasure coursed through her veins, her body responding to his every touch.

His mouth engulfed her nipple, and she let out a soft moan, her entire body trembling with desire. The contrast between his warm mouth and the cool air around them sent shivers coursing through her.

Antonio cupped her other breast, and she gasped as he pinched her nipple. "Do you like that?" he murmured, his eyes never leaving hers.

"Yes," she whispered.

Antonio's touch felt like a drug, and Valerie was addicted. Every time his fingers brushed against her skin, her body arched in response, craving more of him.

"Do you want me?" he asked, his voice low and seductive as he trailed kisses down her stomach.

"Yes," she breathed, eager for the pleasure that he could give her. Her mind was consumed with thoughts of him – his touch, his lips, his body pressed against hers.

Without hesitation, Antonio lowered himself between her legs and gently spread them apart. His hot breath ghosted over her center before he dipped his head lower and began to explore her with his tongue.

Pleasure exploded within her as he expertly flicked and circled her sensitive nub. It felt like every nerve in her body was on fire, building up to an intense climax.

As she reached the peak of ecstasy, Antonio's name fell from her lips in a breathless cry. He continued to pleasure her until she couldn't take it anymore, succumbing to the overwhelming waves of pleasure crashing over her.

As Valerie came down from her high, Antonio kissed his way back up her body until their lips met in a passionate kiss. She could taste herself on him as their tongues danced together.

"I want you," she whispered against his lips, unable to hold back any longer. "I need you."

With that permission granted, Antonio positioned himself at

her entrance and slowly pushed inside of her. The sensation was even more intense than before; pain mixed with pleasure as they became one.

He started off slow and gentle at first but soon picked up the pace as their bodies moved together in perfect harmony. Every thrust sent waves of pleasure through her until they were both clinging to each other desperately.

Valerie entwined her legs around him, pulling him closer as he plunged deeper inside her.

Their bodies moved in perfect rhythm, the ecstasy intensifying with each motion. Antonio's control was slipping, his breaths becoming heavy and erratic as his pace grew more intense.

She moaned his name, her nails digging into his back as she felt the familiar coil of pleasure building within her. "I'm going to come again," she gasped.

Antonio's lips captured hers, tongues dancing wildly as they reached their peak together with a final burst of passion.

He fell onto her, exhausted. Valerie ran her hands gently over his damp skin and took slow, deep breaths until she had calmed down. They held onto each other tightly, not wanting to let go.

She couldn't help but take in the sight of his naked body. The way his muscles rippled beneath his tan skin, the way his eyes looked at her with desire and protectiveness, it was all too much for her to bear.

Antonio's breathing was heavy, and she could feel the steady rhythm of his heart against her chest. She traced her fingers over the well-defined lines of his body, feeling the warmth of his skin beneath her touch. It was like touching fire, yet it didn't burn; instead, it enveloped her in a comforting embrace.

"Again," she breathed, unable to take her eyes off him or the feel of his skin against hers. "I want to do it again."

The sound of Antonio's low chuckle gave her goosebumps. "Give me five more minutes, and I'll be ready for round two," he murmured with a seductive grin. Valerie couldn't resist smiling at his playful charm describing everything that happened.

"I want to feel you inside me again," she confessed, feeling a blush creep up her neck. "Am I being shameless?" she whispered, tracing lines over the ridges of his muscles.

"Never," Antonio reassured her with a gentle kiss on her forehead. "You're my desire, my obsession. I'll make love to you as much as you want, whenever you want, for as long as you want," he promised, his voice low and intimate, sending shivers down her spine.

God… She had never wanted a man as much as she wanted Antonio.

I Love You

Valerie reached between his legs and traced her fingers over the hardness that lay beneath. He twitched a bit as she touched the tip of his penis, feeling its wetness.

He twitched a bit at Valerie's touch, and she couldn't resist teasing him further by running her fingers along the length of his penis, feeling its wetness.

Antonio let out a soft groan and leaned into her touch, his own hands roaming over her body.

"I want you to ride me, Valerie," he rasped.

Valerie straddled him and positioned herself above his length before slowly sinking down onto it.

The sensation of him filling her was both exhilarating and intimate. She closed her eyes and let out a soft moan, sinking deeper and deeper until they were one. Her body felt alive, every nerve ending screaming in pleasure.

As she moved up and down, Antonio's hands gripped her waist, guiding her, his hip thrusts meeting hers in perfect sync.

Her heart raced, matching the rhythm of their lovemaking, and she could feel the pulse of his heart beneath her hands. It was like they were connected on an unseen level.

As the climax approached, Antonio's eyes locked with hers, his gaze intense and full of lust. He whispered her name, and she froze, their eyes locked in a heated exchange.

His hands left her waist, and he began to thrust faster, harder. The pleasure built up inside her, an intense wave of euphoria crashing over her. She screamed his name, her body convulsing around him as she climaxed.

Antonio's hands gripped her hips tightly as he too reached his peak, his rapid breaths shaking her entire being. They collapsed together, their bodies sticky with sweat, hearts pounding in sync.

As they lay there, entwined, Valerie couldn't help but feel like she was exactly where she belonged.

"I love you," she whispered, her voice shaky with emotion.

"And I love you more," Antonio replied, his voice equally soft.

Fifty-Five

Forever

Valerie stepped out into the crisp air and looked around the area. There was nothing but woods all around them.

They decided to have their honeymoon by the lake, away from the city. Nothing fancy, nothing big, just simple peace and quiet. That's what Valerie needed.

Antonio closed the door behind them. Valerie looked around the room, her eyes drinking in the simplicity of the rustic decor, the quilt-covered armchairs, and the braided rugs.

"Feels like we can breathe here," Antonio murmured.

Valerie nodded, feeling the truth of his words settle around her heart. "Are you sure it's okay to leave the children behind?"

It had been two weeks since the incident at the wedding. During those two weeks, Both Antonio and River had their men watch them like hawks. During that time, Valerie felt like a prisoner but she didn't want to risk going outside either.

"No one had attacked the house for the past weeks and we still have them guarded. They will be fine for two days, trust me," Antonio said.

Antonio crouched in front of the stone fireplace and started to light it. He adjusted a log, coaxing the fire higher, and soon, the room started to feel warmer.

Meanwhile, Valerie drifted toward the couch, her feet silent on the worn wooden floor. She sat down on the couch and started to relax a little.

After a moment, Antonio took his place beside her on the couch, the cushions dipping under his weight.

"Are you alright, my love?" he asked in a gentle tone.

Valerie leaned ever so slightly towards Antonio, her shoulder brushing against his arm. "I've been better," she whispered.

The gentle touch of his presence softened her tense body. She turned her head, gaze lifting to meet Antonio's eyes. They were dark and sad.

Forever

"Antonio," she murmured. "I'm scared."

Antonio held her hand. "Don't be scared."

"What if I lose you too like River lost Elle? I just found you. I don't want to lose you already."

"Shh…you won't lose me, cara mia. I am not going anywhere," Antonio cooed.

"How can you be sure?" she whimpered. She didn't want to ruin their peaceful time together, but things were happening too suddenly, and Ellie's death changed everything.

"Valerie. I understand your fear but trust me. I am not very easy to kill," he said with conviction.

Valerie looked up at his face. His scarred yet beautiful face. "You promise?"

"I am very sure. Unless you want to kill me, then I'd be happy to die in your arms," he teased.

"Hmph!" she scoffed.

"I mean it," Antonio said, laughing.

Valerie couldn't help but smile at Antonio's attempt to lighten the mood. His laughter, though strained, was a comforting sound in the quiet cabin. She squeezed his hand, finding solace in the warmth of his touch.

"Just promise me you'll be careful," she said, her voice soft but firm. "For both our sakes. And Landon's."

Antonio nodded, his expression serious now. "I promise. I'm taking every precaution. I want to build a future with you, Valerie."

"Good. Because if you die, I'd be very angry," she declared.

"Ah, I wouldn't want that, my little firecracker," he bellowed.

Valerie smiled and pressed her lips on his, kissing him tentatively.

Antonio responded to Valerie's kiss with a gentle but passionate intensity, his arms wrapping around her as if trying to anchor both of them to this moment of calm.

When they finally pulled away, their breaths mingling in the chilly air, Antonio's gaze softened. "You're the best thing that's ever happened to me," he said softly, his fingers brushing a stray strand of hair from Valerie's face.

Valerie smiled, her heart lifting despite the lingering shadows of their recent traumas. "And you're the most unexpected joy I could have hoped for."

Antonio leaned his forehead against hers, his eyes searching hers for reassurance. "We'll make it through this. We'll find a way to be happy despite everything."

Forever

Valerie nodded. "Yes, we will."

"I'll move out of the country if we have to. We will go where we will be safe. You, me, and our children."

Valerie smirked. "Children?"

"Yes, children. Landon will be happier with more siblings, don't you agree?" Antonio asked coyly, his eyes twinkling.

Valerie raised an eyebrow, a playful smile tugging at her lips. "Is that your way of proposing a big family, Antonio?"

Antonio chuckled, his arms still wrapped around her. "Of course. I'd like more of you running around."

Valerie leaned back, her gaze thoughtful. "And you."

"So you agree with me, eh?" Antonio asked.

Valerie blushed. "Um…I wouldn't mind having…um…more children with you."

She didn't know why she felt so nervous all of a sudden.

Antonio toyed with a lock of her hair. "Well, that settles it then. We can start today."

Valerie's cheeks flushed deeper, her heart racing at Antonio's playful yet serious comment. "Start what today?"

Antonio laughed softly, his eyes dancing with mischief. "Start making baby, of course."

Valerie giggled. "Antonio!"

Antonio's laughter filled the cozy cabin, the sound a welcome distraction from the sadness she had been feeling the past weeks. He pulled Valerie closer, his eyes filled with affection. "We are alone together in the woods, no TV, no form of entertainment. What else do you suggest we do?"

Valerie couldn't help but laugh along, the weight of her worries momentarily lifted by Antonio's infectious energy. "Are you bored? Do you want me to entertain you?" she suggested playfully, not yet ready to surrender to Antonio's teasing proposal.

"I suppose I am," Antonio agreed. "How about you entertain me a little?"

"Hmm? What do you mean?" Valerie asked.

"I don't know. I do believe you mentioned before that you are a good dancer," Antonio said suggestively.

Valerie bit her lip, thinking. "I did. I was good when I used to dance at Julian's club."

Antonio frowned as if remembering something unpleasant. "I am sorry, love. I hope I didn't just offend you. It must've been degrading for you to dance like that."

Forever

Valerie nodded. "It was. Being exposed like that in front of all those men…it was humiliating. I didn't want to do it. I know some of the girls did it by choice, but Julian forced me to do it."

"I am sorry," Antonio repeated. "I won't bring it up again. I won't ask you to dance for me. It was stupid of me to joke about that."

Valerie reached out, her fingers gently brushing Antonio's arm. A playful glint appeared in her eyes. "It wasn't that stupid. Doing it for you is different."

Antonio grinned again. "Are you saying you will dance for me here?" he asked, his voice low and hopeful.

Valerie smiled, standing up. "Here it is different," she said softly. "Here, it's just you and me."

Valerie put some music on her phone and turned back to Antonio, her eyes shimmering with a mix of mischief and affection. "Let's forget everything else," she whispered, her voice barely audible over the music.

Taking a deep breath, Valerie let the rhythm take over. She started swaying slowly, each movement a whisper of silk against air as her body found the soul of the melody. Her arms lifted gracefully above her head as if conducting the flames in their dance within the fireplace. The light caught her features, highlighting her cheekbones and igniting sparks in her green eyes.

Antonio watched, captivated. His eyes trailed down her soft curves.

She drew closer to him, her movements becoming more deliberate. Valerie's hands rested on his shoulders as she guided him to sit back down onto their plush armchair. Now with Antonio seated, Valerie continued dancing before him.

"Do you like this?" she whispered.

Antonio nodded mutely, afraid that he would break the spell by speaking.

She leaned in close enough for him to feel the warmth of her breath against his skin.

Circling around him with the grace of falling leaves, Valerie's fingers occasionally brushed against Antonio's jawline, sending shivers down his spine.

Antonio growled softly as she pressed against his growing erection.

Valerie laughed softly, her breath tickling his ear. "I can see that you do like this," she murmured, her voice laced with playful seduction. She pulled back slightly, giving Antonio a teasing glance as she slowly unbuttoned her blouse.

"What are you doing Signora Costello?" Antonio asked in a husky voice.

Forever

"I am putting on a show for you, Signore Costello," she replied. "Don't you like it?"

"I love it. Please continue," he said hurriedly.

Valerie smiled, her fingers continuing their slow dance on the buttons of her blouse. With each flicker of her fingertips, more of her skin revealed itself to the warmth of the firelight and Antonio's hungry gaze. The sheer material fell away, slipping over her shoulders and pooling softly at her feet.

She stood before him in the glow of the fire, her confidence blossoming with each pulse of the music that filled the cabin. Antonio couldn't help but lean forward, his pants tightening painfully.

"I want this moment to last forever," Antonio breathed out as Valerie stepped closer, now only inches away. His hands reached up involuntarily, hovering just shy of touching her.

"Forever sounds nice," Valerie whispered back, finally closing the distance between them.

Antonio's hands tightened around her waist, pulling her even closer until there was no space left at all.

Valerie tilted her head back slightly, offering Antonio her lips. He accepted with a tender urgency that belied his usual calm demeanor.

Breaking away for a breath, Antonio looked deeply into

Valerie's eyes. "I want you right now," he said gruffly.

"I am yours," Valerie said with a smile.

Fifty-Six

Who Helped You

River's heart pounded in his chest like a caged animal desperate for escape.

"I will punish him for you, Ellie," he whispered to himself, his breath a thin mist in the cold air. His mind was a whirlwind of memories - her laughter, her smile, her touch. But now, all that remained were the haunting echoes of their love, and the bitter taste of vengeance consuming him from within.

"Ellie," he said again, louder this time. "I will find justice for you. I swear it."

The prisoner's silhouette was barely visible, chained to a chair in the farthest corner of the dimly lit basement. River could feel his heart pounding in his chest as he approached.

"Tell me," River began, his voice low but firm, "why did you attack Antonio?"

The prisoner lifted his head slowly, revealing a face bruised from earlier interrogations. His eyes locked onto River's with a cold, unyielding defiance.

"None of your business," the man spat.

River clenched his fists, feeling the anger building inside him. He took a deep breath, trying to maintain control. He knew he needed to be smarter than this, that getting emotional would only hinder his progress.

"My wife is dead," River said, leaning in closer. "So yes, it is my fucking business."

For a moment, he saw something flicker behind the prisoner's eyes – a spark of recognition, maybe, or fear. But just as quickly, it was gone, and the man's face returned to its previous stony expression.

"I had no qualms with her. She was just a casualty."

Just a casualty. River stepped back. His head throbbed with sudden pain.

"Was it money?" River prodded, searching for any hint of a reaction. "Power? Did someone put you up to it?"

"Antonio needed to die. Along with the one he loves," the

prisoner said simply. "I wanted to catch him off guard at his wedding. Kill his wife, but your woman got in the way."

"His wife is my sister," River growled. "Either way, you fucked with the wrong people asshole."

The prisoner smirked, his lips curling into a sneer. "Do you think I care? This is bigger than you or me. Bigger than your precious sister and your wife."

River's jaw clenched tighter with each venomous word that spilled from the prisoner's lips.

"What's your name?" he asked.

"Nolan," the prisoner replied.

"Nolan," River said his name slowly. "Let me show you what happens to someone who dared to cross me."

Nolan's sneer faltered slightly as he watched River closely. There was a calculating coldness in his gaze, assessing whether this emotional display was a sign of weakness or a prelude to violence.

It didn't matter anymore. The thought of Ellie as a mere obstruction in their plan, the reduction of her vibrant life to nothing more than an inconvenience, was more than River could bear.

River found himself moving faster than he thought possible.

His fist connected squarely with the man's face, the impact sending a shockwave through his arm.

Blood spurted from the man's nose, and he staggered back. He fell backward with the chair still attached to his body, his head hit the floor with a dull thud. For a moment, everything was silent except for their heavy breathing.

River stood there, chest heaving, staring at his own trembling hands—hands that had sworn to protect those he loved and failed so catastrophically.

"You think this changes anything?" Nolan spat blood onto the floor and looked up at River with hatred burning through the haze of pain. "You think beating me will bring her back?"

"No," River finally said, voice steadier than before. "But it sure feels good."

Nolan's laughter was a harsh, grating sound, echoing off the cold, damp walls of the basement. "You can break every bone in my body, but it won't change anything," he rasped.

River knelt beside Nolan. "Why?" he demanded.

Nolan coughed, a trickle of blood running down his chin. "Antonio destroyed my family."

River leaned in closer, eyes narrowing. "What do you mean Antonio destroyed your family?"

Who Helped You

Nolan's eyes glinted with a mix of hatred and pain. "Years ago, Antonio's rise to power wasn't clean. My father was one of the men who opposed him. Antonio had him killed and made it look like an accident. His death put us on the street."

River's grip on Nolan's collar tightened. "So you came back for revenge?"

Nolan spat out a mouthful of blood, his expression turning bitter. "Bingo."

River's mind raced. He wasn't heartless. He understood the twisted logic behind Nolan's actions. But understanding didn't lessen his anger or his pain. "You talk about family, yet you destroy another. You're no better than the man you hate."

Nolan's expression hardened. "Maybe not. But at least I'm doing something. What are you doing, River? Besides crying over your dead wife?"

That was it. River snapped. He grabbed Nolan's shirt, pulling him close until their faces were inches apart. "I'm making you pay. That's what I am doing."

Nolan's smirk returned, though it was weaker now, strained by the pain and fear beginning to creep into his eyes. "Do your worst," he said, his voice barely above a whisper. "It won't bring her back."

River's hand twitched, but he forced himself to take a step

back. He couldn't let Nolan goad him into losing control. He needed to think, to stay focused. Beating Nolan senseless might feel good, but it wouldn't get him all the answers he needed.

Taking a deep breath, River straightened and walked over to a table against the wall, covered with tools and implements meant for extracting information. He picked up a small, sharp knife, letting the light catch the blade as he turned back to Nolan.

Nolan's eyes widened slightly, the fear now more evident. River approached him slowly, the knife glinting in the dim light. He leaned in close, his voice cold and controlled. "You didn't do this alone," he said. "Who helped you get those men to attack Antonio?"

Nolan's bravado cracked, a flicker of doubt crossing his face. He tried to mask it with defiance, but River could see through it. "Go to hell," Nolan spat.

River didn't hesitate. He brought the knife to Nolan's arm, pressing the blade just enough to draw a thin line of blood. Nolan flinched, his bravado crumbling further. "Talk," River commanded, his voice deadly calm.

Nolan's breathing grew rapid, his eyes darting around the room as if looking for an escape. "You don't scare me," he said, his voice trembling.

River's jaw tightened, his eyes locked onto Nolan's. The

Who Helped You

desperation in Nolan's voice betrayed the truth: he was scared. River took a deep breath, channeling his anger into a cold, calculated determination. He couldn't afford to let his emotions cloud his judgment.

"You're scared," River said softly. He moved the knife and pressed it against Nolan's cheek. "And you should be. Because I'm not going to stop until I get what I need."

Nolan's bravado faltered again, his eyes widening. "You don't scare me," he repeated, but his voice was shakier now, less convincing.

River pressed the blade a little deeper, enough to make Nolan wince. "Last chance," he warned. "Who helped you?"

Nolan's breathing was rapid, his eyes darting around the room. "Fuck off."

River's patience was wearing thin, but he forced himself to stay calm. He couldn't let his rage take over. Not yet. He pressed the knife harder against Nolan's cheek, drawing a small bead of blood.

"I don't have time for this," River said, his voice a low growl. "Tell me who helped you, or you'll wish you'd never been born."

Nolan's eyes hardened. "What does it matter who helped me? You want to take revenge on me for killing your wife, right? So just kill me."

River's eyes narrowed, and his grip on the knife tightened. He was done playing games. "You're right," he said slowly, his voice deadly calm. "I do want revenge. But killing you won't give me what I need. I want to make sure every single person involved pays for what they've done."

Nolan's eyes flickered with uncertainty, a crack in his hardened facade. River leaned in closer, the blade pressing harder against Nolan's skin. "Tell me who helped you," he demanded again. "Or I promise you, the pain you've felt so far will be nothing compared to what's coming."

Fifty-Seven

Happy Birthday

~~~~~

Valerie settled into her new routine at the mansion. It had been four months, and things had been quiet since their wedding night, and there had been no more problems.

The mansion was still and serene, but there was a lingering sense of emptiness that Valerie couldn't ignore. After a month of living with her, River sent Tiffany to a prestigious boarding school. The decision, though necessary, left a void in Valerie's life. At least he was allowing Lucas to live with her since he was only five years old.

She missed Tiffany's presence. She was so much like her mother, Ellie. But Valerie understood that the school would be good for her. Tiffany needed to be far from where her mother was killed. She needed to heal.

Antonio was devoted to her and Landon as always. He tried to do things to cheer her up, but Valerie still felt gloomy.

"You alright, mi amore?" he asked as he watched her play with her scrambled eggs.

"Yes," she said quietly.

"Are you lying to me?" he asked.

Her eyes snapped up to look at him. "Why would you think that?"

"Because I can see it all over your face. You miss Tiffany, don't you love?" Antonio's voice was gentle.

"And River. I am worried about him, Antonio. He had been distant ever since Ellie died. He would barely talk to me. And he hardly spends time with Lucas." Valerie winced.

Antonio smiled. "He calls Lucas every night. River is a big boy. No need to worry about him. He wouldn't get to where he is now if he wasn't strong."

But still…she worried. He was her brother, after all.

After all they had been through, she longed for the days when they could all be together again, safe and happy.

Days passed in much the same way. Valerie continued with her routine. Waking up, tending to Landon, savoring the

Happy Birthday

moments she had with him and Antonio. Antonio was out most of the day, but he never failed to join her for dinner.

One evening, after finishing their meal, Antonio took Valerie's hand and smiled at her mysteriously.

"What?" she asked him and looked at him suspiciously.

"I have something to show you," he said.

"Where are we going?" she asked, squeezing his hand as he led her down the hallway toward the back of the mansion. Despite living in the Costello mansion for some time now, she had not yet explored this part of the house. After all, it was unnecessarily large and easy to get lost in.

"It's a surprise," Antonio said, his smile widening.

They stopped in front of a door at the end of the hall. She gasped when she saw what was inside.

Valerie's eyes widened in astonishment. "Antonio, this is… incredible."

The room was filled with easels, canvases, and shelves stocked with paints and brushes. Large windows let in the sunlight, making the room bright and cheerful.

"I remembered you mentioned how much you love to paint," Antonio said softly, watching her reaction. "I thought this might cheer you up."

Tears welled up in Valerie's eyes as she looked around the room. She hadn't painted in so long. This was a gift beyond anything she had expected.

"Thank you," she whispered, turning to embrace Antonio. "It's perfect."

Antonio held her close, feeling her relax in his arms. "I want you to have a space where you can find peace. You deserve it, mi amore."

"I love it. But I don't think I am very good at painting anymore," she giggled softly.

Antonio gently pulled back, looking into Valerie's eyes with a tender smile. "Why don't you paint something for me, and I'll be the judge of that?"

She smiled, feeling a warmth spread through her chest. "Maybe I will."

The next morning, Valerie entered her new art studio with excitement. The smell of fresh paint and canvases infused the air, reigniting a spark within her that she thought had dimmed long ago.

Julian never let her paint. He said it was a waste of time and she should be using her time to make him some real money.

She shook her head as if to make his memory go away. She wished she could erase him from her brain completely.

Happy Birthday

Running her fingers gently over the brushes, she picked one up and held it like an old friend. Antonio had arranged everything perfectly: the palette was full of vibrant colors, and there were several blank canvases waiting to be brought to life. God, this man was unbelievable.

As she stood before an easel, Valerie felt the familiar flutter of nervousness mixed with anticipation. It had been years since she last painted.

But then, she suddenly knew what to paint.

As hours slipped by unnoticed, Valerie became lost in her creation.

"What are you painting?" Antonio's deep voice startled her.

She gasped and turned around, covering the canvas with her body. "Don't look!"

Antonio chuckled, raising his hands in mock surrender. "Alright, alright. I won't peek. But I'm curious, mi amore."

Valerie's heart raced, but she couldn't help but smile at his playful demeanor. "You'll see when it's finished," she promised.

Antonio gave her a lingering kiss on the forehead before leaving her to go to work. "Alright, then."

Valerie turned back to the canvas, feeling giddy.

The Mafia Boss's Pregnant Bride

After a few minutes, she heard another pair of footsteps. "Antonio, I am still not done…" she stopped. "Oh, Mary. It's you."

Mary smiled. "A letter arrived for you."

Valerie wiped her hands on a nearby cloth and took the envelope, recognizing Tiffany's neat handwriting immediately. Her heart skipped a beat as she carefully opened it. Inside was a letter from Tiffany, her words filled with excitement and stories of her new experiences at the boarding school.

"Hi, Aunty Valerie,

I hope you're doing well! I miss you so much. The school is huge, and I made some new friends. I think about you every day, and I hope you're doing okay. Is Lucas behaving? Please tell him I miss him and give him a big hug from me. Landon too! Also, thank Uncle Tony for sending me my favorite dessert!

Love, Tiffany"

Valerie felt tears prick at the corners of her eyes as she read the letter. The familiar pang of missing her was softened by the knowledge that she was happy and safe. She carefully folded the letter and placed it on a small table by the window, her thoughts swirling.

Valerie returned to her painting. The hours flew by as she lost herself in the process, the outside world fading away.

Happy Birthday

~-~

Meanwhile, Antonio stared at his computer in his office, a puzzled expression on his face. The numbers on the screen didn't add up, and a feeling in his gut told him something was wrong.

"Salvatore, come in here," he called out.

Salvatore entered, his expression as serious as ever. "What is it, Antonio?"

"These accounts," Antonio gestured to the screen. "Something doesn't feel right. We're missing a significant amount of money."

Salvatore leaned over the desk, scrutinizing the data. "This isn't just a minor discrepancy. It looks like someone's been skimming off the top."

Antonio's jaw tightened. "Find out who it is. Quietly. And when you do, bring him to me."

Salvatore nodded and left the room, leaving Antonio to his thoughts. He rubbed his temples. He was starting to enjoy not getting his hands bloody for a while, but he couldn't let some asshole get away with stealing from him either. He had to make an example out of that fool or his men would never respect him.

Maybe it was time for him to quit this mafia business...

The Mafia Boss's Pregnant Bride

But how could he? His family had been doing this for generations. This life was all he knew.

As Antonio mulled over his options, his phone buzzed with a message from Valerie. "Will you come home early today?"

Without missing a beat, he quickly grabbed his keys and headed home.

"Mi amore, what's wrong?" he asked as he strode into the bedroom.

Valerie looked up at him. "Nothing is wrong."

"Then why did you ask me to come home?" he asked, narrowing his eyes.

Valerie grinned. "I said to come home early. Not get here immediately!"

Antonio chuckled, relieved. "Alright, you got me. What's going on?"

Valerie bit her lower lip. "Nonna told me it was your birthday today."

He raised his eyebrow. "So what?"

Valerie rolled her eyes playfully. "So what!? Antonio, birthdays are special! We need to celebrate."

Happy Birthday

Antonio shrugged, a small smile tugging at his lips. "I've never been big on birthdays."

"Well, that's about to change," Valerie said firmly.

"And how do you suggest we celebrate?" he asked, moving closer to her.

"I thought we could go out to dinner. Or watch your favorite movie or something," she suggested.

"I have a better idea," he said sheepishly. "It involves you being naked."

Valerie giggled, her cheeks turning pink. "You are an idiot."

Antonio laughed. "Hey, I thought it was a good idea."

Valerie playfully swatted his arm. "Be serious."

"I am serious." Antonio pulled her to his chest and kissed her, the sweet scent of her shampoo enveloping his senses.

"Antonio," she murmured against his lips.

"Hmm?" He moved his lips down, kissing her jaw and then her neck.

"I finished the painting," she breathed.

"Oh yeah?"

She moaned as he kissed the crook of her neck. "It's a... present. For you."

He looked up, surprised. "You painted something for me?"

She nodded, smiling shyly. "I want you to see it."

Antonio pulled back slightly, his gaze filled with curiosity and admiration. "I'd love to see it. Lead the way."

Valerie took his hand and led him to the art studio, where the canvas stood covered. Her eyes were sparkling with excitement, and his heart fluttered.

"Alright, here it is," she said, her voice trembling a little as she pulled the cover away.

Antonio's eyes widened as he took in the painting.

Antonio's breath caught as he took in the painting. It was a striking and intimate portrayal of himself, captured with a depth of emotion and detail that left him speechless.

"Do you like it?" she sounded eager.

The piece captured his features with a vulnerability and depth that he rarely saw in himself. His eyes were dark. The right side of his face was scarred like it was in real life, but somehow, she had transformed the imperfections into something almost beautiful. They didn't look as hideous in the painting as they looked at him in the mirror.

Happy Birthday

Antonio reached out to trace the lines of his painted self, feeling a surge of emotions too complex to name. "Valerie, is this how you see me?" His voice cracked with emotion. T

Valerie watched him with tender eyes, a small smile playing on her lips. "Yes. Sorry, I painted your scars too. I just couldn't paint you without them because I find them beautiful."

Antonio pulled her into his arms. "Thank you," he whispered against her hair. "Have I told you I love you?"

"Yes," Valerie smiled. "But I wouldn't mind if you tell me a few more times."

——The End—-

Book 2 in this series

Book 2 in this series

The ENEMY'S Daughter

ANGELA LYNN CARVER

Summary:

Driven by revenge for his wife's murder, River attacks Alexander's house, disrupting Riley's engagement party. Her fianc flees, leaving Riley at River's mercy. Initially cruel and threatening, River is unexpectedly moved by Riley's courage and resilience. As he holds Riley captive in his lair, his intentions shift, and he finds himself falling for her. Struggling with his dark past and realizing their future is impossible, River decides to let Riley go, hoping she might one day forgive him.

Made in the USA
Middletown, DE
14 December 2024